# DEAD MAN'S
# MONEY

# DEAD MAN'S
# MONEY

•

# V. S. Meszaros

*AVALON BOOKS*
NEW YORK

Published by Thomas Bouregy & Co., Inc.
160 Madison Avenue, New York, NY 10016

Library of Congress Cataloging-in-Publication Data

Meszaros, V. S.
   Dead man's money / V.S. Meszaros.
         p. cm.
   ISBN 978-0-8034-9950-8 (hardcover)
   I. Title.

   PS3613.E7886D43 2009
   813'.6—dc22
                              2008048573

PRINTED IN THE UNITED STATES OF AMERICA
ON ACID-FREE PAPER
BY HADDON CRAFTSMEN, BLOOMSBURG, PENNSYLVANIA

To our brother, Terry Meszaros

## Chapter One

The girl was frightened.

Ever since the black-haired man in the dirty flannel shirt boldly eyed her up at the stage station, she had felt the first stirrings of apprehension. That had been in a bustling cow town some thirty miles back with people walking about. Now they were in the middle of nowhere.

Other men had stared at her as well, for she was a very pretty girl dressed in a stylish traveling suit made back East. Those glances had been admiring but respectful. They were the looks of men who were decent around women. The black-haired man's were not. His stares were downright rude.

He had first intruded upon her attention as she had stepped down from the westbound stage onto the box that served as a step. Like other idlers he was watching the stage empty, one booted foot resting on a horse trough. He was a tall man, big-shouldered with a dusty, sweat-stained hat resting on unwashed dark hair. Bold as brass he was, trying to catch her attention as if—she shuddered—she welcomed it.

Instinctively, she recoiled from such open insolence. Thumbs hooked confidently in his leather belt, an over-familiar grin on his unshaved face, he had looked her up and down for a long time as if deciding whether to buy her or not. Deliberately, she had swung her back to him while the horses were being changed. Even then she felt uncomfortable, feeling his unclean eyes boring into her slender back.

There was a sudden scraping as he removed his boot from the trough. Loud footsteps slapped along the wooden boardwalk and for one startled instant, she feared he might approach her. But the footsteps died away, becoming part of the other sounds of the busy street and she stole a glance over her shoulder when she felt it was safe. It was with a feeling of relief that she saw his abrupt departure. Julie relaxed. If she had known the reason for his departure and where he was headed, she would not have been so relieved.

Believing he had finally gone for good, she turned to speak with the only other passenger aside from her uncle, a young man of about twenty with a diffident manner. Julie Carter learned that his name was Jay Paxton and he was on his way home after herding cattle for one of the big outfits in Colorado.

"Mom needs the money," he blushed. "Pa died last year and I got four brothers and sisters. Be good to get back to the farm."

The lovely brunette had smiled at him understandingly.

Uncle John was her only family now. He stood there on the boardwalk in the shade of the station's bleached wooden awning nodding to all, passing the time of day with some of the old-timers slouched lazily on chairs propped against the building. Julie winced as she saw him unbutton his jacket again in the gathering heat, exposing the slight, unnatural thickening in his waist which was his money belt.

"Uncle John," she said quietly but urgently. He laughed and rebuttoned his jacket. Turning, she saw knowledge in Paxton's quick brown eyes. He seemed to read her thoughts.

"Bud Harris is our driver. He's an honest old man and good with his guns," he said, seemingly casual. Julie nodded, feeling more easy. Although she had come from New York she had heard of stages being robbed. It was reported in all the papers back East.

A couple of men further on noticed the money belt as well and exchanged glances. "Trouble," one of them muttered before spitting out his tobacco. "Ain't no need to carry money when ya got yourself a bank to put it in."

"Not unless you can take care of it yourself," the other agreed.

Both of them eyed John Carter doubtfully. A right nice gent but they could tell by his loud voice and excessive gestures that the man was pretty near a fool. Someone else had noticed as well. The black-haired man, Lyle Bodine, had looked first at the pretty girl then at the uncle and his money belt. Now he was making his way over to the telegraph office. He knew some men who would be interested in that money belt. But the girl was his.

Purvis at the telegraph office had read the telegram to

be sent, then looked across at the tall, dangerous man staring coldly at him. He sent the telegram. Only when he was finished did Bodine slam the money down and leave. Alarmed, Purvis knew he had to act. He waited until Bodine had moved away, then came out of the telegraph office wondering what to do next. The sheriff was out of town today and wouldn't be back until nightfall. Harris, the driver, that was the man to tell. This would concern him.

Harris came out of the station and called out to no one in particular, "Time to be gettin'." He carried his rifle in his hand like a man who knew how to use it. A gun was holstered at his waist. A wiry old man of about sixty, he had a pair of piercing blue eyes that sized up his passengers with the knowledge of a trail-seasoned driver. He nodded to himself then climbed up. The luggage was already stowed aboard.

Carter got in and Paxton helped Julie, climbing aboard after her. She was eager to be off.

"Ya got one more passenger!" a hard voice barked. Harris looked down and stared, then he swore under his breath.

Then the dark-haired man got in.

Harris climbed down again and went into the stage office. "Joe, give me an extry box of cartridges." At the inquisitive look from Joe, he jabbed his thumb in the direction of the latest passenger and grumbled, "A man can't be too careful." Shoving the box into his coat pocket, he headed back out. Purvis saw him fling himself up on top of the stage and hurried towards him. Harris flipped the reins and the team stepped out smartly.

"Bud!" Purvis waved as the stage rumbled towards him.

Bud gave him a curt nod but did not stop. His mind was occupied with the new passenger in the stagecoach. He did not notice how anxious Purvis looked nor could he see the piece of paper he waved in his hand. It was addressed to Ed Coolee, Hartsville. It read:

GET REECE BROTHERS. MEET ME AT
BRANSON WELLS. LYLE BODINE.

Purvis looked unhappily after the disappearing coach. Ed Coolee. He'd heard the name. He was some gunfighter out of Oklahoma. The Reece brothers were both locals who never did an honest day's work in their lives. Duncan was the more violent of the two, having killed three men already in his short career.

And they were all going to meet up at Branson Wells— The stage's next stop.

At Branson Wells, which was nothing more than a rude log cabin with a pole corral, three more passengers were waiting to board: Ed Coolee and the Reece brothers. All of them were tough gents who looked like they'd been over the mountain and back again. All of them packed rifles and a gun each. Bud Harris' hard old mouth got harder, but he had to let them board. They had paid their fare.

Now there were four. Julie moved closer to Paxton.

Halfway to the next stop the wheel suddenly broke in two. Harris wanted to swear but didn't in front of Julie. He sharply refused help when one of the passengers, Coolee, offered it with something approaching a smile.

"Stay near your uncle," he had told Julie abruptly as he

reluctantly agreed that the passengers had better make a camp among the rocks for the night. He held back for a moment like he wanted to say more to the girl, but Bodine shot a look over his shoulder ordering everyone to hurry up. His hard, suspicious stare lingered on the driver. Casually, Harris picked up his rifle and stared back. Bodine hesitated a moment then, shrugging, he moved away after the others.

Although Harris had no way of knowing the contents of the telegram Bodine had sent to Coolee, he was shrewd enough to realize that the three rats that had suddenly shown up at Branson Wells belonged to Bodine's pack. One look at Harris' face and Julie suspected it as well. The stage driver was worried and she knew that she should be too.

At first, she spotted the new passengers with eagerness tinged with hope. Perhaps their presence would restrain the black-haired man. It did not. Even though they flatly introduced themselves to the others, Bodine included, she had seen how their eyes met and held. At Branson Wells the four of them went into the stables and talked. When they came out they were smiling.

They knew each other. Julie tried to tell her uncle but he brushed her worries away. They were on a stage. Nothing could happen.

After the wheel broke there was a shifting of power. Bodine was in charge now. He chose the place to camp and ordered Shorty Reece to build a fire and put some coffee on. Shorty made it quickly and without argument as if he had been taking orders from the man for a long time.

Almost on cue, Coolee suggested a game of poker. Carter agreed immediately. He was a gregarious man who enjoyed the company of others. He believed he was merely sitting down to a friendly game with men who were complete strangers to each other. He couldn't see, as Julie did, that the four were together. Together against *him*.

"Deuces wild?" Bodine's words broke into Julie's worried thoughts as they seated themselves for the game. Duncan and Shorty both nodded. Carter did as well. Bodine's eyes swerved to the last male passenger. Paxton had been sitting against a rock somberly drinking a cup of coffee. He was protecting his back. Bodine saw this with annoyance.

"You playing too?" he snapped. He didn't like the blushing glances the young cowboy had been sending the lovely easterner here or in the stage. His anger had a proprietorial edge to it that Julie disliked immediately.

"Nope," Paxton said easily. "Never been one for cards much." It wasn't the response the other man wanted. For a second it seemed as if he were going to make something of it.

"Let's play, then," Duncan said, a slight warning in his voice. Bodine looked sulky but he backed down.

"Deal!" Bodine's voice grated into the silence. Carter shrugged. He found the man's reactions inexplicable and picked up the deck to shuffle. The man was clearly upset about something but it wasn't his business to inquire.

Bodine dismissed the cowboy for the moment and transferred his attention to the game at hand and to one player in particular. His eyes riveted on the man across from him. They narrowed in contempt as he weighed and measured the older man and found him wanting.

While Shorty and Duncan sat at the game with Bodine,

the last man, Coolee, sauntered out into the gathering darkness—to help with the horses, he said. He gave a slight nod to Bodine as he left. Bodine grunted.

Carter picked up his cards. He was an honest man and a friendly man but he was not an observant man. Unlike his niece, he had not seen the sly smiles as he put down his money. And he had plenty more, they knew, plenty more. Enough for everyone.

After a few hands, it penetrated even his bluff and hearty exterior that he was not enjoying the game very much. Through a blur of cigarette smoke, he glanced up quickly from his cards and his smile wavered. He had caught the tail end of a look Bodine was aiming at his niece sitting behind him. Those eyes, smouldering with ugly lust slid past Carter's shoulder and honed in on the pretty girl in her fitted suit. Carter could hear the nervous rustle of her skirts and knew instinctively that she was trying to avoid the look. He moved over slightly to shield her from Bodine's penetrating gaze. Bodine couldn't mistake what that meant: His prey was getting skittish. He chuckled softly at this and studied his hand again.

Carter suddenly felt unsure of himself. Briefly, he wondered if he should say something. Very slowly, his eyes traveled around the ring of men. The leather-tough faces were not encouraging. Carter decided to let it ride. He concluded that it was just their awkward way of admiring a pretty girl. There was no harm meant. None at all!

Carter tried to concentrate on his game. He had come from the East where there were rules and laws that people followed. It was taken for granted that the people out here were just as law-abiding even though they were days away from a sheriff or judge. The older man's eyes bounced off the guns so prominently displayed and away again as if he were afraid to stare at them. It was odd that in stark contrast to their rumpled clothing and unkempt hair, their weapons were clean and well cared for. Vaguely, Carter remembered that he had a gun in his valise. He never loaded it.

Bodine shuffled the cards and then reshuffled them. It was done with quickness and expertise. It was done like a professional, not like a ranch hand passing the time away. All three men played well together, merely nodding as if they needed no words. As if they had played together before. All professionals. All friends. Carter's heart beat a little quicker.

As Carter reluctantly collected his cards, Bodine raised his eyes above his own hand and watched the nervous Easterner. He noticed his hands shaking slightly. Beads of moisture dampened his forehead; he licked his dry lips.

He was onto them. Yep, he was onto them all right. It didn't matter in the least to Bodine whether the older man suspected or not. What was going to happen would happen. Every man knew that when they had boarded the stage. He saw Carter's eyes dart past him worriedly scanning the darkness for the driver. Bodine didn't even bother to look to see if the driver was there. He knew he was not. Coolee had gone out to meet him.

"A mite warm this evening," Carter commented, running his finger around his collar. All of a sudden it was too tight. Bodine smiled, but the smile didn't reach his eyes. Like chips of ice they reflected the firelight but shone no inner warmth of their own. He was actually enjoying the Easterner's discomfort, much as a cat would when a mouse suddenly realizes he's being tailed.

Where she sat near the fire, Julie slid her hand down to her purse that lay at her feet. Unobserved, she picked it up and placed it in her lap. She gave a little sigh as her hand closed over the hard form of the derringer hidden in there. Back in New York when she had asked Uncle John to buy her a gun he had laughed and told her she had read too much about the wild west. Good-humoredly, he had bought one for her anyway. Now she was glad to have it. Dipping her hand into her purse, she silently removed it and slid it into the pocket of her skirt. Her uncle, she knew, had a gun but he was not wearing it.

"It gives people the wrong impression," he had told her amiably. "Makes it seem like you're hunting trouble. I'm not." Maybe so, but trouble had certainly found them.

A sudden commotion from beyond the camp's perimeter caused everyone except Bodine to look up, startled. Stones rattled and something heavy seemed to fall out there in the gloom. Then there was silence.

The young cowhand came to his feet quickly and took one step towards the noise. Julie also stood up, peering nervously into the darkness.

"Don't go out there, Paxton," Bodine's terse voice cut in, halting him in his steps. "Coolee is out there with the driver. No use both of you bungling around in the night. Sit down!" Paxton noticed Bodine's hand resting lightly on the butt of his gun and made himself lean back against a tree. If it came to a gun battle, he was no match for Bodine and his men. He could shoot pretty accurately if he had the time, but somehow he didn't think he would get the time. Tentatively, he touched the butt of his own gun and saw Bodine's eyes light up with interest. He dropped his hand back down to his side. Bodine returned to his game.

Julie went over to the fire and poured out a cup of coffee. With determination she walked in the direction where the coach had broken down.

Irritated to have his game interrupted again, Bodine flung out, "Where do ya think you're goin'?"

Julie put her chin up as she made a move to pass him. "The driver might need a cup. We haven't even offered him one."

Bodine grinned. "I need one more than he does." He grabbed the cup from her and took a swig. "Sit down!" he rapped out, coffee dribbling down his chin. He wiped it away with his filthy sleeve. Julie obeyed him not because she wanted, but because she was afraid her uncle or Paxton might object to his tone.

Paxton's frank, honest face was frowning. He was definitely edgy. Carter was restless, too, but he was an easygoing man who was used to shrugging off unpleasant things. He had noticed Bodine's roughness and crudeness, but he supposed it was the man's way. He didn't see how often those sharp eyes slashed over the Easterner's gullible face. He didn't see the detestable smile.

"What do you want to do, Carter?" Carter lost his concentration. Maybe he had been staring at the cards too long in the dim light of the fire. "Are you playing or folding?"

Carter wished now that he hadn't agreed to a game of poker in the first place. Come to think of it, it had been Coolee's idea and he wasn't even playing.

"I'll raise you," he said finally, pushing forward another dollar into the pot. Carter's smile wavered. The men didn't smile back. All eyes flicked to his breast pocket where his billfold was kept. Carter pulled the pocket flap down firmly. His worries began to let up a little when he saw, to his surprise, that he had won the game with a straight flush.

"Not bad, Carter. You're a pretty smooth player," Bodine said. His voice had a mocking edge to it. "Duncan, your deal." Duncan gathered the cards to him while the others greedily watched Carter scrape up his winnings.

The next hand, he won again. This time Bodine was riled. His face flushed red as he snapped out, "Ya know, Carter, you got a real bad habit. You don't bet straight out. You wait to see what we do before you make your whole bet! That's real sneaky!"

"Why I do no such thing!" Carter looked confused.

Duncan stared down at his cards but his shoulders started to shake. He tried to keep the amusement from his face and couldn't.

"Was I you, John"—he drawled the name with excessive familiarity—"I'd try not to win so much. Lyle, here, has a short fuse when it comes to poker. 'Course, you wouldn't know that, would you?"

Carter looked at the circle of men around him. A sinister cunning lurked in their sharpened features. Suspicion finally penetrated his brain. He wanted to push it down but couldn't. Not this time.

Things were moving too fast for him, and he got the feeling that he was being stampeded in a direction he didn't want to go. They were implying he was cheating! He looked at Duncan, who had dealt him the cards. Dazed, he wondered if Duncan had slipped him that pair of aces on purpose.

Julie rose from where she was sitting. Paxton carefully put his mug of coffee down. Things were coming to a head now. They could both feel it. Coolee suddenly appeared out of the dark.

"Everything okay?" Duncan asked.

"Yep," Coolee drawled.

No one spoke. No one asked if the wheel was fixed or where the driver was. Coolee's eyes swept the place as if checking where everyone stood. His hand remained at his side near his gun.

"You almost done here?" he asked.

"Practically," Duncan said.

Paxton moved closer to Julie who was clutching her bag so hard that her nails bit into her palm.

Duncan noticed the movement and warned, "Watch it, Lyle, or that young sprout is gonna steal away your filly!" His laugh, thin and reedy, was irritating. Shorty slapped the table and laughed. Coolee turned to look at Carter to gauge his reaction.

Carter felt as if he'd been kicked in the stomach. The almost crippling fear that had been building inside of him was suddenly turning to outrage. He rose to his feet.

"That is my niece you're talking about, sir! She is a lady and I will not tolerate—"

"Take it easy, Carter!" Bodine reached out and shoved Carter back down. "Before you start in makin' trouble, we got a game to finish." He added ruthlessly, "And think of this: Who's gonna take care of sweet little Miss Julie if you're not around to do it?"

Carter's jaw dropped. Suddenly his throat constricted with fear. He swallowed hard. His back was against the wall and he knew it. Too late he realized that he had been their target from the very beginning.

Cold and aloof Coolee added, "You know, Carter, it's not a good idea to rile Bodine. He gets kinda crazy sometimes. A mite trigger happy, ya know?" He stroked his stubbly chin and considered the man across from him through slitted eyes. He had branded him for a coward and thought he knew his man. "'Course, if you was to lose this pot . . ." Coolee nodded towards the stack of coins and bills, roughly forty dollars' worth lying loosely on the upended trunk being used as a table. "Let's just say it would go a long way to smoothin' things over." The men around him grinned. "Well, Carter?" Coolee leaned forward. "How much does your life mean to you?"

There it was, out in the open. The words seemed to hang there, stark and threatening. The gauntlet had been thrown down, and Carter was too weak a man to pick it up.

The air was shocked with tension. Every man waited for Carter to act. It was his hand to play alone. How would he play it?

Julie took an impetuous step forward, but Paxton's hand reached out to stop her. If there was shooting, they wouldn't balk at killing her as well.

Coolee's long, stone-like face was watchful. His hand was poised over his holstered gun, barely touching it. It was clear he was eager to curl his fingers around its smooth surface.

The four men sat so still, cards clasped in their hands, that they seemed to have turned to marble. Carter's stomach felt like lead. He knew he was staring death in the face. He had never done a single harm to any man, yet for the money he carried so carelessly he was probably going to die, here and now, in this awful place. No matter how he scrambled about in his mind, he could see no way out of this. A nighthawk called in the sagebrush. The men waited.

Bodine laughed. It was a harsh sound that shattered the stillness.

Shorty sniggered. "Well, Carter, what do ya think? You won't miss that money anyway. Look how much ya got stashed away in that money belt." Carter drew in his breath hard.

"The way I see it," Bodine drawled, "you might as well just hand that money over now. We're going to get it any-way."

"That's right," Duncan agreed. "Just hand it over now and you can walk away alive." He lied.

Carter knew he lied. Seconds ticked away. Carter looked at Julie. What had he gotten her into? Perhaps if he bargained with them to let her go . . .

"Make up your mind. You got about ten seconds to de-cide," Bodine warned.

"Ah, the hell with this!"

Always an impatient devil, Coolee raised his hand and his gun spat lead. The bullet tore into Carter's chest. He was dead before he tumbled to the ground. Blood covered the front of his new vest and saturated the gravel where he lay, eyes open but sightless.

Julie screamed and tried to rush over to him. Paxton held her back. His hands were empty when Coolee spun around and shot into his body. The boy fell backward.

Julie screamed again and knelt beside him. It took only one glance to know he was not going to last.

"Sorry, ma'am," he whispered as she bent over him. "Sorry to leave ya alone with these men. My mom . . . my mom woulda wanted me to—" Paxton went limp, his head falling to the side. A nice young man, Julie thought dully, who just wanted to return home.

She got up, her skirts spattered with blood. The other four were grinning and scraping up the winnings.

"Hey, Ed," Bodine said, stuffing his pockets full of dollar bills. "Get me that vest the old boy's wearing. It's new and I like it."

Julie ran over to her uncle and knelt down next to him. "Leave him alone!"

"Face it, Miss Julie, he's a goner," Bodine pointed out. "He tried to draw on Ed, here, and got what was coming to him." The other three tittered.

Julie stared at them. "Liar! Draw on him? He didn't even have a gun!"

"Is that so?" Bodine pretended surprise. "Ed? Didn't he have a gun? Sure he did." Bodine took one of his own and tossed it near Carter's lifeless body. "There it is. I can see it as plain as day. Don't you see it?" Coolee said he did. Shorty and Duncan agreed solemnly as well. "Yep. Tried to draw on Ed, here, and him minding his own business. That's what comes of cheatin'!" Coolee grinned at Bodine's words.

Furious at their cruel mirth and scared of what would happen to her, Julie grabbed up the gun with both hands and pointed it at Bodine. His lips twitched with amusement.

"Hooey! Lyle, she sure hates you!" Duncan howled. "She'll shoot ya right between your eyeballs sure enough!" He slapped his thigh.

"I'll bet ya ten bucks she'll wound ya," Shorty said gleefully.

"Twenty that she misses," Coolee put in.

"She won't shoot," Bodine drawled. "Will ya, little Miss Julie? She's a lady." He mimicked her dead uncle.

Julie pulled the trigger. Duncan and Shorty dived out of the way. Nothing happened. She pulled it again and again. Nothing but a loud click. The gun was empty. Bodine jumped now and jerked it from her hand.

"I knew it! I knew you'd try it! Think I'm stupid enough to give ya a loaded gun?" Grabbing her by the arm, he hauled her to her feet. Pulling her arm back, she slapped him openhanded across his grinning face. The hard smack echoed in the night. Bodine's grin turned into an ugly snarl.

"Don't ever do that again, missy, or you'll be the sorrier for it! You better be glad that all that money's put me in a good mood!" Instead, he gave her a hard push and she fell backwards on the dusty ground. She heard the caustic jeers behind her.

As she regained her balance she felt something heavy pulling down in her pocket. It was her derringer. She drew it out and stood up, then she turned to face them. The men were laughing and reaching for Carter's money belt when Coolee saw her eyes first. He saw the gun second.

"Watch out, Lyle!" he warned but did not go for his gun. This was Bodine's business. If he wanted the girl so badly, he should take all the risks.

Bodine spun around just as Julie fired. He jumped aside and Shorty, who was eagerly counting out his share of the money, was struck above the hipbone in the fleshy part of his side. Howling with pain and rage, he dropped his money and clamped his hand on the blood rushing out.

"Ow! What the hell ya shootin' me fer?" Shorty yelled. "Oh no!" he groaned when he saw the blood oozing through his fingers and staining his shirt and pants. "Duncan, give me a hand!" Duncan bolted over and helped.

Bodine kicked the valise out of his way and rushed her, snatching her wrist just as she got off another shot. It slammed into the rocks and ricocheted off.

"Little hellcat!" he snarled. He squeezed her wrist with an iron grip as he twisted it painfully backwards. The derringer fell from her numb fingers. "Now you're gonna pay for that!" Bodine lifted his bunched fist to strike her.

## Chapter Two

When Jim Wyatt had gotten out of prison three days ago he had quietly taken his property from the warden, then went to collect his horse from old man Pike.

"Here he is, son." Pike had patted the horse fondly, but looked searchingly at the tall, lean man who was bending over, tightening the cinch. Jim looked the same but Pike could sense the difference. The green eyes were still level and direct, yet there were shadows in them. The well-cut mouth was set grimly and his whole manner was wary. Pike noticed that he threw a look over his shoulder several times.

"No one knows that horse of yours is here," Pike promised, interpreting that look. Jim gave him a smile. It wasn't warm and fulsome, but it showed Jim was still game. The old man had heard that prison could sometimes break a man, especially someone as proud and respected as Jim had been.

19

"How much do I owe you?" Jim asked, shoving his hand into the pocket of his worn jacket.

"Don't be an ass," Pike said irritably. Jim shot him another small smile. The older man abhorred thanks. "No one's been askin' about you neither, if that's what's botherin' you," Pike guessed shrewdly. "I've been keepin' a lookout for any strangers. Nothin' suspiciouslike that I seen. Don't have to worry about anyone on your tail for a while, I reckon."

"Good." Jim prepared to mount his horse.

"Come in and have something to eat. Don't be in such an all-fired hurry to git."

"Thanks, Amos, but Laban's been taking care of business for me. He might need my help." Laban Kettering was Jim's foreman and best friend.

"Last time I heard, he was doin' jest fine. Filled one of March Newton's hired hands with buckshot. Had to find a doctor to git all of the pieces out." Pike took his pipe out of his mouth. "He'll be hard pressed to sit astride a horse fer a while."

This time Jim's laughter was genuine. "I didn't hear that. Laban's not one to brag." He shoved his rifle into its scabbard. "He only wrote me a handful of letters."

"Surprised he even writ them!" Pike commented, disappointed that the young man seemed determined to go so soon. "He always said he's jest this side of literate." He held onto the bridle for a moment. "Now you stick to the high country and you should be all right. Fewer coyotes up thataway—the two-legged kind I mean."

"I intend to. I want to get back to the Flying W before Newton knows I'm out." The tall young man sat easily in his saddle, but Pike noticed the first thing he did was to clean and load his guns. Jim always was careful.

"Got enough money?"

"Sure."

"Dang it! If ya need somethin' let me know!" Jim grinned at the old man's irritability. "I'll git you some bacon." Pike stomped off and came back with bacon, beans and coffee. "There now, stop bein' so durned independent! Got enough ammunition?"

"That I have. That's one thing I made sure of." Pike relaxed as Jim showed him his supply.

"Well, at least you got some sense."

"I'll be all right." Jim leaned down and squeezed the old man's bony shoulder, touched by his concern. "I've had a long time to plan this all out—every single night I lay in that bunk, in fact. I know exactly what to do. So long, Amos." He shook the old man's hand, and Pike watched as Jim rode slowly away from the house.

Pike shook his head. He had no faith that Newton wouldn't hear of Jim's release. That man always had his ear to the ground. Sooner or later Newton would make his move, damn him!

Jim started his trek towards home. For a while he enjoyed the scenery and the freedom of going wherever he wanted after the harsh prison regime. Just feeling the fresh breeze cool his face was enjoyable. There had been breezes in prison, too, but they had been in the hot, dry sun while he worked away at the granite rock piles.

Jim had done his time without complaint. Now it was time to set things right—if he were permitted the chance. Jim figured he'd have about five days before he'd have to start worrying. That's how long it would take Newton to hear the news of his release, and act on it. Jim knew Newton would have to act. It was that or allow the truth to come out. Newton couldn't afford that. Yep, five days. But Jim still kept a look over his back just the same.

It turned out he wasn't even granted five days. The very next evening Jim came upon the stage. For some distance he had seen a dark object in the road and had approached it carefully. He was stumped when he edged closer and saw the stage lying askew. No one was in sight. Circling widely, he rode to the base of some hills and slipped silently from the saddle.

Tying his horse among some trees, Jim scaled the rough terrain until he could look out over the vista. He climbed warily, silently, careful of a trap. It may have nothing to do with him but it was best to be alert.

At the edge of a high, rocky ledge, Jim hunkered down and scanned the twisting landscape. Even as the sun began to dip out of sight, it didn't take him long to locate the seven passengers. They were immediately below him, camped among a scattering of boulders. A fire was burning and four men were playing cards. Jim's brow furrowed in puzzlement and worry. He still didn't see the stage driver. All he saw were the six men—and the girl, of course.

Jim had noticed her right away. She was pretty and slender, and by the cut of her clothes, an Easterner. Moreover, she was as skittish as a colt. Even from this distance he could sense that. It was no wonder, seeing the company she was with.

Jim's handsome mouth tightened as he recognized two of the other passengers: Duncan and Shorty Reece. What in blazes were they doing here? They were a violent pair. Their reputation as thieves and cattle rustlers stretched throughout Wyoming into the southern plains. Their names had been associated with several bank holdups and the disappearance of small herds of cattle. If they were here in this desolate spot, it was for a purpose. It wasn't just to pass the time away playing cards. Or was it? Jim's face was thoughtful as he saw how the four men played the game with barely restrained eagerness.

At that moment a dark-haired man with black eyes and dirty shirt looked up from his cards right at the girl. Jim saw her swiftly turn her head away, and he felt a hot anger rise up in him. It was plain to see what held the man's interest, but what of his other friends? Shorty Reece was sipping coffee. Like a hawk, Duncan was watching the older man with the graying hair as if he might get away from him. A tall, long-faced man with icy eyes and a dangerously calm exterior leaned nearby, looking on. He was not playing. An unpleasant smile clung to his lips as he viewed the proceedings.

Duncan wouldn't risk anything for a woman. Neither would Shorty. What about the long-faced man? It was hard to tell. Jim's sharp eyes probed Bodine and Coolee. He recognized neither of them, but from the way they exchanged looks with the Reeces, it was apparent that all four men had the same agenda. Four against one girl? At first it didn't make sense.

Then Jim's attention went to the older man playing cards. It was at that moment that he spotted it: A slight thickness about the man's waist. There were also some silver dollars stacked in front of him winking in the firelight.

Judging by his clothes he was an Easterner as well. Jim guessed that he and the girl were together. His eyes cut back again to her and read the worry crossing the pretty face. She understood the fix they were in. The older man did not. What a hell of a problem for her!

Finally, Jim studied the last man there. He was just a naive boy who looked as apprehensive as the girl. Jim knew his type: A young lad, probably a cowpuncher, who had ended up in this company by the merest chance. He kept looking at the girl but Jim didn't question his intentions. It seemed as if he wanted to protect her, but didn't know how to go about it.

Ordinarily, Jim didn't interfere with other people's business. After all, he had enough on his own plate. If a man was so foolish as to put himself into danger by wearing a money belt . . . well, it was Jim's philosophy that he ought to get himself out of it again. Out here, a man didn't look to others to fight his battles especially when he was perfectly capable of doing it himself. That is, Jim corrected himself, if he had the wits to comprehend his danger. This damned Easterner obviously didn't. He didn't even have a gun on him. The others did. They were all packing plenty of muscle. His life was ticking away. Each hand he played was like a constricting noose around his neck. How long would it be before someone trumped up a reason to shoot him and relieve him of his money? Not long.

Jim's eyes went back to the girl. She was his main concern. That girl knew the score. She was looking mighty fidgety, gripping her handbag and trying to avoid the black-haired man's hot stares. All the while she was watching the easterner uneasily.

Jim had seen enough. He backed off the ledge and slid down the rocky ascent to where his horse waited. He yanked his rifle from its scabbard and silently led his horse down the slope for a closer look. Jim didn't have any plan. The boy was armed but the older man wasn't. He'd take it from there.

Jim strained his eyes now to find the driver, Bud Harris. Jim had known him for years. Bud was a good old man and an honest one. He would never have let the situation with the passengers get out of hand if he were alive. He would have gotten his rifle out and started shooting. Going against the likes of the Reeces wouldn't have slowed him down any. In fact, it might have sweetened his disposition. Bud had known the Reeces and disliked them as much as everyone. He would never have let them touch the pretty brunette.

Jim learned what had happened to Bud when he reached the level plain not far from where the stagecoach stood disabled. Behind a screen of brush where shadows spread out growing into darkness, he came across the stage driver. He was bleeding from a wound to the chest. Injured he might be, but his eyes and ears weren't impaired any.

"Who's that?" an old voice growled. Jim saw the shaggy head turn alertly towards the rocks. "Come any closer and I'll blow you to hell!" In the lowering sun Jim could see the orange rays glinting off the shiny rifle barrel pointing directly at him.

"That's a mighty interesting proposition, but I've been there already, thank you." Jim chuckled softly.

"Who is it?" Bud peered into the dark. That voice sounded downright familiar.

Jim kneeled down so Bud could see his face. "It's Jim Wyatt," he said quietly.

"Jim!" There was relief in the voice but the relief was mingled with pain. "Son, am I glad to see you! That danged Ed Coolee got me. Offered to help me with the wheel, then he up and stabbed me. Couldn't even git a shot off myself." He sounded weak yet he could muster enough strength to cuss himself out for his own stupidity. "Shoulda seen it comin'! Shoulda knowed he was up to somethin'." In the dim light, Jim made out the weathered face, strained and white from loss of blood. He reached out to examine the wound.

"Never mind about me." Bud pushed the hand away almost impatiently. "I'm a goner, boy. I knowed it when them four sidewinders got on my stage. Thought I could make it to the next stop without a fracas, but they knowed that now was the time to git rid of me." Spent from his sudden outburst he leaned back. The wind stirred and rustled the brush that grew all around. Bud's heavy rasping drowned out the gentle noises. Jim, ignoring his low protests, did his best to stanch the flow of blood.

"You lost a lot of blood," he observed narrowly.

"Danged right I did! When Coolee struck me, I fell to the ground. He musta thought I was dead. Kicked me a few times, then walked off leavin' my carcass to fry in the sun. Then I crawled off to hide. Figger they won't bother with me once they git what they came for."

"And what did they come for?"

"Money, son," Bud said bluntly. "There's twelve thousand dollars tucked in that thar money belt of Carter's."

Jim whistled softly. He didn't figure it would be so much, but it made sense.

"Dang fool showed it to me right in the open. Asked if it'd be safe on the stage. Hah! Safe! And him a sayin' it so loud everybody and his Aunt Fanny could hear it! I told him to put it in the bank but he jest laughed." Bud shook his head in disbelief at such stupidity, then wished he hadn't. He groaned. "That Coolee is one mean hombre. I think he cracked a few ribs." He touched his side tenderly. "Sure feels like it." He then proceeded to tell Jim what he thought of his attacker and his underhanded tactics.

"And then that durned wheel had to break." He smouldered as Jim held up his canteen to the old man's lips.

"Tough break," Jim said casually.

"No such a thing! That thar wheel was tampered with. Cut almost clean through. They probably done it whilst I was eatin' at Branson Wells. I seed it right off. That's when Coolee sidled up to me and give me one with that blamed knife of his. They knowed they had to git me outta the way," he said with some satisfaction. "If I'd a had my gun to hand, I'd have blown Coolee wide open. Yep, they had it all planned out. Even takin' me outta the way." He laughed bitterly.

"Coolee," Jim murmured, tying the wound loosely, "I've heard of him."

"You better watch your every step, son. I wouldn't tangle with him myself 'cept for that girl. Did ya see her?" Jim nodded. "I'm gettin' mighty worried about her and her uncle." Jim's lips tightened. He understood very well what the old man was trying to say.

"Saw him from above," Jim said, helping Bud into a sitting position so he could lean against a big rock. He caught his breath but couldn't be silent.

"Them murderin' polecats!" he snarled between gasps of pain. "They'll have him killt afore long. Then what'll happen to the girl?" He paused and looked up almost slyly at Jim. "That girl's as pretty as a speckled hen!"

Jim couldn't stop the grin from tugging at the corners of his mouth. "Aw, she's prettier than that!"

"Ain't no one to help her if her uncle gits it."

Jim's face became serious again. "Don't worry, you old buffalo. I'll see she gets away safely."

"Knew ya would. Can't think of a better man to handle things." Bud closed his eyes tiredly, then they flew open again as if he'd just remembered something. "When did you git back?"

"Two days ago," Jim said shortly, not liking to speak of it.

"Better git yourself over to your ranch smartlike. Soon as ya left, that Newton feller saddled up and rode out to your place."

"I know. Laban wrote me a letter or two."

Jim tied another knot in the bandage to secure it. Bud flinched at the sudden stab of pain.

"Take it easy, boy," he said with a twinge. "That there's mortal flesh you're tormentin'—and it hurts!" For an instant Jim flashed an apologetic look at the old man. His mind was obviously elsewhere. Before he could put that look into words, Bud spoke again. "Don't you bother with me. I ain't long for this world."

"That's what you said last time you were shot," he said,

gently chastising him. But he had to admit even to himself that Bud looked damned bad.

"That wound was in the leg. This is a sight worse. Now you git goin'. I don't know how long I was out, but they ain't gonna wait long to do their mischief. Ain't exactly a patient bunch over there—especially Coolee."

"You should be safe hidden here, Bud. I'll send help for you when I can. I don't think I'll have time to take you with me right now."

"Don't reckon you will," he agreed humorously. "Now don't worry about me. The stage'll come through sometime and maybe they'll send someone out when they find I ain't made it to the next station. They can collect my earthly remains." After a moment he continued, "Lyle Bodine is there. You mind him," Bud warned as he saw the determined look on the young man's face. "That Bodine will start talkin' and then he'll start shootin'. Don't wait for him to finish no sentences."

Jim gave him a slight smile. "Wasn't plannin' on doing any oratin'." He gave the old man an affectionate pat on the shoulder. "Stay put because if I see anything move, I'm shooting."

"Don't plan on gettin' up even if I could." Then he blustered, "Dang Coolee! I coulda taken five—no six—of him before breakfast if I'd a been more awake!"

"It happens. Now listen, Bud, I got a party to go to and you'll be more help if you'll stay alive and tell someone what happened. I'll take over from here." Nodding, Jim turned and disappeared into the night's vastness. Bud listened closely as the light footsteps, barely whispers in the dust, died away. Then he was alone. He gave a sigh of self-pity. Too bad he couldn't go to that shindig. He enjoyed a shootout as well as the next man!

On soundless feet, Jim ghosted through the night in the direction of the circle of rocks that enclosed the camp of stranded passengers. He could see the fire flickering eerily through the sparse trees, throwing its yellow color everywhere. As Jim moved silently from bush to boulder, he speculated about the four dangerous men whose acquaintance he would be forced to make.

Two were a known commodity. Jim knew exactly what to expect from the Reece brothers: Get the drop on them and they'll behave like choirboys; get sloppy and let your guard down for one instant, and you're a dead man.

Ed Coolee was a name Jim should know. He was a man who was handy with a knife, with eyes as cold as death. He wore only one gun and ironically it was a Colt Peacemaker. Apparently, the man thought one was enough for him to get the job done.

Of Bodine, he knew nothing. He knew only what he observed and he thought Bodine the worst of a bad lot. Any man who would look at a girl like that—!

The harsh crack of a bullet shattered the silence. Jim was yanked back to the present with a hard jolt. He swore under his breath. He was too late!

Jim could hear a rushing of feet and voices raised in shock. A second bullet rang out almost immediately. A woman screamed . . . there was a popping sound and a man groaned. The groan dwindled to a whimper. Then it was silent.

Jim raced over the hard-packed sand to the opening in the rocks.

Bodine's fingers bit cruelly into the white-faced girl's wrist as he pushed his face into hers.

"Turn your back on me, will ya?" He loomed even closer. Struggling to free herself, Julie stumbled backwards tripping over her entangling skirts. The black eyes held no mercy and she shrank inside at what she saw in them. Her knees were buckling as Bodine's fist moved to strike. For a fleeting instant Julie glimpsed Duncan's grinning face over his shoulder.

"Smack her one, Lyle!" he baited him.

"I don't think ya ought to hit a girl. It ain't right," Shorty muttered uneasily. "Even though she did shoot me."

Coolee stood by, a queer gleam lighting his flat, colorless eyes. He didn't seem to object. The point of his tongue touched his lips as he waited for Bodine's fist to crash into that puling face. Julie could do nothing but squeeze her eyes shut and wait.

"Let the girl go—now!"

The order rang in the taut air. For a second everyone froze. Julie's eyes flew open. A little cry escaped her lips. Who had uttered those words?

"What the hell?" Bodine grated out and swung his head sideways. Startled now, Coolee and Duncan straightened up and spun around. Too late they saw the stranger standing there in the opening, feet planted apart, his Winchester trained on them.

Grouped together the way they were, it would be an easy

kill. As they all stared in angered distraction the rifle barrel moved a fraction and leveled on Bodine's chest.

"Let her go!" the voice rapped out again.

Bodine's release of the girl was sudden and she slipped to her knees. Lightning quick, Bodine's hand lowered to gun level. A bullet whipped past his head and shattered a slab of stone.

"Don't even think about pullin' on me! Now get your hands up!"

Unwillingly, Bodine raised his hands.

Coolee didn't move, eyeing the intruder insolently.

"Now Coolee! Or the next shot won't miss!" The words were ground out.

For a second Coolee's eyes blinked as the stranger used his name. So he knew about him, did he? His reputation had preceeded him. Coolee liked that. Grinning like a wolf, Coolee slowly, very slowly raised his hands.

As they stood still, all four squinted into the dark trying to see the man behind the gun. It seemed he could see them as clear as day with the firelight revealing them and their every move. Annoyingly, they couldn't see him. Nothing of the man was visible except the twin guns riding his hips, the worn jeans and boots—nothing to give away his identity. The voice was hard and capable. Where the shadows were less dense they could just make out the shape of his head, the wide shoulders, the powerful, lean body of a fighting man—tough and rugged. Another thing they caught in the tone of his voice was that he wouldn't give a damn about gunning them all down if someone made a wrong move.

Shorty impatiently asked, "Who are you, mister?"

Jim ignored the question. "Unbuckle your gunbelts with your left hand, then kick them over here. And no tricks. I can bring you all down in a split second!"

Somehow they didn't doubt him as they did as he ordered. It was as Jim reached down for the belts that the firelight caught his features for an instant. Coolee stared, trying to remember. There was something about him . . .

"Get your things together, miss. You're comin' with me." It was a terse order. Julie had been staring open-mouthed ever since the man entered the camp. Now she could scarcely believe her ears. He was taking her with him, away from this horrible death scene. She nodded quickly. It took her only a second to grab up her carpetbag and the money belt Duncan still clutched in his hand. She gave it a hard, angry tug and he was forced to let it go.

"Aw, hell," he muttered as he encountered her accusing eyes.

Julie saw the derringer lying at Bodine's feet where it had slipped from her fingers during the struggle. Poised in front of him, she looked quickly into his ruthless face and paused. His mood was ugly. Dark eyes narrowed to pinpoints of anger and frustrated desire as he glared back at her. She needed that gun!

Leaning forward an inch, he ground out for her ears only, "You little—!"

Lunging down quickly, Julie snatched up the gun and hurried to the safety of the stranger. Before Jim could start backing away, Coolee spoke up.

"Wait a minute! I know you! You're the man who killed Ralph Garvey. You're Jim Wyatt. What are you doin' out of prison?"

Jim heard the girl close at his side catch her breath, suddenly looking up at him as if seeing him in a different light. He knew she was wondering if she were jumping from the frying pan into the fire. There was no time for explanations now even if he had wanted to give any in front of these outlaws. He shoved her behind him, out of his line of fire. She moved reluctantly.

"Turn around all of you!" he ordered.

"Why? So you can shoot us all in the back like you did to Garvey?" Coolee taunted. He looked at the girl, pleased, when he saw a touch of fear mount her face at his deliberate words. They were not enough, however, to stop her from throwing in her lot with the stranger. The unknown was not as bad as them. She knew what she'd receive from the Bodine gang. At least she had a chance with this man. Julie took a few steps away then waited, uncertain what she was supposed to do.

Jim didn't flinch at Coolee's words as he once had done. He knew he was innocent and one of these days he'd be able to prove it—but not to these men. Considering who they were, it just wasn't worth it.

"That's right, Coolee, I'd shoot you! Front, back, any which way you want it just ask me and I'll oblige! You're the expert when it comes to shootin' innocent people." The cool green eyes flickered over to Carter's body. "You sound mighty self-righteous for a killer who just gunned down an unarmed man!" Jim gave him his own brand of smile. "Reckon they'll come after you with a rope for that."

Coolee's face darkened with fury. Before, he had wanted to push this man to the edge so he would draw on him. Now it was Coolee who hesitated. He could still go for his rifle or pull his knife but he didn't. Something held him back. The stranger was primed for action. He was too edgy, too confident, too willing to shoot it out and let the devil decide the outcome. Coolee stopped himself from going for a weapon. The stranger's eyes noted the small action. It just made Coolee angrier. Right away he glanced at his comrades, but they seemed in no hurry to back him up.

Jim started moving off, back into the shadows. "Head for the horses," he whispered to the girl. Julie didn't take long to decide. In an instant she was running through the rocks and across the sagebrush flat.

As the girl left, the men surged forward. Jim let off two shots right in the middle of them. The time it took for them to jump away, Jim was already gone, following the girl into the night.

"C'mon!" Coolee made a grab for his rifle and ran to the opening where Jim had disappeared. Once away from the fire he could see nothing in the dark. At a slight noise he lifted his rifle to make a wild shot in that direction. Immediately, a bullet screamed out of nowhere ripping a groove across the stock of Coolee's rifle. As the bullet scorched his hand, he dropped it with a yelp and swore harshly.

The other three vaulted behind the rocks as the shots smashed into their midst. When they saw that Coolee was still standing, they came out cautiously. Pounding hooves met their ears and a few more gunshots that sounded several hundred feet away.

"What the hell's he shootin' at now?" Bodine yelled, puzzled. For precious seconds they stood there listening.

They all realized at the same time that there were more than two horses riding off.

"The stage horses!" Shorty groaned out loud. Sure enough, the remaining three horses were off and running.

In a flurry of curses and rushing footsteps, the outlaws ran into the open waving their hats into the air as two of the horses veered toward them. This served only to scare them off as a string of coarse words floated after them. For an hour the men tried to chase them down, but every time they came near the horses took off.

At last Bodine called for a halt. He was in a foul mood and everyone was aware of it. He'd lost the money, he'd lost that girl, and now those damned horses were giving him grief.

When they got back to the camp, Bodine had a slug of cold coffee which further exacerbated his mood. The other men were quiet. Even Coolee knew when it was not politic to annoy Bodine in this black humor.

After a while Duncan spoke, "Well, Lyle, what next?"

"Next? Next we track those two down and put a bullet in both of them. Tomorrow at first light we go after them horses. They'll be lookin' for water then."

"Where do you reckon Wyatt is headed?" Duncan wanted to know.

"How the hell should I know? Damned if I know anything about him. He has the girl and one of them will leave some kind of tracks."

"We've got to get them before they talk to anybody," Coolee warned, almost calmly now.

"We'll get them," Bodine promised. "They can't get far.

That girl will slow him down plenty." He seemed pleased at this. "Lots of open spaces to get him in this country."

"What about me?" Shorty sat up. Duncan had tied an old shirt around his brother's wound to stop the bleeding. It wasn't doing much good. Shorty was looking pale and weak.

"What about you?" Bodine asked with distaste. Another aggravation to deal with, he decided.

"I . . . need . . . a doctor."

"Well, don't look at me! Think I'm gonna waste time finding you a doctor? You ride with us or you stay—them are your choices." Bodine looked hard at the wounded man. Shorty moved uneasily.

"He'll probably be better tomorrow," Duncan spoke up. "The bleedin' will stop by then and Shorty can come with us." He spoke with confidence although Shorty looked worried. He was feeling worse by the minute.

Bodine gave a curt nod. He didn't believe it at all. He was leaving tomorrow to get those two and he didn't intend to be slowed down by anyone—anyone! He gave Shorty a sharp look before rolling up in his blanket.

Perched on one of the stagecoach horses, Julie followed her rescuer blindly. He led her through gorges, across cool streams, and over rocky piles. They seemed to crisscross back and forth until Julie wasn't even sure in which direction they were headed anymore. Only the gray light from the half-formed moon partially illuminated the country. Up ahead of her, Jim's dark form moved steadily onward. All she could see of him was the tall, broad-shouldered outline and occasional chiseled profile as he turned his head to listen or look at the land. After a while she lost interest even in that. She was physically and emotionally exhausted.

Seeing her uncle murdered right in front of her eyes without warning had left her shocked and still going over it in her mind with disbelief. Evil had intruded into her quiet world. She'd seen her share of grief and sorrow when her parents had died and their money vanished, but this was different.

Uncle John had been marked for death as soon as Bodine had seen that money belt. That was all it had taken: One greedy, grasping look and Uncle John's fate had been decided. Hers as well, if it came to that. Her job now was to try to gauge what kind of man had saved her. His name was Jim Wyatt and he had shot a man in the back. At least, he had not denied it. He had been in prison. He had also saved her life. That was enough for now.

Onward they went while the weak moon rose and traveled along with them. Julie no longer had the strength to speculate about where they were going or what would happen when they got there. It was all she could do just to hang onto the horse and keep plodding ahead in Jim's wake.

In the morning's early hours, he found a place to stop. Past a creek was a small cave the wind had ripped out of stone. As Jim unsaddled his horse he could see that Julie had fallen asleep again. Quickly he spread out a ground sheet and then lifted her down. When her feet touched the dirt she came groggily awake.

"Why did we stop? Are they coming?" Half asleep she might be yet her fingers went unerringly to her derringer.

Grasping it in her hand, she looked about her. Nothing seemed familiar.

"No, Miss Carter, you don't need that derringer yet. We're just stopping to take a few hours' rest. You look like you need it and I know I do."

"I can go on," she insisted, swaying on her feet.

"Sure you can," he said easily, steadying her as he led her to the cave. He took out his blanket and spread it on the ground for her. "You wrap yourself up in that and get some sleep."

"Where are you going to sleep?" she frowned, trying to think as the sleep pulled at her consciousness.

"I'll watch the trail for a while."

Julie sat down and pulled the blanket around her. She ought to stay up and watch the trail with him. Four eyes were better that two and she really didn't know Jim at all. She would just lay here quietly, keeping an eye on both him and the trail. Clutching her gun under the blanket, Julie prepared to do just that. Two minutes later as Jim shrugged into his jacket, she was already asleep.

Jim sat alone in the coldness, pulling his collar up around his ears. He knew that come morning, Bodine and his men would be after him and the girl like a passel of banshees. Then the fun would really begin.

Twice the small sounds of the night awakened the girl. Each time, she opened her eyes to see Jim in profile, stoically keeping guard over their camp. How could he keep going without sleep?

Julie would have been surprised to know that Jim had managed to catch a few hours of light sleep, but a few hours was all he could spare either of them. Before the sun's rays blasted their way above the skyline, they were mounted up with several miles behind them and a long way to go.

Although she had been able to sleep, Julie still found her fragile strength ebbing away with each mile. Parts of the country were quite pretty with groves of trees, streams, and even fields of flowers. Julie saw none of it.

Few words passed between them. Both were busy with their own thoughts. They put in a grueling day before Jim finally called a halt in a stand of poplars. On the horizon the sun was beginning to dip slowly in the orange sky. As the intense rays lessened, a slight breeze played across the plains.

Jim helped Julie down and she stretched her cramped muscles. While Jim watered the horses, she came up to him. It amazed her that Jim's mind was alert and his eyes as keen as ever, even after endless hours in the saddle. He gave her a slight smile and patted the horses as they drank.

"Do you think . . . do you think we've lost them, Mr. Wyatt?" she asked, running her hand down the horse's neck. Her hand touched his and she moved it away.

"No." His tone was unequivocal.

At once Julie's spirits dropped. "But we haven't seen them all this time! I know you've been looking and so have I."

"Ma'am, they want that money. They're not going to give up so easy. Besides"—he watched her consideringly as if weighing up how much character she possessed—"they've done murder. And we've both witnessed it. They'll be after us for that as well."

Her face went white. "You mean they *have* to kill us?"

"That's the way I figure it, ma'am." His voice was gentle. "If we can outrun them we'll have a chance; if not—"

"If not . . . what?"

"We'll have to fight them where they find us. So we have to make sure they find us in a place we can defend." Their eyes met for a long while before Julie was forced to turn away from the intensity in them. She dipped her hand into her pocket to feel the derringer again. It seemed to give her great comfort. As for Jim he didn't feel safe even with his Winchester, two pistols and a hundred rounds of ammunition. If they ran into the Bodine gang he'd have his work cut out for him.

Jim didn't impart his thoughts to the pretty girl in front of him. After the long ride she was on edge, exhausted and high–strung. She couldn't take any more bad news just now. It was enough that he had honestly told her the facts. You didn't have to spell things out for Julie. A sober warning was sufficient. Even now she was busy scanning the hills behind them, something Jim had already done.

How different she was from Anne! Anne was soft and helpless. She would expect to be protected while doing nothing to help herself. By contrast, Julie was determined to do her share. Jim liked Julie very much. He admired people who didn't quit.

After their meal, Jim turned in while Julie insisted on keeping watch.

With the darkness and only her morbid thoughts to keep her company, doubts about her rescuer's intentions began to loom in her mind. What if he wanted the money himself? What if he wanted—she forced herself to finish the question—her? How was she to know if he wasn't as bad a lot as the Bodine gang? She only had his word that they were following. Perhaps they'd given up. Jim and she had covered a good many miles. How could the others possibly find them in this churning, desolate land?

She turned to try and pry behind his seemingly honest face to divine his real thoughts. Unfortunately, his face gave away nothing. It was relaxed and almost boyish in repose. If there were any evil impulses underneath his candid exterior, they were not evident to her. For a second she toyed with the idea of taking off by herself, but she knew she wouldn't get very far. Julie had no idea where she was nor how she could go about finding the nearest town. At last she decided the best thing to do was to bide her time. She'd go along with this Wyatt person, but if he tried to take her money she knew exactly what to do. Julie took a firmer grip on the gun and looked again at him sleeping.

"Thinkin' of leaving, miss? I wouldn't if I were you. Not with those four men out there some place," Jim drawled, still with his eyes shut.

Julie jumped with surprise, then turned pink. She hadn't realized he had felt her prying eyes studying him so carefully. "I was not thinking of leaving," she stammered. "I was merely taking stock of the situation."

"And what did you come up with, ma'am?" He opened his own and turned his head towards her. Stretching a little, he clasped his hands behind his head and leaned back comfortably.

"I have few options," Julie admitted ruefully.

"That's right, miss, you do. And I'm one of them. The best one," he admitted modestly. "Besides, I promised

Bud Harris I'd take care of you. He was mighty particular about making me promise that."

"Bud Harris? The stage driver? What do you mean? I thought he was killed?"

In as few words as possible he explained what had happened.

"I'm glad he's not dead." He had been a courteous old man and tried to warn her about Bodine. "Do you think he's all right?"

"Sure, he's a tough old coot. The authorities will go lookin' for him and bring him to town. He's probably layin' in a soft bed right now, wolfing down hot cakes and pretending to be sick." There was a pause. "Sure could go for some flapjacks myself just about now."

Julie could too, but all she could say was, "So you only helped me because he told you to do it?" She was a little deflated.

He suppressed a smile. "Reckon I would have thought of it myself. Even though you are mighty handy with a gun, I couldn't see you handling the Bodine gang all by your lonesome. I wonder, now, if you have the stamina to see this through?"

"I certainly do!" she replied, stung.

"That's good."

This time she saw his grin and refused to continue the conversation, clamping her lips shut. Jim closed his eyes again, still grinning. He could pretty much guess what she was imagining concerning him and her money, and it amused him. He heard a slight rustle and knew she was feeling for her derringer. He let out his breath and started to doze.

*V. S. Meszaros*

Before he fell asleep Anne crept into Jim's mind again. She had occupied that place for a whole year. It was hard to break the habit. Anne was all blond-haired, blue-eyed sweetness. She always needed a man to lean on. Jim turned over and yanked his blanket over his shoulders from the cold night air. He dropped off to sleep with Anne's gently smiling face fading away.

## Chapter Three

Julie and Jim reined in their horses and sat shoulder to shoulder, looking down at the sagebrush rangeland spread wide before them.

It was a vast space, open and barren, that stretched out until it ran into the mountains far off. The mountains hunched there in sharp chains as if they had cut through the earth thousands of years ago to take their rightful place in this wild, untamed country. Massive white thunderheads crowded above their peaks contrasting with the sky's blue brilliance. Even at this distance there was muted murmuring as lightning cracked over the peaks throwing its white light down in bursts of anger. But while the storm raged in those distant heights the plain below remained quiet and untouched. It was a savage, beautiful land. Some found it unrelieving and austere. Jim Wyatt loved it. He even loved the loneliness.

He glanced at Julie quietly sitting her horse. It was

difficult to determine what she was thinking. Was she see-ing its beauty or was she hating it because of the turn of events that now left her at its mercy?

Anne Garvey hadn't found pleasure in the land or the ranch. She preferred to concentrate her attention on her home. Her father, Ralph Garvey, had made it very com-fortable, sending back East for its rich furnishings, want-ing to please his only child.

Jim's own house was built on more modest lines for room to expand in case he had a family. It just occurred to him now that Anne would never have wanted to move to his home when they married. Well, that was one problem Jim would never have to face. Considering that Anne had not contacted him since his arrest, he was fairly safe in as-suming that the engagement was at an end. She had prob-ably started to build a future with March Newton.

Jim's thoughts harked back to when Newton had first come to Dautry. He had ridden in four years ago, took a look around and liked what he saw. He had bought him-self a piece of land and put his cattle on it. At first, people were glad to see a new neighbor. Gladness soon turned to fear.

Not content with what he had, he proceeded to devour all the land around him. He was not a fair man, he was a greedy man. He told the small landowners in no uncertain terms that they could take his price or get out. Many of them went. When a man has a family, he can't afford to make too many enemies, especially of Newton's ilk.

Next, Newton had turned his eyes on Jim's land. Jim had a nice beginning of a herd and had carefully chosen land that had water on it all year round. Higher up in the fertile hills he had planted crops to feed his cattle in winter. Newton appreciated the setup and decided he wanted it for himself. He had made Jim a ridiculously low offer which Jim firmly refused.

He did what Jim expected him to do: He started riding him. But Jim was ready. When Newton's men tried to drive off his cattle, they got themselves shot up. When they tried to destroy his crops, he was waiting with an ambush.

Newton was irate. He was used to being the winner. Those small landowners like Jim were dirt under his feet. If they didn't have the money and acres to match his, they simply didn't deserve to exist. It infuriated him that Jim wouldn't budge.

Such hostilities might have turned into an all-out war if Ralph Garvey hadn't intervened. He gave Newton to understand that Jim's enemies were his enemies. For the time being, Newton backed down. If Newton had respect for anyone, it was old man Garvey. So Newton sat back and waited for his chance. He was still determined to get Jim's ranch. It was not that he particularly wanted it just then, but he wanted to grind Jim into the ground and humiliate him, especially in front of his girl, Anne Garvey.

That was another reason for Newton to hate Jim and listen to Ralph: He wanted Anne for his own. She was beautiful and blond and had thousands of acres attached to her. So what did Anne think of it all? It had annoyed Jim that, while she professed her love for him, she still seemed to admire Newton. Ralph didn't like Newton at all, though he was civil enough to to him. He wanted to see his only daughter engaged to Jim.

Then one black day Ralph was found dead with a bullet

in his back. Jim had come across the body. The old man lay facedown in the dirt. He must have known his killer as a friend for him to turn his back to him the way he did. Ralph had been a savvy man and kept his gun handy. He wouldn't have shown his back to someone he didn't know or trust.

There was something else peculiar about the killing: Ralph hadn't drawn his gun. It was still in his holster with no bullets fired. It looked as if he hadn't even attempted to draw, so he was unaware of any danger when he was shot.

When the sheriff rode out to examine the murder scene, he found only Jim's footprints. That was not unusual since there was a lot of caprock around where a person could step and leave no sign. Not a mile from where Ralph lay, the sheriff found twelve steers with their brands crudely worked over from the Garvey brand to the Flying W brand. The cattle were hidden in a draw on Jim's land.

The sheriff had been suspicious and in no hurry to arrest Jim. However, Newton and his men at once had demanded an arrest. Afraid that there would be a lynching, the sheriff had jailed Jim for cattle rustling. Newton was mad clean through and demanded Jim be tried for murder and hanged to the nearest tree, preferably of his own choosing. He even offered to skip the trial and go right to the hanging. The sheriff had refused to surrender his prisoner and put a bullet into the hide of one of the rancher's men when he tried to take matters into his own hands.

Anne hadn't come near Jim. She hadn't even visited him in jail before the trial to ask him what had happened. It was as if she had already judged him and found him guilty. Jim would sometimes see her from the jail window, walking about with Newton. Easy to see who had influenced her.

Laban, Jim's foreman, wanted to help him escape. "Easiest thing in the world," he assured Jim. "They're bringing in a herd of cattle at the end of the week. Everyone in town will be drinkin'."

"No." Jim's mouth had tightened. "That would be like admitting I did it—and I didn't!"

On the day of the trial, the jury was packed with Newton's men. He had seen to that. Newton was very careful to point out to the good citizens of Dautry that anyone who sat on the jury and found Jim Wyatt innocent of murder would, alas, become his enemy. Everyone knew what that meant. They wanted to do the honest thing, but they were afraid to accept the responsibility of serving as juror.

Witnesses were likewise discouraged from coming forward to testify on Jim's behalf. Newton's men went personally to visit each witness. It was astonishing how many people declined to take the stand after that.

In the end, ten of the twelve jurors selected had been Newton's paid men, one was a drunk they hustled off a passing stage, and another was a gunslinger who had been hired by Newton right before the so-called trial began.

It was no surprise to anyone when the jury found Jim guilty of murder and cattle rustling. The drinks supplied to the jury while they debated Jim's innocence had been thoughtfully provided by Newton as a gesture of his commitment to his civic duty.

The judge, irate at Newton's manipulation of the legal system, refused to accept the verdict since Jim wasn't being tried for murder. Instead, he sentenced him to one year in prison for cattle rustling only—the most lenient sentence he could hand down. The judge hated doing even that much.

Hearing this, an infuriated Newton whipped his men into a frenzy and tried to storm the jail, but the sheriff had been clever. He had smuggled Jim away in the stagecoach that was just pulling out. Before anyone realized Jim wasn't there, it was too late to do anything about it.

Three days later, the sheriff was found shot to death in a ditch on the outskirts of Dautry. No one dared ask who did it.

With Jim and Ralph both out of the way, Newton launched a campaign against Laban Kettering and the Flying W. Several of Newton's men tried to go calling and all of them ended up regretting it—that is, the ones who lived. It soon got around that he would shoot anyone who stepped onto the ranch.

Even a parson, Brother Arvel, had been dispatched with a bullet in his hat when he tried to reason with him, urging brother Laban to give himself up. The self-proclaimed parson, who was a well-known drunk in other parts of the country, assured Newton that the Almighty would punish brother Laban in his own good time but this evidently was not the time. He departed for more friendly climes less saturated with flying bullets.

For a whole year Newton had been frustrated at every turn in his attempts to acquire Jim's ranch. The last straw came when Laban put a few Shoshone bucks on the payroll to herd cattle. Unlike the other hired hands, these boys weren't hesitant about going after trespassers with a vengeance. They were disappointed when Newton's men began to give the ranch a wide berth.

About Anne, Laban told Jim little. She was in good health and had moved into town after her father's death. Newton ran both spreads now. She wouldn't have allowed that if there wasn't an understanding between them, Jim figured. He did not doubt that Laban had tried to smooth things over between them. He wouldn't have been able to resist. Apparently, he had been unsuccessful.

Jim shrugged away these memories impatiently. Anne could do what she wanted. His mouth tightened—and so could he. If that meant unmasking the man she now loved as a murderer, then he would do it.

A touch on his arm brought him out of his meditations. He found Julie watching him with concern.

"May we stop for a while?" she asked shyly.

"Sure." He smiled agreeably.

As he got a meal going, Jim watched as Julie gathered firewood and took out the utensils. She was calm now, as if she had studied the situation and accepted it.

Impossible to believe that such a desirable girl was still unmarried. Next to Anne's blond features, Julie's wild rose beauty stood out. Even the tragedy and the hardships of the last few days couldn't dim it. Her lovely face also held strength of character. She had followed Jim every inch of the way and hadn't even complained. He smiled slightly. The wind and the sun filled her hair with grit and turned her pretty suit dusty, but she still clung to her poise. As he watched her, he saw Julie bend hesitatingly over a log to move it into the shade.

"Let me do that." With alacrity, Jim got up from the fire and pulled it into a better position for her to sit on.

"Thank you," she said gratefully, sitting down on the comfortable log. He didn't notice that she was looking consideringly at his bare head while he leaned down. Nor was he aware that she was fingering her derringer again as if she were making up her mind about something. Turning his back to her, he knelt down by the fire.

In fact, Julie was observing him closely. If Jim had looked up at that instant, he might have been uneasy as to just how closely. He would have also noticed that she had, unhappily, decided upon a course of action. This was reflected in her very expressive face. She liked Jim; she really did. However—she checked again to make sure her derringer was loaded—some things just had to be done. And done now.

When the meal was finished Jim handed her a plate of food and a cup of coffee.

"Thank you, Mr. Wyatt." Her voice held sorrow and a touch of guilt. Jim didn't notice. A man who knew more about women would have been suspicious.

Happy to have done his duty as a host, he sat himself down and started to eat. When he looked up, he saw Julie's dinner plate next to her on a rock along with the cup of coffee.

"Is there something wrong?" he asked, puzzled, at last seeing the look on her face.

"There is something wrong, Mr. Wyatt." As he watched, she took the derringer out of her pocket, placing it gently in her lap.

Jim's eyes sharpened. He watched the gun with the same

fascination one would a snake. Damn fool! he thought to himself. Caught with a plate in one hand and a fork in the other! Green eyes lifted to her face.

"Before we proceed any further I believe we should have a little discussion, don't you, Mr. Wyatt?"

Hell! There he was, caught flat-footed with no gun to hand! His face was grim as she smiled at him benignly.

What was she playing at?

Slowly, Jim lowered his plate to his knees. The bright eyes of the girl followed his hand with keen awareness as he set his utensils aside.

"Yes, Miss Carter? What would you like to talk about?"

"First of all, I want to know our destination." She was most polite and Jim tried to match that politeness.

"I was going to take you to my ranch if that's all right with you, of course." He raised one eyebrow. Julie considered this carefully.

"Why not the nearest town?"

"The nearest town is Dautry. Ten miles from my ranch. If I rode into there, every nickel-plated gun-for-hire would be taking shots at me."

"You're not well-liked, then, Mr. Wyatt?"

"Not by March Newton. He's—"

Jim paused to halt the flow of curses that rushed all too easily to his lips at the mention of Newton's name. "He's the big landowner around there."

"But it's more than that," she observed shrewdly. "Why would he employ men to kill you?"

Jim told her everything. Why not? It was public knowledge. It was only a matter of time before the pretty

Easterner found out who her traveling companion was. Jim gave her the raw facts about his arrest and conviction. He didn't mention Anne.

Julie listened carefully, hearing the edge of bitterness in his voice. She accepted his story as the truth. After her unfortunate brush with the Bodine gang, she could readily believe that some men out here corrupted the law to benefit themselves.

"And who is this Ralph Garvey?"

"He owned a big spread about twice as large as Newton's."

"Who inherits this Mr. Garvey's land now that he's dead?" There was something here she didn't understand and was trying to find it out.

"His daughter, Anne," came his reply crisply. Julie noticed the change in his voice. Being a woman, she would. Her attention was caught.

"Did you know her well?"

"I was engaged to marry her," he returned shortly. Julie felt her stomach jolt a little although she didn't know why. It was probably fatigue.

"Is she pretty?" she couldn't resist asking.

Jim had to smile at her priorities. "I was engaged to her."

"That's no answer."

"Yes, Miss Carter, she was pretty. Probably still is. Blond hair, blue eyes, small and dainty—yes, she was very pretty. Some might even call her beautiful," he added with a touch of humor.

"I see." Julie did not smile back. Indeed, she didn't appear to receive this last little bit of information with overwhelming joy. Several times during the trip she had seen him staring off into the clouds, a soft, rueful look on his face. She knew he had been thinking of a woman—she could tell. So this was the explanation: Anne Garvey—beautiful, rich, and alone in the world. Julie decided she didn't like the name.

"Are you still engaged to her?" She had been quick to hear the past tense in his words.

"I seriously doubt it." He was honest. Even if he said it emotionlessly, she sensed the hurt and anger there.

"What happened?"

"Jail happened. After I was arrested, she didn't come near me."

"You mean she didn't even want to hear your side of the story?"

"Apparently she wasn't interested in it." Then he couldn't help adding, "She spent most of her time with March Newton."

"I see." And Julie did. The other man was moving in on Jim's territory. "Did she write to you?"

"She didn't write, she didn't telegraph, she didn't visit, and she didn't send me a cake for Christmas."

"Then you're well rid of her," Julie commented wisely. "What happened to your ranch while you were away?"

"Laban Kettering, my foreman, is running it for me—if he's still alive." Jim lapsed into silence which neither broke for a long time.

As Julie stared off into space, her hand resting lightly on the gun in her lap, Jim began eating. No use letting good beans and bacon go to waste.

While Jim ate his bacon Julie looked over at him, wondering if he had any evil intentions towards her. In the short time they had been together he had treated her with kindness and consideration. Nevertheless, there was still her money. Twelve thousand dollars was enough to tempt a saint and Julie was sure, for all Jim's gallantry, he was no saint. For a year he had been in prison. When he returned home, there might not be a ranch waiting for him. Her uncle's money could buy him a very nice place. She frowned at the direction her thoughts were taking her. She fervently hoped his plans weren't along that line.

As Jim looked up he caught Julie's fine eyes probing him, analyzing his story from all four corners. He finished his beans and bacon and took a long drink of coffee.

"Well, what's the verdict, Miss Carter?"

She flushed a little at the touch of sarcasm, but she believed she had earned it. She had been remarkably underhanded. Julie cleared her throat.

"I like you, Mr. Wyatt, and I'm very grateful to you for saving me. I don't know what I would have done if you hadn't arrived in time. Moreover, I don't believe you stole cattle or killed Ralph Garvey."

"That's on the plus side," he observed. "Do I still detect some hesitation?"

"I don't think you would hurt a lady. So I believe my person is safe. However, money is an entirely different matter. Although I almost trust you I feel it only fair to warn you that I still have my derringer." She waved it about in case he was blind. "And I will use it if anyone tries to harm me or take my money. I deplore using brute force but sometimes it's necessary."

"I was wondering when you'd get around to that derringer again." There was a hint of a smile in his deep voice. "I knew it was only a matter of time."

Somehow her derringer seemed to amuse him. Julie didn't know why. Shorty Reece hadn't been amused. As far as she could see it had done the job quite effectively.

"I find nothing to laugh about being shot with a derringer." Her manner was stiff. It was rather annoying that he wasn't the least bit afraid of her.

Suddenly he stood up, all six-feet-two of him. Julie leaned back a little, intimidated by his great height, especially as she still sat on her comfortable little log that didn't seem so very comfortable all at once. He covered the ten feet between them swiftly. Julie's heart quickened. She was bewildered by his intentions. In one fluid movement he was down on one knee in front of her. His eyes were level with hers now, and he was so close she could see the dark green flecks in their depths. Julie couldn't move. Her back was against a wall of rock. Her heart raced in sudden consternation.

"What—what are you doing?" Her voice quavered as she felt his knee brushing the twill of her skirt.

"A derringer is all right," he confided to her, "but if you really want to get the job done—" His hand went down to his hip and he yanked out the six-shooter. She looked at it, then she looked back up at him. His eyes glinted. For a second he held the revolver in his hand and twirled it about expertly.

"It's Duncan Reece's. The man may be a criminal, but he sure knows guns. Here. You take it." He held it out to her. A stray lock of brown hair fell over his bronzed forehead giving him a devilish air. "I guarantee if you'd have hit Shorty with this, it would have been a lot more to the point."

Indecisively, she looked into his face. She saw that beneath the small smile was a grim sort of truth. Tentatively, she touched the butt of the gun just to see if he really meant it. He did, even magnanimously offering her the bullets. She pulled her hand away hurriedly, shy again at his nearness.

"No, thank you. At least not right now. Maybe later." After a moment she added, "It's awfully heavy."

He unbuckled the gun belt from around his own narrow hips and slung it around her slim waist. She sat still in surprise at his sheer audacity. As he leaned down to tighten it, his wavy brown hair was only inches from her face.

"You may not have time to ask for it later if they come on us all at once." Fear doused her warm skin like icy water.

"I don't think I could actually kill a man," she admitted.

Jim's eyes widened in mock disbelief. "You were sure talkin' big a minute ago! And what about Bodine? I kind of got the feeling you were ready to send him to perdition back there. Too bad your aim wasn't better." He leaned his forearm across his knee but didn't move back.

"That was in the heat of the moment," she confessed. "Now, I just want to go to the law." She tried to lean farther away but there was no room.

"I'm the law out here, Miss Carter." Her expression was startled. "And so are you, and every other citizen who has some wrong done to them. Can't ride hundreds of miles to get justice. You have to take care of your own problems." He leaned forward and took her small chin between his thumb and forefinger. She could feel the calluses on his warm hand. She had heard that convicts worked on the rock piles. "Besides, I have a feeling that you won't be running if they attack. You've got spunk." Julie felt a little breathless. "I like that in a girl." He let go of her chin.

"I—thank you." Then, just in case he was trying to lull her suspicions, she added with inspiration, "I can shoot you with this just as well." Julie referred to the six-shooter.

"No, ma'am, you can shoot me even better. And you'll need to because I'm a hard man to kill," he told her almost confidentially. "Many have tried but few have succeeded." His voice was whimsical. "But you'd better wait until we get clear of the Bodine gang before you start taking aim at me. You'll need someone to take care of them for you."

At these close quarters she could see the web of laugh lines etched into his suntanned skin. She tried to avoid his direct gaze which was very direct indeed. She wouldn't be a woman if she hadn't recognized there was admiration in his look as well.

"I'll remember that," she replied distantly, her eyes sliding away from his.

"I know you will." Grinning, he stood up. Julie could breathe easier now. "Is there anything else?" he asked her.

Julie hesitated. "There is . . . just one more thing." She glanced up at him as he watched her narrowly. Slowly she picked up her plate and held it out to him. "Do you think you could warm up my beans again, Mr. Wyatt? They're all cold."

After the situation was straightened out to Julie's satisfaction, the meal continued in a much friendlier atmosphere. Contented now that everything had been explained to her, she bestowed a warm smile on her rescuer and helped him repack. The log was once more comfortable and she was reluctant to leave it. However, she now possessed two guns and this seemed to cheer her.

She was also feeling optimistic about their chances of survival. Jim was glad. He was not, however, as positive as he appeared but saw little advantage in frightening the girl unnecessarily.

For all his lighthearted talk a while ago Jim was worrying. Having both the girl and the money along was like perching on two kegs of dynamite. Either one was sufficient enticement to draw the unwanted attentions of men like Bodine. Together, Jim felt that the slightest wrong move on his part would be as a spark to tinder. He'd just have to hope he could either shake off or eliminate the four men who dogged his steps.

Jim glanced back but the trail was clear with nothing for miles. It didn't make him less vigilant. They were out there, all right. Bodine would not give up—not when there were easy pickings to be had. This was a perfect breeding ground for Bodine and his type. They roved around like wolves across this empty land prowling for victims. Sometimes they hunted alone. Other times, like now, they came together as a pack to attack their prey.

Jim had no doubt that it had been Bodine's idea to track and kill John Carter. As Jim had watched their camp below, he had seen how Bodine took command. How the others, even the savage loner Ed Coolee, had let him call the shots. It would be like him to do something as bold as disable the stage, kill the driver, then do away with the other passengers.

It must have left a bitter taste in his mouth to find that everything had gone as planned except that now he had no girl, no money, and two witnesses had slipped through his fingers. There would be no quit in him after that. Bodine had to find him and Miss Carter before they could tell anyone what had really happened. Bodine also wanted the girl.

Shorty Reece was down with a bullet in him and Jim had no way of knowing how badly hurt he was. Still, Jim was not counting him out. Besides, he had his brother to help him.

Duncan was known to possess a real mean streak. He had not been particularly interested in Miss Carter, but he had been in the golden coins John Carter plunked down. He'd killed for a few dollars, how much more would he do for twelve thousand? Jim didn't know, but he didn't think Duncan would hesitate killing a woman.

All of them wanted the money belt and Bodine wanted the girl as well. Jim's mind shifted to Coolee, who had a reputation for being rough on women. Perhaps he wanted the girl, too, yet Jim figured he'd never let on to Bodine. When the time came he might just try and take her and have it out with Bodine. But a bigger problem loomed for the outlaws and it dealt with the horses.

Jim assumed they had caught the rest of the team. Hunting them down would detain them a bit, but not as much as Jim would have liked. Even so, that left three horses and four men. To him the math would be simple: Someone had to go. It certainly wouldn't be Bodine or Coolee. Shorty was wounded. Shorty couldn't defend himself. Jim wondered when they'd get rid of him.

Duncan? Would he help his brother or stand up for him? Jim remembered how he chuckled when Julie had risked a shot at Bodine. What was going through his mind then? One less man to share the pot? Would he think the same about his brother?

As he wiped the sweat from his forehead with his sleeve, Jim's keen eyes skimmed over the plains stretching to west. It was necessary to leave the sagebrush flats as soon as possible and move into higher elevations. Up ahead were some hills and brush canyons that Jim knew well. One canyon in particular came to mind. He'd like to show that canyon to Bodine and Coolee. He grinned to himself. He had a feeling they'd appreciate it—if they lived long enough inside of it.

A plan was forming in his mind. The idea of the Bodine gang traipsing through that particular canyon appealed to him. It appealed to him a lot!

## Chapter Four

Heddy Gibson was lying flat on her stomach in waist-high grasses, her thoughts closed off to everything but the deer delicately nibbling on a bush not one hundred yards off. She had seen it fifteen minutes ago as it topped the slight rise. Hovering there, silhouetted against the sky, it had looked around suspiciously before coming closer. Heddy smiled to herself. She had not moved a muscle since then, knowing it was only a matter of time until it ambled over to the lush grasses nearby.

Very slowly she lifted her rifle to her shoulder and sighted down the length of barrel. Flicking a long strand of brown hair behind her ear, she seriously contemplated the shot she was about to make. The deer was sure to come into easy range in just a few more minutes now. She could wait. Heddy was a patient girl. She was too patient, her brother had derided her.

"I can get it first time," he had bragged. "By the time

you get around to pullin' that trigger, I could dance a reel with all the girls around here!" It was an exaggeration of course. But then she was not, she generously admitted, as good a shot as Joss or her father. But *she* was here now, not Joss, and sometimes being patient paid off. Like today. All morning she'd been searching for sign of game. Tired of not finding anything, Heddy had plunked herself down atop this low bluff and waited. Her wait had been rewarded. Tonight Ma would have fresh meat for the supper table, the first in over a week since Pa was down with the fever and Joss had a broken leg.

Heddy shifted slightly, for her arm was stiff from being held in one position. A little closer . . . come on, she silently urged the deer along.

The slow minutes ticked by. The ground's warmth and the sun on her back lulled her. Hugging to the gentle contours of land all around her, a slight breeze passed over the grasses with a soft rustle. A small smile tugging at her lips at what her brother would say, she closed one eye and eased back on the trigger.

Suddenly the deer's head came up and it braced itself, frozen to the spot. For a long minute it stood poised, staring in her direction.

Should she risk a shot now? The deer just might take off at the least motion. If she didn't, that would be a whole morning wasted and they needed meat so desperately. Once again she squinted down the barrel, her finger hesitating on the trigger.

All senses were intent on the shot as she waited for the right moment. If it were a few yards closer she would be sure of hitting it.

Suddenly the deer bolted. The animal bounded off over a slight swell directly in front of her and vanished. Heddy made a small moan of frustration. She should have risked the shot—she should have!

For a long minute she remained in that position, the gun held rigid against her shoulder. All at once before her startled brown eyes, a gloved hand came out of nowhere and quickly closed over her rifle. The hard body of a man pressed itself next to her, partially covering hers. Immediately the other hand shot around her head clamping her mouth shut, and pulling her close in a smothering hold. Heddy's first instinct was to scream. At the inspiration of breath a masculine voice whispered urgently in her ear, "Quiet! Indians! Don't shoot!" Her body went stiff in that iron grasp.

Heddy's eyes flicked around and saw nothing. It was a trick! At once she started to squirm and struggle to break loose from the man's hold. It didn't work so she bit his hand. He let go of her with a muffled cry of pain.

"Stay still, you little wildcat! You'll get us both killed." It sounded like a young voice, but she couldn't see his face. She craned her head sideways and made out only a sun-bleached shirt sleeve.

"I don't see anything, now let me go!" she hissed. Instead of releasing her, he clamped his hand over her mouth again, even tighter.

"Listen!" he ordered. She stopped fighting and held still.

She thought she heard a noise and immediately became very quiet. There was something moving out there, but the sound was barely discernible, so vague that she began to doubt she was even hearing it. While she listened with all of her attention, the man took the rifle from her slackened grip. Gradually she became aware of a slight tremor in the ground beneath her. The hair on her head prickled a warning.

A flock of quail exploded from the brush. Her body jumped with shock from the sudden roar of wings so near. Worried now, her anxious eyes restlessly scoured the land in front of her but she saw nothing—only grass and sky.

Then came a silence that was utter and complete. The feeling of menace was so thick it could be cut with a knife. Her ears perked up as she strained to hear something, anything, some indication of what was happening.

There was that swishing noise again like the wind rippling across a grassy expanse, except the rustling sound was roaming closer now, growing louder as it came. She knew that sound. It wasn't the wind at all. It was the whispering sound horses make when they are being walked through tall grasses—a great many horses.

"Oh no . . ." she murmured against the hand. She was breathing fast now, her eyes growing wide.

She stared at the small hill to the left from where the sound was coming. That's where they would first appear. She could feel it in the pit of her stomach.

Sure enough, at the very place where she was watching so fearfully, an Indian appeared. Then another. Then another. The three riders crested the hill and stopped. Unhurriedly, their eyes prowled over the vast land before them. Heddy flattened down instinctively, pressing her cheek to the grass. She stopped breathing. The man at her side yanked off his hat and covered the glinting metal of the rifle with his arm.

The Indians sat there a long while. At last satisfied, they nudged their ponies forward at a sedate pace. Heddy let out her breath. They had not been seen—so far!

A whole column of warriors swung into view behind them. Slowly, deliberately, they approached, their battle line stretching out over the broken terrain. In a matter of minutes the small plain was alive with them. Heddy became aware of the stranger's hand at her back keeping her down. No doubt he had felt her fear and was afraid she'd try to run.

Some forty Cheyenne bucks were there, mounted on their best war ponies, arrayed on the plain before Heddy's terrified eyes. The ponies moved along kicking up clouds of dust that clung close around their feet. Forty pairs of eyes roved in different directions searching for some diversion. Heddy closed her eyes as one young buck's gaze came back to the low bluff.

"Don't move," the man's voice warned. Her reply was to freeze in place. The buck took one more look then moved on. Others took his place. The pounding of unshod hoofs grew thunderous, shaking the earth as the moving line of warriors rode directly at the place of concealment. So close were they that when she opened her eyes she could see the warriors dressed in their battle regalia, colored beads adorning their necks, hatchet features streaked with paint. Leather creaked, bridles rattled, a horse shied and stamped its feet. Brash sunlight reflected off lance points and brass tacks studding their rifle stocks.

On they came and the earth thundered under them. Even the leaves on the bushes were shaking crazily about.

"They're going to find us! They're coming!" she

breathed. In a state of panic she grabbed the man's arm and squeezed it tightly. Now she could have run like a jack rabbit except it wouldn't do any good. If she broke cover now, they'd run her down and kill her!

They were almost upon them. The solid, protective chest pressing against her shoulder was her only cover. She tried to burrow her slim body under his.

"Be still." His lips were pressed to her ear.

Heddy's eyes stung from the dust as she stared, mesmerized. It clogged her throat and she almost choked.

Through a dust cloud she saw an Indian level his gaze upwards where they hid. Just then, hands that were strong and capable silently took her rifle and lifted the barrel slightly. It poked through the sparse ground cover. The man would shoot if the buck raised the alarm.

Heddy was sure the warrior could see them there behind the wisp of brush. For one breathless second she thought their eyes met. The fierce, black gaze seemed to penetrate dust and brush, and drill into her brain.

Then she remembered what her pa had told her: If you look at an Injun too long, he'll feel your presence. She squeezed her lids shut so as not to draw his attention. When she looked again, the buck was staring straight ahead once more.

A war whoop split the air and Heddy's eyes flew wide. Miraculously, the line of warriors suddenly wheeled their ponies at a right angle carrying them away from the low bluff upon which they hid.

Away they rode like cavalry on a parade ground. Eyes straight ahead, they never looked back. The column mounted a slight land swell then disappeared where the land features dipped down into a dry wash. Soon they were gone from sight and the accompanying sounds became muffled with distance. All was quiet again. The teeming plain was now empty. The ground–hovering dust cloud slowly dissipated and the air was clear once more.

Heddy stared at the plain for several long seconds. She hugged the ground tensely, her heart beating like a war drum in her chest. She let out her pent-up breath slowly.

She was alive! Breathing deeply of the clean air, she went limp with relief. The steel grip around her loosened. She trembled a little as she realized how close to death she had come. If the stranger had not stopped her when he had . . .

Heddy turned her head to see who her rescuer was. She was startled to see that he was not much older than her own seventeen years. His hair was light brown and his gray eyes studied his surroundings carefully to assure himself the Indians were really gone before he looked down at her. Although he was young, an air of seriousness sat upon his shoulders. His mouth was much too firm, like someone who had responsibilities thrust upon him at an early age. Joss was more carefree, almost arrogant. This young man seemed older and more reliable than her brother who was five and twenty.

"Thank you," she swallowed hard. "I almost—I was going to—"

"I know. I saw you." His voice was gentle and kindly. "Didn't think I'd make it here in time to stop you." A sudden smile lit up his face and made it good-looking. "You sure took an awful long time to shoot. Thought you'd turned to stone."

She turned pink. "I was just waiting for the deer to come close. I'm not a very good shot."

"Good thing you're not."

"Did I hurt you? When I bit you, I mean?"

"Not at all. But you almost broke my arm off, you were grippin' it so hard." He grinned again at her embarrassment. "We'd best get going. There may be more Indians around."

"Our ranch is about five miles from here and you'd be very welcome—" She stopped short when she saw the look on his face. "Joss is down with a broken leg and Pa has the fever. And Ma—! I must go!"

"They're gone!" he told her, grabbing her arm firmly.

"Gone?" Her eyes began to tear. "What do you mean, gone?"

"I rode past your ranch a couple of hours ago. The place was deserted. Horses, livestock, everything. I saw hoof prints all over the ground. The horses were shod. It's my guess a column of cavalry out of Fort Ewell came by and rounded up all the settlers in the area. They must have heard reports from their scouts about roaming bands of Cheyenne hereabouts. Your family is probably with them now and are on their way to the fort. There was a buckboard trailing along, too, to carry out the sick and wounded."

"They wouldn't leave without me!"

"Have to. Orders are orders," the boy said bluntly.

"I must get to Fort Ewell then."

"No, miss, we can't go that way. The Cheyenne war party will cross the Army's trail. They'll follow behind and harry the stragglers. Anyway, that war party may be joining up with other bands in the area. We'll head for Dautry instead." Her face fell and he rushed to add, "When it's safe to return I'll take you home myself. I promise."

The decision to go to Dautry was a logical one to make, but it saddened her to be separated from her family.

"All right," she said softly.

"I left my horse with yours. Let's get going." He held out his hand to her. "My name's Jesse Altman."

Heddy hesitated an instant, then took it. "I'm Heddy Gibson."

## Chapter Five

Lyle Bodine was mad clear through. He stood there drinking tepid coffee, frustrated anger flushing his face. Most of the day had been spent chasing down the stage-coach horses. Bodine could still taste the dust in his mouth from the wild rush across the bleached-white flats. Exhausted and thirsty, the men had returned with only three horses. When they searched the stage they had found a couple of canteens missing and the water from the barrels leaking onto the ground.

With three men mounted up and Bodine on foot, they took off after Wyatt and the girl. The long afternoon had been spent trailing them under a merciless sun that beat down relentlessly. Bodine swore and swore again. The soles of his feet were burning from having walked mile after mile over baked ground.

Bodine smelled sour from dried sweat and he hated it. He hated the grindingly slow progress. He hated the back of his collar, stiff with crusty sweat, chafing against his neck. Right then he hated just about everything and everybody.

Even though he had his turn to ride, by the time they made camp late in the day he was in a filthy mood. One thing was clear to all of them: He was damned tired of eating Jim Wyatt's dust!

A man who was fastidious in his planning, Bodine liked everything in a neat package with no loose strings. The plan had been simple enough at first: Disable the stage and driver, take the money and the girl, and get the hell out of Wyoming Territory to a place where they were unknown. Everything was moving along according to schedule, then Wyatt showed up and his plans went haywire. Hate seethed in him for the man who had done this to him.

Now, the only witness to the killings, the girl, had gotten away. That girl could tell everything. No matter where she went—to the fort or to any of the towns—a rope would be waiting for Bodine and his men if he didn't catch them in time. He hadn't intended to keep her alive long anyway.

Reward posters would be circulated all over the territory. After what he'd tried to pull the posters would read DEAD OR ALIVE. People would take that for a DEAD. There were a lot of men who would try to cash in on that, including some of Bodine's old "friends."

When things didn't go right, like now, Bodine made sure everyone felt his wrath. Not one to take responsibility himself, he blamed Coolee for their predicament and had no hesitation in telling him to his face.

"Ya should of just shot the driver instead of breaking a

wheel!" he shouted bitterly. Coolee was bone-tired and on edge. He wasn't about to take a browbeating from someone like Bodine; not after a defeating day like today.

"You thought it was a good idea at Branson Wells," Coolee responded flatly. Shorty's gun, which Coolee had appropriated, hung on his hip. He had taken it out of Shorty's waistband when he was asleep. Shorty wouldn't need it and it had been underhanded of him not to share it with the others.

Fed up with Bodine's bickering he allowed his right hand to linger near the holster. Bodine saw it and got even madder. There was an undercurrent of reckless anger in Coolee. He was always in a hurry to draw at the least provocation.

"Stop it!" Bodine snapped, leaning forward with belligerence. Dammit, he was running this show. After all, the Easterner had been his pigeon. He saw him first and had generously cut the others in.

Coolee's hand relaxed but his stance showed that he was still ready. The heat and the uncertainty had them all on a short fuse.

"And where did the driver go to? And where's the food he was packin'?" he questioned testily. "The beans and bacon are almost gone and the coffee is watered down!"

In scorn Coolee stared back, disdaining to answer. Bodine was really walking a razor-fine line with him. He'd shot men for much less.

Suddenly, Bodine's attention was drawn elsewhere. Coolee still watched stiff-jawed as he followed Bodine's glance. Bodine's black eyes slanted to Shorty who was ravenously scraping up forkfuls of beans and washing them down with the coffee. He didn't seem to mind that it was weak.

Like the cylinder of a revolver being rotated from chamber to chamber, Bodine's mind clicked methodically as he considered the situation. They had to reduce the number of men here, and he had a pretty good idea who was expendable. This was a big land. People got lost. People disappeared. No one ever learned what happened to them. What was one man more or less? Especially a man like Shorty Reece.

Eyes still on Shorty, Bodine gulped down the last of his coffee. His gaze shifted then to Duncan Reece and rested there so long that Duncan felt his stare. Reece looked up slowly, saw his look, and gave him a cold, tight smile. Bodine wondered if, when the time came, Duncan would stand up for his brother—or not.

Right now Duncan might put up an argument with his rifle. He might change his mind later though, when he did some walking in the sweltering sun himself, when his flesh was burned and rubbed raw, or when Shorty became too heavy a burden. Bodine thought that the likelihood of Reece coming around to his way of thinking would occur when they were close to getting the money. It wouldn't hurt to see where he stood now.

After all their work, they had recovered only three horses. Three horses, four men.

Bodine waited for Shorty to nod off, then drew Duncan aside. "That brother of yours sure eats a lot. Hurt pretty bad and won't be able to do much ridin' or fightin' when the time comes. If he was a horse, I'd shoot him."

"But he ain't a horse. He's my brother," he said flatly.

"That's right. That sort of makes him your problem." Bodine would let him think about that for a while. "Don't seem fair," he added just to help him along with that thinking, "that he should get one quarter of everything and him doin' nothin' but eatin' and drinkin'." Bodine left it at that.

Duncan Reece moved over to his brother's side. He looked down at him exasperated. Somehow this partnership with him wasn't working out so well. He'd only taken him on a little over a year ago. He'd promised his ma he'd take care of Shorty, yet all he seemed to do was get in the way. It had taken some time to tend to his wound and now his supper was getting cold.

Maybe there was something in what Bodine said. Duncan had given him this great opportunity to get three thousand dollars and what does he do? Gets himself shot. What did Duncan have? A wounded brother and a plate of congealing bacon. And three horses. He was coming to the same conclusion Bodine had come to and it wasn't making his temper any sweeter.

Shorty was resting easy now, his drawn face settled into relaxed lines. A while back he'd looked pretty bad and Duncan had thought he wouldn't make it. Swaying unsteadily, fevered eyes constantly fluttering shut, he had managed to stay on the horse's back. At day's end they had finally made camp next to a stream where they found signs of Wyatt's encampment. It seemed there wasn't enough water in the stream to slake Shorty's thirst.

When Duncan examined Shorty's wound he found it dirty and inflamed. It must have gnawed at his side all day long causing him to groan with pain. Duncan cleaned the wound and bandaged it. Slight though they were, his ministrations helped and had eased Shorty's pain quite a bit. Looking down at his face, Duncan could see he was sleeping peacefully. The fever had abated somewhat. For Shorty's sake he hoped he'd get better.

"How is he?" Coolee's voice sounded at his shoulder.

"Good as can be expected." His answer was dispassionate.

"That ain't damn near good enough!" With slow anger still simmering in Coolee since the bustup with Bodine earlier, he turned on Bodine once again.

"It was you that girl was mad at back there, Lyle. You should be layin' there with a bullet in your side, not Shorty." Coolee's voice had a sly edge to it.

Duncan turned his head and watched Bodine's face working. Coolee's expression, as always, showed nothing.

Coolee was trying to stir things up and he was satisfied to see resentment flare in Bodine. The two were always at each other's throat. But Duncan knew that when it came around to disposing of Shorty, the conniving pair would be on the same side. And where did he stand? They would probably both be watching him to see what he would do later.

Disgusted with the whole situation, Duncan flung himself away, sat down, and swallowed his cold supper in silence.

Next afternoon, Bodine dismounted for what seemed the hundredth time, studying the ground for sign: There was none. Once again Wyatt had eluded him. He mopped the sweat from his face and damned Wyatt to perdition. None of them was much of a tracker so it was left to Bodine to choose their route. Hour after tedious hour he had been merely feeling his way blindly, picking the more likely trail. Screwing his face up toward the hills, he now tried to decide which route Wyatt would take that girl.

"Did ya lose the trail again? That Wyatt is too smart for you, Lyle." Duncan's smile was meant to be nasty. It was payback for Shorty. Stung, Bodine whirled around.

"Shut your stupid mouth!"

"Or what?" Duncan sneered.

"Cut it out!" Coolee's voice intervened. "We got enough problems without you two goin' at it."

"I don't see you helping none!" Bodine returned violently.

Coolee took off his hat, wiped his forehead and put his hat on again. He looked about him coolly, then settled his gaze back on Bodine. Aware that he was irritating the hell out of him, Coolee said slowly, "He can either go to Fort Ewell or one of the towns to the west or northwest. And I'm pretty near certain he ain't goin' to the fort. So that leaves the towns. Dautry is the closest."

"How can you be so sure, huh?" Bodine's voice was belligerent. "Ewell is a damn sight closer. It'd make sense for him to go to the fort, especially with that girl."

"You think you know him so well?" Reece put in. "Since we ain't found his sign, what makes you so danged smart?"

"'Cause I been usin' my eyes while you've been usin' your mouth," Coolee returned with an unpleasant smile. Before Bodine could explode, Coolee got off his horse and motioned to the other two to follow. He led them to a place where the low hill they stood on fell away to level plains. There were markings all over of unshod ponies. At least twenty warriors had passed by, traveling fast and light. They were headed in the direction of the fort.

"They passed here about two days ago so Wyatt must have seen them too. Even if he wanted to go to Ewell, he can't."

Bodine stared at the churned up earth. His mouth went dry when he thought of how he'd almost missed it. He was about to give the order to head towards Ewell. If he had, they would have met up with them bloodthirsty heathens, sure enough. He changed his mind and decided on a northwesterly direction.

They got back on their horses. He pointed out the trail they were to take, ignoring Coolee's knowing smirk.

"We should be running into canyon land again. Be a good place to ambush Wyatt."

"Yeah, if we can find him," Duncan muttered but Bodine was too far ahead to hear.

They kept riding from place to place. The fact that Duncan was right about Wyatt outsmarting them rankled Bodine. Bodine thought for sure they would come on some sign by now, but Wyatt had disappeared leaving little trace of his passing. Yesterday, they had found one of his campsites. For a while they had followed his tracks, but to Bodine's chagrin the trail petered away. He expected Wyatt to make it hard for them yet he hadn't counted on him being so cagey.

Who was he anyway? At first he figured him to be just another down-at-the-heels cowboy like that Paxton kid, only just lucky enough to catch them unawares.

Involuntarily, Bodine's mind flashed back to the face he had seen illuminated briefly in the firelight. Wyatt's eyes had been like cold steel, but Bodine had thought it was a bluff. Now he was not so sure. What would Wyatt do when they finally cornered him like a wolf with its back against the wall? Would he talk truce or go down fighting? He didn't know the answer to that and it irritated him. And now he couldn't find sign of him again! Bodine's mood blackened.

Coolee broke into his thoughts. "I figger we'll come upon his tracks again, Lyle. Bound to eventually, now that we know where he won't be headin'."

"Maybe so." Bodine nodded, still smarting from Duncan's taunts. Turning his head, he looked back at Duncan who was plodding along leading the horse Shorty was riding. The corners of his mouth twitched. That was more like it. He tried not to laugh outright as Duncan, his throat dry, spat on the ground. His turn to eat dust! Enjoy it!

Duncan's head was down. His shirt was wringing wet from sweat and his feet were swelling in his boots. On wobbly legs he shuffled along through the blazing afternoon. He glared up at Shorty, then stumbled and righted himself. A sharp rock dug painfully into the thin sole of his boot.

"Damn Wyatt! Damn him to hell!" he muttered.

## Chapter Six

Even as the sun burned through his thin shirt, Jesse went cold when he thought of how close he and Heddy had brushed with death. They had been lucky, plain lucky. And now he was escorting her home. After traveling with her only a short time, Jesse was already deeply attracted.

Heddy Gibson was cute as a bug, and had pluck down to the backbone. Even in her old clothes a man could see that. Jesse had little experience with girls but he found it easy to converse with her right off.

She had looked him over mighty carefully when he suggested she come with him. He didn't blame her. A body had to be careful out here, especially a lone girl, and a pretty one to boot. She had searched for traces of character in his face and he hoped she found them. Anyway, she had agreed to come along and had been pleasant and intelligent company. Not meaning to be disrespectful, Jesse acknowledged to himself that Heddy was nothing like his mother. He remembered long ago his ma telling him, "If you find a girl like me, son, consider yourself lucky."

Heck, if he found a girl like that, he'd run in the other direction and count himself fortunate for missing out on a load of unhappiness.

Although she was his mother and he loved her, she hadn't made life easy for his pa. To be fair, he couldn't blame it all on her. Bad things just seemed to happen. Pa tried, but he never seemed to have much money. It wasn't because he didn't work hard—he did, darn hard, from morning until night. It wasn't until they headed out West that his hard work came to anything. They got the ranch and paid off their debts. It seemed as if their luck had finally turned.

That was seven years ago when Jesse was only thirteen. That was the day robbers entered the town and held up the bank. They wounded the bank clerk, took the money, and fled. Carl Altman, Jesse's father, was just entering the bank. After three years of hard, backbreaking work rounding up stray cattle and laboriously building up a fine herd, he had sold them for a good price: Four thousand dollars. It was the first real cash money the Altmans had had in a long time.

"Your mother deserves it," Carl had told his son. "She hasn't had a new dress in years and women like pretty things around them." Although he had built her a snug cabin, the curtains were plain, like the furniture he had made himself for her. Mrs. Altman was a pretty blond, and more than one man had looked admiringly in her direction. Now she would have everything she'd always told Carl she wanted.

Under Carl's arm had been a length of blue fabric for a new dress for his wife. In his pocket was the four thousand dollars. Two minutes after opening the bank door Carl Altman lay dead in his own blood, the fabric trampled by the fleeing thieves as they shoved their way past and hurled out of town on their horses. If they would have known the money was there, they would have taken it as well.

Kate Altman grieved for her husband but she was a woman who needed a man around. Jesse was only a child and although he worked hard, she needed someone to tell her how pretty she was. There were plenty of men in town who were willing to do that, particularly when the blond widow had a nice ranch and money to spend.

With his father gone Jesse had taken over the work. From sunup until sundown he worked the cattle, herding them from watering hole to green grass. His mother always had a good meal for him, but after several months Jesse began to notice that she paid less and less attention to the ranch and home and more attention to her appearance. She made up several new dresses including the blue fabric his father had bought her. It seemed like every time Jesse came back to the house, she was dressed up either going to or coming from some place. The news came a year later when Jesse, then fourteen, arrived home tired and dusty from rounding up strays.

"Jesse"—she swallowed hard then smiled defiantly— "I'm getting married again. You're going to have a new father."

Jesse had been dumbstruck. It had been barely a year and his father had been a good man. He hadn't been handsome or witty or even talkative, but he had been honest and a good provider. Jesse couldn't think of a single man around there who could have replaced him.

"I'm marrying Lee Jenkins."

A shocked Jesse had stared at her, then his shock turned to anger. "Lee Jenkins? Why, you know Pa didn't trust him! He'd throw him off the ranch if he'd stepped foot on it!"

It was the wrong thing to say. Mrs. Altman did not want to be reminded of Carl nor did she want her happiness dimmed in any way. She had wept and told Jesse he was hardhearted like his father. Neither of them wanted to see her pretty and happy. Lee did—and that was that.

"What about the ranch?" Jesse had asked tersely. Kate had turned red with guilt.

"Lee will be taking it over. You won't have to work as hard." There had been a pleading in her voice. "Lee has got some men he hired—"

"Gunmen!" Jesse had spat out. Even at fourteen he knew the world better than his mother ever would. "Scum and worse. I thought you had more sense, Ma." Smart about the world he might be, yet Jesse didn't know a thing about women. His mother stiffened up and became cool. If she had felt guilty about her engagement, she was no longer.

"That's the way it's going to be, Jesse." Her voice was hard. It had never been hard before; not while Pa was alive. "Lee is anxious to make something of this ranch."

"Pa and me did. We made something of it. It was only prairie before. We culled the hills for miles around to round up unmarked steers and brand them for our own. He and I built this house and the corrals. It's a good ranch now, thanks to Pa."

Her lips had tightened. She was happy, and here was her son ruining it all for her. "As to that, Lee didn't want to say it but thought maybe your pa took the cattle that didn't rightly belong to him—"

"They had no brand. They were wild—"

"And he said some of his were missing and he didn't like to say anything—"

"Pa was no thief! Those cattle are not Lee Jenkins'. He didn't have a tin pot before he started out courtin' you!"

"I won't have another word said against him! I'm marrying him, and nothing you say is going to change that. Now you be polite and nice to him." She started to cry. "I don't know why you're doing this to me! I thought you would want me to be happy. Your father would."

"Pa didn't know that the money he and I worked for would end up in Lee Jenkins' pocket and you with it."

There had followed hard days after that. A silence grew between them, thick and heavy. When they spoke to each other, their words were tainted with bitterness. Jesse couldn't understand how a woman who had had Carl Altman for a husband would think that a weasel like Jenkins would be a good replacement.

Of course, Jenkins had to know about the four thousand dollars. Ma just couldn't keep quiet about that. She never did have much common sense. Jesse sighed. If you didn't want everyone to know your business, it was best not to tell her. He was sure Ma had told Jenkins what he had said. Jenkins had been sneering and insulting to him before; now he was openly rude. Ma didn't reprimand him, though. His rudeness and arrogance were a sure sign of strength to her.

They had gotten married and Jenkins had proceeded to

make life miserable for Jesse. First, he suggested that Jesse get out of his bedroom in the house and stay in the barn. A married couple needed their privacy. Ma didn't object. On the contrary, she seemed almost relieved to have Jesse's accusing gray eyes out of her sight.

Jenkins' men, of course, taunted him when they weren't loafing around. The final test to Jesse's patience came when the cattle were rounded up and Jenkins gave all his men good, hefty bonuses—and Jesse doing all the work!

"No need to pay Jesse," Jenkins had smiled maliciously. "He's your son and you don't pay family. 'Sides, he's got room and board, and has no right to ask for more." Ma didn't object. She had bought a new lamp, some more material to make dresses, and a pair of red shoes. Jesse didn't need much more than the clothes he stood in, she had thought vaguely, if she thought at all.

That night Jesse packed up to leave. If he was going to labor all day long he might as well get paid for it. Let Jenkins and his men try to run the place without him. All they knew was how to sit around on their backsides, eating and drinking.

Jesse had felt a slight twinge of guilt towards his mother. His father had always made him promise that if anything happened to him, to take care of her. But his staying here didn't make any difference anymore. Ma was ruled by Lee Jenkins, but Jesse was damned if he would be as well!

Ma had come in just as he was tying his pack on his horse.

"Where are you going, son?" she had asked bewilderedly. "Not on a trip, are you? Lee says there are more cattle to be combed out of the hills tomorrow, and you know you're the best one to do that."

He manfully refrained from pointing out that he was the only one who did it. "I'm leavin', Ma," he told her bluntly, avoiding her face. "I can't stand this place anymore." She was shocked.

"How could you? How could you leave like this? Lee won't like it. And your pa—"

"Pa would agree with it," he cut her off. "He would be the first one to say I have no place here anymore." He looked at her directly. "All you care about is Lee." She had turned red, then white. There followed, as he knew there would, tears and reproaches. First, she tried to persuade him to stay by clinging onto his vest and weeping into it. Almost, Jesse weakened. Then he thought of Jenkins and all the thankless work he was doing for him and he stopped himself from agreeing to stay.

Ma saw his firm young face toughen and she became angry. He was just like his father! When Carl made up his mind to do what he figured was right, there was no talking to him! Both Altman men were stubborn.

"Well, go then! I don't care! Lee is trying to do his best for you, even though you aren't his kin. I would think you'd at least owe him some gratitude," Ma had sputtered.

"Gratitude for what? Allowing me to stay in a home I helped build? Paying for the little I eat with the money I earn? I'm sorry, Ma. I love you and I'd like to have stayed and help run the ranch, but there's no future for me here. For your sake, I hope Lee and his men start doing something."

"They always work all day long," she informed him

coolly. At last realizing that he was actually going and that she might not see him for a long time, she asked in a trembling voice, "What are you going to do?"

"Don't know yet," he said, securing the flap of his saddlebag.

"Do you have anything to eat? I'll get something." She hurried out, and came back with some bread and cheese, bacon and coffee. Jesse thanked her.

"Oh, you're so stubborn! Here, then!" She handed him a hundred dollars. "You'll need something to live on for a while." Jesse was touched, especially when she kissed him.

"Thanks, Ma," he said sincerely, almost smiling at her. She wiped her tears on her handkerchief.

"Oh, go on with you then. You'll see what a harsh world it is. You'll be back. But maybe we won't be here," she told him, her tears drying quickly. "Since you won't be here, maybe we can sell the ranch and move to the city." She brightened up. Her sorrow at seeing her son leave was already evaporating in visions of a new, exciting future.

"Ma! You wouldn't! Not sell Pa's home that he built for you!"

"I would. The past is gone, Jesse, it's the living that matters now. I was a good wife to your father," she insisted. "Now I'd like to have some fun myself. I'll go to the theater, eat at a real restaurant—not at Lou's place in town." She shuddered, thinking of the cramped, shabby dining room off the saloon. "Then I can *buy* my dresses! And live in a hotel room and—"

"I gotta go, Ma," Jesse interrupted, not able to bear the thought of her abandoning the ranch so willingly.

Ma stopped, taken aback at his abrupt change of voice.

"I hope everything works out for you," he said seriously.

"It will!" she had shrilled defiantly.

Jesse's smile was sad as he mounted up.

"If you need me, send a message through Bud Harris. You know, the stage driver. I'll probably meet up with him sometimes. He's always around to the different towns."

"I won't need you," she promised. "And if you have to come home, you may," she primly added, "despite how you've wounded me. But don't be too long or I'll be heading back East."

Jesse waved good-bye. He hoped everything would work out for her but he sort of doubted it. Ma couldn't afford to live in a hotel for long. When the money ran out, what then? Somehow he didn't see Jenkins holding down an honest job. Would he just desert her? Jesse sighed and continued down the road. He glanced back once, but his ma had gone in the house. No doubt she'd forgotten him already.

One day, Jesse mused, he'd have his own ranch and family. He'd build something for himself that no one could take away. He hoped that in the future he'd run into Jenkins alone. Jesse shrugged his wide shoulders and balled his hands into fists in anticipation. Jesse was big enough, strong enough now to take him on and Jenkins had it coming. Someday . . .

"Jesse, look! Riders!" Heddy interrupted his thoughts. Instantly, they swung their horses into cover and watched the approaching horsemen with wary eyes.

"Maybe we can join them. It would be safer traveling with four other men. Should we wave them down?"

It had been risky so far passing alone through Indian

country, but they had made out all right. Jesse just wasn't ready to forge headlong into company he might not want later on. A man couldn't trust just anyone.

"No." His suspicion was already up. "Just sit quiet. We don't know anything about them." A discerning glint in his steel-edged gaze, Jesse sat easy in the saddle with his rifle, fully loaded, across his saddlebow. Very young yet very confident in his knowledge of men, he observed the riders strung out along the trail. He liked the look of them even less as they came nearer.

A coarse-looking foursome, it appeared as if they had just ridden out of some kind of fight. One of them was hurt badly. He was slumped over on the horse. The others didn't pay him any mind. Rough and hard-bitten, they were driving themselves and their horses at a punishing pace. One man was on foot and jogging along to keep up. With reckless disregard for the wounded man's condition, they pressed on in one big hurry.

Maybe someone was following them. Jesse thought it more likely that they were doing the chasing. The dark-haired man in the lead could barely restrain his eagerness. Like a bloodhound on the scent, he had his eyes trained on the trail ahead. The second man kept searching the ground around them for prints, Jesse thought. He pitied the man they were after.

"Jesse," Heddy spoke softly at his side, "those men are riding bareback. What happened to their saddles?"

"I know . . . I wonder where they got those horses from." Jesse watched till the men were out of sight, then turned to Heddy. He was well aware of the danger they had just sidestepped by her timely warning. He rested his hand on her shoulder and squeezed it gently. "That was real sharp of you to spot them."

Heddy smiled, pleased at the compliment.

He continued, "If they'd seen us first, we'd be walking or we'd be dead. It depends on who they are and why they're in such an almighty hurry. We'll keep a smart distance from them. Looks like they're heading for Dautry too. I hope we don't meet up with them again."

## Chapter Seven

Shorty was trying desperately to stay on the horse. He knew if he fell off one more time it would invoke an explosion of wrath from either Coolee or Bodine.

The deep, throbbing pain in his side matched the one in his head, and combined with the jolting of hoofs as the oppressive heat beat down on him. Barely conscious, he slumped over and hung onto the bridle. His body braced each time the horse swayed back and forth. Several times he had blacked out, but Duncan's hand had propped him up until his vision cleared.

"We're nearing the river. We can rest a while." Duncan said it for Shorty's benefit as much as his own. Bodine and Coolee had set a killing pace, and Duncan was exhausted.

"Rest? The hell we will!" Coolee let loose, turning his head to glare at the both of them. "Wyatt's gettin' farther away and you want to stop to play patty-cake in the water. We ain't stoppin'!"

"Listen, Coolee, we all need rest and not just Shorty. The horses need water so we're stoppin'!" Duncan said grimly. "Wyatt can't be that much ahead, handicapped the way he is with that Carter girl. We can afford to rest a bit!"

"Handicapped? Look what we got! When Wyatt's good and dead, then we can rest. Until then, we move on. I say so!" Coolee's eyes flashed fire. If the Reeces weren't his associates, he'd have drilled them a long time ago. He figured he had put up with just about enough from them. He had a certain code of ethics when dealing with acquaintances but he was considering abandoning it right now since his turn to walk was coming up.

"No." Shorty opened his eyes and spoke weakly, his voice barely audible. "Don't fight, Duncan. I can keep up. I can . . ."

"Cut it out, you two!" Bodine turned in the saddle, skewering the men with his menacing look. "I've had enough of you both!" The dark eyes went to Coolee's hand which was beginning to curl around the butt of his gun.

"Coolee! Put it away!" Bodine's command cracked like a bullwhip. "Now!" The air was filled with tension. Duncan's scalp tightened as he read the threat in Coolee's face. "Damn you both!" Bodine's voice rose to a shout. His hand tightened on the reins. "We almost have Wyatt! We found his tracks, now don't do anything stupid!" Coolee hesitated a moment then let his hand drop to his side.

"Leave the kid alone. We all need each other," Bodine warned Coolee. "We'll take a quick rest at the river and fill our canteens." Angrily, Coolee jogged his horse and continued along. Bodine turned to Duncan who was watching it all, stone-faced.

"I'll go up ahead. You bring Shorty. Take your time," Bodine added as insurance against Duncan's waning loyalty.

Duncan nodded, but admitted to himself to feeling as angry as Coolee. Shorty *was* a burden. It was hard enough traveling across this dry-as-dust land without having to look out for someone else as well. Shorty didn't seem to be trying at all to get better. At first, he ate and drank ravenously. Now, he didn't eat anything much. Duncan didn't know why that should worry him more.

Bodine's fury seethed within him. Damn Coolee! This was no time to rile Duncan. They needed his gun. It would be a hell of a lot easier to take Wyatt with three men rather than two. Bodine caught up with Coolee at the river. He had drunk his fill and was ready to move on.

"What are you gonna do about Shorty?" he asked him bluntly as he kneeled down to drink. "I ain't walkin' today or any other day."

"Just leave it to me," Bodine snapped back.

"I'll leave it to you—for a while, but you better do something soon or I will." Coolee bent down and scooped up another cupful of water.

Duncan had just arrived with Shorty. He sent Coolee a cold look and tended to his brother. He didn't dare help him from the horse. He was doubtful whether Shorty could get on again.

"Ed, go find where Wyatt's tracks lead on the other side of the river. Wait for us over the hill," Bodine said casually.

Coolee sent him an intense look full of meaning. He straightened up and mounted. Throwing one last look at the Reece brothers, he trotted through the river and climbed up the other side. Soon he had disappeared from view.

Duncan expelled his breath. He didn't realize he had been holding it so long. "Thanks, Lyle." He managed a small smile. "That Ed's crazy. He'd kill anyone. Thanks for stopping him. You're the only one who can control him."

Bodine's nod was barely noticeable. His attention was on the wounded man. Shorty was breathing heavily and barely drank the water Duncan urged upon him. Feeling Bodine's eyes on his brother, Duncan said, "He'll be fine." Even Bodine noticed that Duncan was not too enthusiastic. He'd probably be glad to unload Shorty as well, Bodine figured. It was hard enough to haul your own carcass over this rough terrain, but even worse to drag a dead weight along with you.

"Tell you what. I'll see to Shorty for a while." Bodine clapped Duncan on the back. "You go on ahead. We'll catch up."

Duncan stilled. For a long moment there was silence. Bodine's voice sounded like a death knell. Duncan didn't think he possessed the patience to take care of Shorty. Hell, even he, his own brother, was becoming impatient. What was Bodine planning?

"I don't know . . ." It was not only Bodine's words that made Duncan falter but the chill edge to his voice even when he tried to infuse it with warmth and concern. It all sounded hollow to his ears. He looked into Bodine's granite-hard face and saw no give there at all. Still, Duncan reminded himself, he had come to Shorty's aid. Coolee would have killed him sure enough if Bodine hadn't stepped in. Maybe Duncan was too suspicious.

"You been taking care of him all along. Now it's our turn."

Duncan didn't quite like the way he phrased it, but it was a fact that he was tired of nursing Shorty. He bit his lip and looked directly at Bodine.

"If anything happens to him—"

"It won't be by *my* hand," Bodine promised. "If I wanted him dead, I'd have let Ed do it." That made sense to Duncan, who was anxious to find a reasonable explanation.

"Okay, Lyle." Duncan gave Bodine a long, hard look, then his eyes went to his brother. Something told him to stay with Shorty, but his aching back and blistered feet urged him to get on the horse and go. He mounted up. "I'll see ya later, Shorty," Duncan said. Then before he changed his mind he cantered away. Shorty didn't even notice at first.

"Duncan?" he murmured, looking around confused. Shorty's eyes at last focused on Bodine. He was too ill to notice the cool appraisal in the dark eyes. The boy was sick as a dog. He probably wouldn't last long.

"I'm taking charge of you now, Shorty. Time for you to go." Bodine took up the reins and led the horse and rider in the direction Duncan had taken.

Reaching the river bank, Bodine halted. A breeze from across the cold water was refreshing against Shorty's flushed face. It revived him enough to force his eyelids open to see where they were. Mustering enough strength to speak, he asked dully, "Where's Duncan?"

Bodine waited a moment to speak while he scanned the river's bank. Duncan had not decided to return. Bodine was afraid he might. After surveying the crossing he answered the wounded man almost absent-mindedly.

"He's up ahead with Ed looking for Wyatt's trail. Looks like it's just you and me, kid." He smiled icily up at him.

"Lyle . . . thanks . . . for not letting Ed shoot me."

"Why sure, kid. No one's gonna shoot you. You have my word on that."

Shorty smiled tiredly. He gripped the horse harder as a dizzy spell came upon him.

Bodine noticed. He turned his attention to the high walls of the canyon surrounding them. It was devoid of any movement or sound. They were entirely alone together.

"Okay, kid, let's go." Bodine took up the reins, then skittered down the steep bank to the river's edge. With horse and rider trailing behind him, he waded into the swift, ice-cold current to where the river was knee-deep. Partway across the freezing water, he halted. Now was the time. Struggling for a foothold on the slick, rocky bottom, he shot a sideways glance at Shorty. His eyes were closed and he looked to be asleep. So much the better.

For one last time Bodine looked quickly around. No one was in sight. Suddenly, he reached up and grasped Shorty by his shirt front with two fists and hauled him from the horse, tossing him into the water. With one swift movement, he grabbed the reins and vaulted onto the horse's back.

"So long, Shorty!" he yelled, riding his mount across the broad expanse of water. On the other side he glanced over his shoulder. Shorty's head had disappeared underwater. Bodine turned away and kicked his heels into the animal's sides. He galloped over the ridge and didn't look back again.

Bodine caught up with Duncan and Coolee a few miles later. As he rode into view, Duncan stared to see Bodine astride the horse and Shorty nowhere in sight.

"Where's Shorty?" he asked tersely.

Bodine pulled his horse to a stop a few feet from Duncan.

"I left him back there."

Duncan made a movement as if to go back.

"Leave him!" Bodine's voice rang out. "He's better off where he is. We're heading into the canyon lands. You know he'd never make it."

Duncan considered this and had to admit Bodine made sense. "Is he all right? What did he say?"

"'Course he's all right. I left him lying under a tree, real comfortablelike. He's got his canteen and some food. He'll be fine. As a matter of fact he was glad when I left him there. Felt real bad bein' so much of a burden on you."

Duncan relaxed a little. That was something Shorty would say. He was always apologizing.

"And he'll feel a lot better when he gets his share of the money," Bodine said heartily. Duncan's ears perked up.

"You mean he's getting his three thousand?" This seemed to ease his conscience.

"Sure he will! We're partners!" Bodine met Coolee's poker face. Coolee knew Bodine was lying. Duncan didn't. All he thought about was three thousand dollars. Maybe he'd even end up with six thousand if Shorty didn't make it.

Duncan hadn't noticed that none of the food was missing, and the canteens were all present and accounted for. His mind was consumed with the idea of all that cash just waiting for them to go and collect. Duncan looked back at Bodine, a slight flash of doubt crossing his features. Bodine noticed.

"You have anything else you want to say to me?" Bodine asked. It occurred to Duncan that the smile he thought so friendly a moment ago had turned wolfish—or had it always been wolfish? Apprehension about his brother crowded his thoughts. Coolee's and Bodine's dark faces seemed to tell him to get rid of those thoughts—or else! Duncan let them go.

"No," he finally answered, "I guess not."

Bodine heard the note of submissiveness in Duncan's voice and eased back.

"Then let's go." Coolee gave a tight-lipped smile and followed Bodine. Duncan brought up the rear. He took one last look over his shoulder. There was no Shorty on their back trail. Duncan couldn't help that. There was nothing he could do. Shorty was better off where he was than going farther into this hellish land. And at the end of the trail, he'd get his share of the money anyway. Of course, it wasn't fair for him to get it all. Duncan thought Shorty might be entitled to, say, one thousand dollars, and

## Chapter Eight

Jim picked up the pace. He had formulated a plan as they had ridden along and now he was prepared to carry it out. He had realized all along that it was imperative that he slow down the Bodine gang. He needed a chance to, at least, get Miss Carter to safety. That canyon, now, kept coming into his mind. Abruptly, they turned south.

"Where are we going?" Julie pulled her horse alongside Jim. She glanced uneasily in the direction they were heading. "This looks like canyon land."

"It is. I aim to get shut of them here."

"Do you think they've found our trail?"

"Bound to," he remarked almost casually although Julie knew him well enough by now to know that he was not. "They're coming up on us."

She glanced about her but saw nothing. "How do you know?"

"I can feel them. We've had it our own way for a while, but the time will come when we'll have to turn and fight. Meanwhile, I'm going to buy us some time."

"Can you, Mr. Wyatt?" She tried to read his expressionless face but was unsuccessful.

"I can try." He glanced at her. "It will mean that I'll have to leave you alone for a bit."

"Absolutely not!" her voice rose, alarmed.

"Have to. I want to lead them away and you'll—" He searched for a kindly way of putting it.

"I'll be in the way." She finished up for him dryly.

He heaved a sigh of relief. "That's it, ma'am. Not 'in the way' exactly, but you will slow me down a mite and we have no time to waste." His voice was apologetic.

"I understand." There was a moment of silence. "Are you going to tell me your plan?" she asked stiffly.

He threw her a quick grin. "Sorry, ma'am, I'm not accustomed to telling people things. I kind of got used to doing things on my own. Not a whole lot of people to confide in in prison."

"I imagine not."

"The way I'm thinking is that instead of trying to hide our prints, we let them find them." At her startled look he went on quickly. "Not a lot of them. That would make them suspicious, and there aren't two more suspicious men around than Lyle Bodine and Ed Coolee. No, we'll just leave a little bit to use as bait: A partial print maybe, or some broken twigs. They'll think themselves real clever to find them and be after us in a minute. Only they won't find us because you'll be hidden up in the hills while I lead them into the Furnace."

"The Furnace?"

"It's a box canyon I know of. There's only one entrance. I figure on leading a trail in. They'll follow it all the way through searching for me. By the time they find out they've been tricked, we ought to have a good head start on them."

"Why do they call it the Furnace? Is it hot?"

"Hot as Hades," Jim responded cheerfully. "And no water. Even if they make it back, they'll be in pretty bad shape."

"How will you get out?" Julie asked worriedly.

"There's a place up along the ledges. I don't think anyone knows about it but me. Leastways, I've never heard anyone mention it. I'll leave through there. It's about a quarter mile from the entrance. When I'm finished, I'll come back to pick you up." He smiled at her, then his smile vanished. "Here they come."

Frightened, Julie turned her head. Far off, faint wisps of dust were visible in the flatlands. They *were* coming. Every time she had turned around she had expected it, and now they were almost upon them.

"They're miles away yet," she pointed out hopefully.

"And we'll need every mile."

"It might not be the Bodine gang."

"It is." He sounded very sure.

She squinted her eyes. "It looks like only three riders."

"Probably got rid of Shorty. I didn't think they'd drag him along once he got hurt."

"You mean because I shot him?" Julie had not thought of that.

"Yes, ma'am, and it's too bad you didn't get a few more while you were at it. Still, you did cut down their numbers.

It will make it that much easier." He seemed to admire her for that.

"What do you think they did with him?" she asked a trifle guiltily.

"Well now, that depends. If his brother, Duncan, stood up for him he might still be alive. That means he'd have to face down Bodine and Coolee. I don't know how much brotherly affection there was between them, and I don't reckon Duncan has the makin's to take those two on. My guess is he's dead." He changed the subject. "There it is up ahead: The Furnace. Let's give them a taste of what they can expect in the next life!"

As they hurried along, Julie, suddenly frightened of being abandoned, tried to reason with the young man.

"You know, we could make much better time if I went with you."

"No, we couldn't." He was leading them along the river.

"I'm sure we could. You wouldn't have to come back for me," Julie persuaded, but her words seemed to have no effect on him.

"It's not out of the way."

"And if you got caught and had to shoot your way out?"

"You wouldn't be there to get hurt." They turned to the left around some rocks.

"I was going to say"—her voice was breathless from keeping up with him,—"that I could use my derringer and the six-shooter."

"Up here." He pointed out a trail that she couldn't even

discern. He dismounted and lifted her down. Holding her hand firmly, he urged her up the steep rock pile. Reluctantly, she accompanied him. Eventually, they came to a dark, gouged-out cave. It was small, but at least it provided her protection from the sun and was back far enough from the narrow ledge that no one could see her from down below. Julie stopped and looked about her unhappily.

"Stay here and don't make a sound. Don't move or even look for me. They'll be here soon and before they go into the canyon, they'll take a good look around. I don't want them finding you when I'm not here." He was ready to go but turned back at her melancholy expression. "I'll try to be as quick as I can but I can't hurry."

"I know."

He took her hand in his. Julie looked up at him through her lashes. "I am coming back. I'm not deserting you. We get through this and we'll have a good head start. And one more thing."

"Yes?"

He met her eyes. They were beautiful: Big and blue. "You take good care of that six-shooter. I've grown mighty fond of it." Giving her a gentle smile, he turned and then disappeared down the hill accompanied by the rattling of loose gravel.

Soon all was silent. Julie sat down tiredly. Before she did, she withdrew her derringer and placed it on the ground next to her. If anything happened she was ready. But all her thoughts were with the dark-haired young man still out there. What he was doing was dangerous no matter how he downplayed it for her benefit. Clasping her hands tightly together in her lap, she prayed that he would make it back alive—to her.

At the canyon's mouth the horses balked at the heat and Jim tugged on the lead lines. "Come on, boys," he urged them on. "It won't be for long." He needed both horses in order to convince Bodine's men that Julie was with him.

Soundlessly, they moved over the sandy canyon floor leaving a trail that was easy to read. Too easy? He would soon fix that.

Jim looked up at the mighty walls of towering sandstone. Their great height gave them the false impression that the serrated crests were leaning inward like giant teeth. Their steepness didn't prevent the sun from pounding down oppressively and baking to burnt brown everything on the canyon floor. The endless stretches of red walls were dotted with small stands of spruce and junipers that had boldly taken hold in crags.

Piles of boulders lined the twisting trail, providing excellent places wherein a sniper could take cover. Jim knew that when Bodine saw the canyon for the first time, he would have that thought in mind: Ambush. Good. It would make him wary, and that very wariness would slow his pace to a crawl. His mind would be busy anticipating Jim at every turn. By that time, Jim thought with some satisfaction, he would be long gone from this hellish place.

A quarter mile into the canyon, the sandy ground lost itself to gravel and stony rubble. Jim's tracks ended here as he knew they would. Bodine would assume that Jim had continued down the length of canyon, but he would find out too late that he had not.

Jim did not intend to go through the whole canyon. He was not a fool. When he reached an ancient outcropping of boulders he left the canyon floor. Riding directly to the north wall, he headed to some low-growing brush till he found the remnants of a trail. Then he began a switchback ascent up the side of the cliff where the trail consisted of a mere two-foot-wide shelf angling upward.

Higher he climbed, scaling the massive rock sheet. He mounted a tilted slab that was slick to stand on. The horses, struggling for a footing, slipped and stumbled up the sloped surface.

At each turn, Jim squinted down into the canyon to see if anyone was following. Each time only shimmering sand met his eyes. Yet he knew they were coming.

Two hundred feet above the floor the climb shot almost straight up for another dozen feet. When the horses scrambled up the dangerous chute, a startling spray of pebbles rattled over the edge and echoed loudly in the stillness below.

The horses lunged forward in enormous leaps to finally come level on a ledge. It had been a wicked climb that left the animals badly winded. The heat was draining their energy rapidly. For a few minutes he allowed the animals to catch their breath. He couldn't spare more time even now. He was worried about Julie being left alone.

Jim led the horses along the ledge. Then an opening appeared in a fold of rock. A narrow gash tucked away between two mighty columns gave way to a tunnel-like space just large enough for horses and rider to squeeze through. Without hesitating, Jim urged his mount through the opening. In a short while they emerged from the Furnace and were descending to the river once more. Another half mile and he would be back at the cave.

With a surge of relief he knew he had done it. Jim figured he and Julie would be halfway to Grand Mesa by the time Bodine worked his way to the end of the box canyon and found it empty!

Duncan Reece reined in and waited for Coolee and Bodine to catch up. Coolee's horse had been limping so Duncan had ridden ahead.

A few miles back they had picked up Wyatt's trail and lost it again. Now, after casting about for signs, here were partial hoofprints of two horses deeply imbedded into the sand. Every once in a while even someone like Wyatt got careless. This was one of those times, he exulted.

Bodine came abreast of him and Duncan pointed triumphantly to the trail leading into the narrow canyon off to the left.

"They went in there."

Coolee came up and dismounted. He walked to the mouth of the angry, red-walled canyon. A spiteful jolt of hot air struck out, almost suffocating him.

"Aw, hell! It's like a damned oven in there! Ain't there another way we can go?"

"No!" Bodine spoke over his carping. "Wyatt knows this area. You can bet he's taking the fastest route to wherever he's going, and I ain't risking losing his trail again!"

Duncan added, "When he came through this morning it was probably cooler."

"Cooler than what?" Coolee spat out. "Molten lead?"

Bodine studied the deep indentations going straight

into the canyon. There was no doubt Wyatt had come this way. "Mount up," he ordered testily, annoyed by Coolee's outburst.

Coolee squinted into the burning sun. "You go ahead. I'll catch up to you. My horse picked up a stone. He's been limping for a while. I can't let him go lame." Bodine gave him a piercing look. "Unless you want to take turns walkin' again!" Coolee snapped at Bodine's skeptical look. He stared until Bodine finally looked away.

Without another word Duncan and Bodine followed Wyatt's beckoning tracks into the canyon. Coolee watched till they swung around a twist in the passage, then he turned to his horse. He picked up the horse's hoof and carefully pried out with his knife point the stone that was lodged there. Afterward, he led his horse to the river to drink of the refreshing water.

As the horse drank, Coolee was doing some thinking. For the past few days Wyatt had gone out of his way to hide his trail. All they could find were bits here and there, leaving them to piece together where he had gone. Now, of a sudden there were prints. They were mighty clear prints too. They were just parts of prints, of course, but there for the seeing just the same. Reece and Bodine had leaped on them, determined to follow them. Now maybe Wyatt just didn't have the time to cover his tracks. That was a possibility. Coolee was not so sure. He'd let those two huckleberries go into that hell's oven. He was going to try to bypass it. Maybe one of these other trails would take him someplace.

Consideringly, his eyes lifted to the rude trail Wyatt had taken. Something moved at the corner of his eye and his head turned sharply. There was a scratching noise, and Coolee's hand reached for his gun.

A tumbleweed detached itself from the other low-lying growth and slipped from a ledge to go bounding off a boulder. A playful breeze tossed it along down the face of the shelf. It rattled past a black gash in the rock and continued down. Coolee's stare honed in on the black gash, ignoring the tumbleweed as it continued on its way. From here, the gash looked like a dark recess.

Coolee's eyes paused. Something was not quite right to his way of thinking. He scratched his dirty fingernails over the black stubble on his jaw.

He had himself a hunch. He started up the slope.


Duncan Reece kept looking over his shoulder and tried to focus in this unbearable heat. An hour had plodded by, and there was still no sign of Coolee. Why wasn't he here, suffering alongside of them?

"Where's Ed?" Reece's voice was sharp.

Bodine shot an indifferent look at Reece and shrugged his shoulders. "Maybe his horse went lame and he had to walk all the way. Serve him right." His voice held ill humor. He and Reece seemed to be going nowhere and without another sign of Wyatt. That, and infernal heat, was making him short–tempered.

Trudging through the white-hot afternoon, they had been forced to get off and lead their horses. It was too much for the animals to carry the weight of their riders.

Reece screwed up his eyes and swore as sweat ran down his face. Hot sand had worked its way into his boots again, and he stopped to empty them. The sand was hard enough to slog through, but when the ground covering became rock it was like stepping on hot coals. They burned right into the worn soles of his boots. First thing he'd do when he got that money was to buy a new pair—maybe some fancy Spanish ones with big roweled spurs.

There was no shade in any form to provide even a moment's relief from the smothering heat. No rock, bush or ledge beckoned to them with cooling shadows. The dry heat seemed to singe their nostrils and lungs with every breath. Reece felt as if he couldn't breathe. Even if they had the strength to hurry, they couldn't do it. It was enough that they were still on their feet and moving.

Every time they rounded a corner, Reece expected to see Wyatt or the girl. The girl surely couldn't hold up under the sun's intensity. She'd keel over, for sure. Reece grinned momentarily through cracked lips as he contemplated this eventuality. Sure she would. She wouldn't be able to take it like men did. Why, the money was almost in their grasp.

This thought was all that kept Reece going through the long day as he kept his eyes fixed on the glaring red rocks. Just a little further . . .

His head was bowed at the neck. It felt as if his brain was cooking in his skull. Reece looked over at Bodine and saw he was in the same bad shape. With shaking fingers Bodine pulled his kerchief from his neck and mopped his face and scalding eyes. Once a brightly patterned affair, almost gaudy, it was now a dull gray color and soggy with sweat. Doggedly, they continued on in silence. They hadn't even strength to speak.

Six relentless hours later, Reece and Bodine shuffled

around the last curve in the canyon and came up short with a jolt. An incredulous Bodine stared. His red-rimmed eyes followed the steep cirque of cliffs blocking what should have been the way out of the canyon. They were boxed in!

Reece's jaw dropped. He turned slowly around and looked at their backtrail. Nothing. Legs wobbling with weariness, he slumped down in the hot sand.

A flood of curses hurled out of Bodine's sunburned lips which only partially relieved his fury. Driven by the need to punish someone or something he flung rocks at the impassive walls. A lethargic Reece watched as Bodine then proceeded to unload his rifle into every crevice he could see. After he'd exhausted himself, he threw his rifle into the sand and collapsed next to Reece. The sun was heading for the horizon and it was beginning to cool off slightly.

"A trap!" Bodine spat out bitterly. He was as close to defeat as Reece had ever seen him.

"Ed ain't caught up yet," Reece said slowly, thoughtfully. After a moment he added, "Probably ain't gonna."

"No, he probably ain't gonna!" Bodine mimicked nastily. "We'll have to spend the night here. The horses can't make it back unless they rest." Bodine stared at the ground. "But if Ed thinks he's taking off with the girl and my money, he'd better be watching his back 'cause I'm gettin' 'em." He glanced up and saw Reece's eyes upon him. "We're gettin' 'em."

Reece relaxed. Yeah, that was more like it.

From a distance Jim saw the three figures hovering around the mouth of the canyon. They had found his tracks. With a little smile of relief he saw them start in. By the time he worked his way down to the canyon opening, they had all vanished. Now to get Julie and get out of there.

Then he noticed the tracks. There were only two sets of tracks going into the canyon. His jaw clenched and the muscles in his body stiffened.

A horse whinnied. Slewing around in the saddle, rifle ready, he looked frantically for the source of the sound. One of the stagecoach horses was hitched to a cottonwood. Riding over, he saw the bootprints heading up to the cave and his scalp tightened with fear.

"Julie!" He swore under his breath. A woman's scream ricocheted off the rocks above.

Obediently, Julie sat within the cave's protective walls waiting for Jim. For a time she looked out into the dazzling sunlit perspective, but she soon grew tired of that. All that was visible were the high, rocky cliffs. The trail in front of her was empty and the canyon floor was impossible to see. She could only hope that the men would follow Jim's trail, and that he would come back to take her away. At this point she did not even care where that was as long as he was with her.

Of course, there was the distinct possibility that the outlaws would not be lured into the canyon. They might come up here, past her cave. What would she do if they discovered her? Her heart leaped in fear; a pulse pounded in her head. She knew what she would do. She'd fight until Jim came back—if he came back. They might kill him, then there would be no one left in this world who cared what happened to her. Haunted by a mounting sense of danger she moved restlessly about.

The sullen minutes dragged by as the sun neared the noon mark. A horrible scenario played over and over in her mind, always ending with her being captured by Bodine and Jim being gunned down. These thoughts of Jim with his warm green eyes, his bold kindness in rescuing her, his grit and determination in tackling the outlaws, made her turn cold even though the cave was stuffy and hot.

All at once a faint rattling came from outside, high on the slope. Julie held her breath. It was reminiscent of dry bones clicking together. She got to her knees, dodging nervously into the shadows. Scarcely breathing now, she kept her eyes fixed on the opening waiting for what might happen. In each tight fist she clutched a gun.

The noise stopped for a second then started again. It seemed to move in stops and starts like an animal scampering from boulder to boulder. Closer and closer it came, scratching against hard rock as it advanced. It was almost at the cave opening. Firming her lips, she lifted her guns.

The next moment a tumbleweed rolled past carried by a gust of wind. As if mocking her fear it threw itself at the opening then clattered its way downhill. Another tremendous roll and it was out of sight.

Julie started to giggle nervously. Her laugh had a hollow echo. It would be a fine thing if she started shooting at the tumbleweed and brought the whole Bodine gang down on her head! Relieved, she put the guns down and moved closer to the cave entrance. Jim would be here soon. She must just take a quick peek to see. Feeling a little braver, she leaned forward on one hand and craned her neck. Disappointed, she could still see nothing.

"HAAA!"

The loud noise was almost in her ear. Julie froze for a second. It was all that was needed. From out of nowhere a man's hand suddenly shot out, grabbing her wrist. She cried in terror. The dirty hand tightened, pulling at her. The next instant her eyes grew wide in shock, for the head that poked around the corner of the ledge and shoved into her face belonged to Ed Coolee!

At once her free hand groped around for the derringer. A grinning Coolee saw it and slapped it away. Yanking her hand from his sweaty one, Julie managed to crawl into a corner. Both guns were out of reach. She searched the dark walls frantically for an escape, but there wasn't even a place to hide.

Coolee swung himself into the cave and stood up. His massive bulk seemed to fill the place.

"Well, well, well. Lookee what I found! I knew Wyatt wouldn't take you into that canyon. I knew you was about here some place. Let Reece and Bodine go chase their tails. You and me, girlie, are gonna have some fun." His eyes shifted to the small pack lying against the wall. "That the money?" Julie was mute. "I'm having it—all of it. And you're comin' with me too."

Suddenly his head tilted like he was listening. His eyes honed in again on the terrified girl.

"Did he leave ya? Naw, he wouldn't do that. Not without taking that money. So where is he, girlie?" Julie clamped her lips together and Coolee lost his good humor. "I asked you a question and I expect an answer!"

He lunged at her, his fingers digging around her forearms like pincers. As he dragged her to the cave entrance

Julie deliberately went limp, but he merely lifted her up and pushed her against one of the walls.

"Where is he, damn it? Don't you be foolin' me! I got ways of dealin' with women and you won't like it. None of them ever did!" As his face darkened with an ugly look, Julie screamed again and kicked out wildly. He commenced to shake her. He shook her till her hair came loose and whipped around her shoulders. Unable to break free, she bent her head down and sank her teeth into the fleshy part of his arm. Coolee howled with pain.

"You'll pay for that, you little hellcat! Wait till I take care of Wyatt. You'll be next!"

A sob was torn out of her, then choked in her throat. Someone suddenly came up behind Coolee. Terror kept her still. Her fear blinded her. All she could make out was a dark shadow.

"That's more like it." Coolee's voice was satisfied by her sudden submission. Unaware of the presence looming there, he pushed Julie down. "Now we can have us some fun."

As she fell Julie looked up and saw Jim's face over Coolee's big shoulder. Raw fury blazed in him. Green eyes spat fire. He clapped his hand down on Coolee's shoulder and spun him around. Jim's powerful fist ripped through the thin air and slammed into Coolee's unprotected gut. Coolee's stomach caved in and a grunt was torn from his lips. His eyes flared wide with shock.

"You!" Coolee managed to get out before the other man threw an uppercut that snapped his head back and made his teeth crunch together.

Before Coolee had a chance to recover, Jim brought his

shoulder down against Coolee's solid chest and rammed the tall man into the wall. Coolee's skull bounced against the stone with a dull thud. Head reeling, he reached down automatically for his knife.

As the sharp blade arced swiftly upwards Jim jumped back. Lightning quick, his hand shot out and captured Coolee's wrist. He smashed Coolee's hand against jagged granite. He kept slamming it down until Coolee's hand turned bloody.

"Drop it!" Jim snarled, "or I'll break your damned hand!" Coolee gasped as Jim, true to his word, slammed his hand against some pointed rocks protruding from the cave wall. It was too much even for the obstinate Coolee. Pain made him lose his grip, and the knife thudded on the dirt floor.

Julie, who had been watching fearfully, instantly came to life. She leaped to grab the knife away from his vicinity. Coolee's furious eyes warned her that she would pay dearly for that later. Julie didn't care. But she did scoot away to the opposite side, flattening herself against the cold wall to get out of the men's way.

Like two big cats thrown together in this cramped space to fight it out, they circled each other. Shoulders bunched warily and knees flexed, they sized each other up. Each probed for the other's weakness. His nerves tightened to a razor-fine edge, Jim waited for Coolee to strike. It came.

Getting his wind back, Coolee suddenly pushed forward and swung a vicious right hook at Jim's head. Jim slapped it away with his left and ground his fist into Coolee's stomach. Blanching, Coolee struck out grazing Jim's cheek, while his other fist swung wildly. He was not used to fighting without a weapon. Jim dodged back a few steps and Coolee once more swiped at him.

The air was close and musty. Both men were breathing hard. Then Jim stepped in and jabbed at Coolee, battering his head and face with quick, hammer-hard blows.

Julie dodged away from the grappling bodies and swinging fists. She feared they would trample her into the dust, so intent were they on tearing each other apart.

Coolee's nose began to gush. He smeared the blood away with his hand before furiously shooting a right cross at Jim's jaw. Jim rolled with the punch and Coolee's ire began to mix with frustration. A blast of light blinded him as he stepped back to continue the fray.

"Ah, hell!" he snarled, blinking rapidly. He made a quick decision. Instead of staying to fight it out he pushed Jim hard with his shoulder and bolted for the entrance.

Afraid Coolee might get away, Jim barreled his lean, rugged frame into him. The force of the blow caught Coolee in the back. He let out a small cry as the loose debris underneath him made him lose his footing and hurled him over the rim of the cliff. Arms flailing, he flew through the air like a rag doll and crashed onto the rocks below.

Jim almost went careening down with him, but scrabbled for a handhold at the last second. Julie threw herself out of the cave and grabbed his one wrist with both her hands. Using all the strength he could muster, he pulled himself back, breathing heavily. He saw the knife lying beside him and took it without a word. Hauling himself up onto his feet, he staggered down the slope to where Coolee lay. If necessary, he would finish the job.

There was no need. When Jim reached the bottom he

found Coolee sprawled on his back, his head at an awkward angle. His skull was crushed in and he had broken his neck. Jim fell to his knees and rummaged through Coolee's pockets for extra ammunition. Tiredly he stood up, slipping Coolee's knife into his own boot. Coolee wouldn't be using it on anyone else. Julie had grabbed her things and followed Jim. She was there when he turned around.

"Is he . . . is he dead?"

"Yes." What would she think? Being from out East, would she turn from him after she had seen him kill a man?

Julie let out her breath. "Oh, Jim. I thought he was going to kill you!" She threw herself into his arms and he held her close for a few seconds.

"Come on," he mumbled into her hair. "We've got to get out of here. There's no telling if the others heard anything."

Julie pulled reluctantly out of his arms. "I'm sorry for screaming. I didn't expect him."

"I should have," Jim said grimly. There was a sudden urgency to leave this place. "Let's go. The others just might get fed up and come back." They went down the hill and collected Coolee's horse. Now there was an extra rifle for Julie.

It had been a good day's work. They had gained time. More important, Coolee was out of the picture. Now there were two left.

## Chapter Nine

Bodine and Reece found Ed Coolee's body the next afternoon. Exhausted, they stumbled out of the canyon. When they spotted the body, they rushed over to see who it was.

"It's Ed, damn him!" Reece cried bitterly. "Greedy swine. Tryin' to steal a march on us. I knew it!" He kicked his erstwhile pal in the side for causing them so much trouble.

"Yeah, greed's a terrible thing." Bodine nodded, his eyes touching on the cave above, and the piles of debris that had fallen down with Coolee. It covered his boots and turned his hair a dusty brown. "Looks like he fell."

"Yeah?" A disinterested Reece shrugged.

"Or was pushed," Bodine added musingly.

Reece looked a little more interested, but not much. There was something more important to be done here. Kneeling down, he went through Coolee's pockets and deftly extracted forty dollars, Coolee's poker winnings. "Lookee here!" he chortled, holding them up. Just as nimbly, Bodine swiped it from the careless hands.

"Hey!"

"It belongs to me." Bodine tucked it into his own pocket. "Ed wasn't your friend, he was mine. 'Sides"—he patted the pocket—"he woulda wanted me to have it."

"Well, ya ain't gettin' this." Duncan felt around and brandished a cigar he took out of Coolee's vest pocket. "They didn't get his stogie." He placed it under his nose and sniffed with appreciation. He grinned at Bodine. "Maybe Wyatt don't smoke but I do."

Reece looked down into Coolee's stiff, staring face and said reproachfully, "Ed, you was holdin' out on me. Now, that ain't nice. I recollect askin' you for a smoke yesterday and you said you ain't got any. Don't you know you can go to hell for lyin'?"

"This place is close to it," Bodine said dryly. "Wyatt took his rifle and horse. Ed shoulda stuck with us. Three against one. We coulda taken Wyatt." Realizing how close they had been to that twelve thousand dollars made Bodine kick out furiously. His toe came in contact with a rock, and he immediately regretted it.

Reece continued to reprimand the corpse. "Ya see, Ed, that's what ya get for tryin' to get the jump on your old friends." He looked at Bodine and asked reluctantly, "Should we bury him?"

"Do you want to hang around here digging in this heat or go after that cash?"

Put like that, Reece made the obvious choice. "Let's go. Got me lots of plans for that money."

Ed Coolee was friendless in life. Without his stogie and poker winnings, he was friendless in death as well. His partners didn't notice his passing except to kick some more dirt on him as they mounted up and got the hell out of there.

## Chapter Ten

Lee Jenkins was there when the stage swung down the main street of Pawnee Bluffs and rolled to a stop in front of the stage office. He watched, mildly interested, as the driver jumped down and hurled himself into the open doorway. At a shout from him the clerk at the desk rushed out and together the two removed a wounded man from the stagecoach. Jenkins craned his neck from where he stood in front of the saloon with other onlookers. He saw that it was Bud Harris, one of the company's drivers. Immediately, he lost interest.

"Bud Harris," Jenkins muttered to himself. "Old fool."

The arrival caused a lot of commotion in this usually quiet place. People hurried from their businesses to see what was happening.

Curiosity finally got the better of Jenkins and he summoned up enough energy to go over and loiter on the fringe of the growing crowd to see what the big to-do was.

Bud was speaking in ragged gasps. Jenkins caught the gist of the story the driver was telling as he was being carried to the musty, cramped doctor's office above the Feed and Grain. He said that it was Ed Coolee and the Reece brothers, led by Lyle Bodine, who had deliberately disabled the westbound stage out of Branson Wells. They killed and robbed two passengers. There were shouts of outrage when it was told to them that a young lady had been aboard as well.

A man had ridden into that hornets' nest—a man by the name of Jim Wyatt! Single-handedly, that young fella had faced up to those outlaws—just him and his Winchester— as cool as you please. He got clean away with the girl. He was probably heading for Dautry this very minute with the Bodine gang hot on his trail!

He gasped. So Wyatt was out of prison!

Jenkins smiled to himself slyly. This news was as good as money in his pocket, and right now the only thing in his pocket was the lining. It was a golden opportunity he couldn't pass up. He knew what he would do. Before the townspeople could even think to get up a rescue party, he would ride the fifteen miles to Dautry and tell March Newton.

This was something Newton would want to know, by sugar! He might even offer so high as a ten spot for the information. Jenkins was in a bad way for cash. Things would be different, of course, if he could only sell that ranch. For now he had to do what he could to make a dollar.

Yes sir, Newton would be plenty interested, all right. Even he knew there was bad blood between him and Wyatt. Now Wyatt was out of prison, and Newton had his girl.

It was a mighty interesting situation, and one Jenkins knew must end in somebody's death. He didn't particularly care whose as long as he made a little something along the way.

Money was the thing, and he was about to go get himself some. He hurried out of the saloon to the hitching rail and untied his horse. Swinging onto the dun's back, he tore out of town to Newton's ranch.

Jenkins rode right into the ranch yard and dismounted in front of the house.

"Came to see Newton," he called out as he swaggered over to the foreman. "Got some business to transact with him."

Arms crossed, the foreman took a stand in front of him, blocking the way. "What business?" Pete Gillens challenged, spitting tobacco juice contemptuously onto the ground near Jenkins' feet.

"He ain't got time to see ya. Can't go around seein' every tinhorn thinks he's important."

Jenkins got angry. "I tell ya, I got somethin' to tell him! Somethin' he'd better know!"

Gillens moved forward to confront him. "And I tell ya—!"

"Who the hell are you?" A metallic voice cut Gillens short. "What do you want with me?"

Jenkins knew Newton by sight but even more by reputation. Newton was a good-looking man in his thirties with unreadable brown eyes, a square stubborn-looking chin, and a face that warned you that you'd better not be wasting his time. His manner was always brusque and impatient.

Jenkins brushed past Gillens and came to a halt in front of Newton who stood, hands on hips, on the stone steps of his home. From here he could look down on Jenkins. He liked it that way.

"Got some information I thought ya might be lookin' for. Somethin' I *think* will be interestin' to you."

"What is it?" Newton's voice was curt. His eyes raked the tall, lanky man with the worn pants and faded blue shirt. Another small-timer who thought he was somebody.

Jenkins blurted out, "Well, I thought I'd be paid for it!"

Newton snorted disgustedly. "Paid for what? I don't have time for you—now get outta here!" He turned abruptly. Jenkins was alarmed. He spoke quickly as Gillens strode towards him to toss him off the ranch.

"I just thought you might be interested in the where-abouts of a man named Wyatt!"

Newton halted. His shoulders bunched as if he'd been struck. He turned back slowly. Gillens stopped in his steps and looked questioningly at his boss. Newton's flinty eyes had narrowed as he yanked his black cigar out of his mouth.

"Wyatt?" he barked sharply.

Jenkins relaxed. Now he had his attention.

"That's right. Fella by the name of Jim Wyatt. I heard you had some sort of feud with him—"

"Never mind about that! What do you know about him?"

Jenkins stalled. Should he ask for money again? He looked at Newton's face and decided to count on his generosity to name an amount.

"Well, it's this." Jenkins stuck his thumbs into his belt. "He's out of prison." He had the satisfaction of hearing

Newton exclaim angrily. "There was some problem with the stage out of Branson. They brung the stage driver in. He was knifed. Man name of Coolee done it—him and Lyle Bodine and the Reece brothers out of Texas."

Newton shrugged. "So?" he said as if he couldn't care less, and Jenkins hurried on with his tale.

"Seems some pilgrim and his daughter come along on the stage. The Bodine gang killed the man and was planning to take off with the girl and the loot from the robbery." He paused for effect. Newton's eyes widened but he said nothing. "Afore they could do it, this here Jim Wyatt comes in, wounds one man, and takes the girl with him."

"So now he's kidnapping women." Newton sneered, his eyes faintly amused. "I'm not surprised!"

"Bud Harris, he said Wyatt helped him and was helping the girl," Jenkins added apologetically, as if hating to ruin Newton's dark picture of Wyatt. Newton had formed his own notion of Wyatt and if the facts didn't fit his notion, he'd make them fit.

"I don't believe it!" Newton rapped out. "He's probably in on it!"

"Could be—him bein' an ex-convict and all. Anyways, he's headed thisaway to his ranch," he added helpfully.

"Is he?" Newton swore long and hard. He had wanted that ranch of Wyatt's bad. Real bad. Not so much for its intrinsic worth but more as a trophy of a vanquished enemy. He had hoped something would happen to Wyatt in prison or before he came back home. It seemed it hadn't. Now it was up to Newton to see that it did. He chewed his cigar thoughtfully for a few moments as he culled through his options.

"Pete!" He turned to his foreman, his mind made up. "I think it's the duty of every law-abidin' citizen to do what he can to save this girl."

Gillens grinned. "If Wyatt ain't killed her already."

Newton ignored this. "We'll get a posse together to go after him—*our men*," he instructed. "No need to get the town involved. "You!" He looked at Jenkins. "Do you want to earn fifty dollars?" Jenkins did indeed. He nodded eagerly. "You can go along with my men."

"There'll be some shootin'," Gillens drawled. "Someone may get killed." He looked at his boss. "Maybe Wyatt will get killed."

"I think he just might." Newton's smile was unpleasant.

"That girl might get killed, too," Gillens said consideringly. Newton balked. Where should he draw the line? "Her bein' a witness and all to everything," Gillens added.

"Well, we all hope that won't happen," Newton said, condoning the idea in a backhanded way. "But it *could* happen. We have to expect that when you have a felon like Wyatt involved."

Jenkins looked uneasy. Stealing was one thing; killing was another. He'd killed a few men but they'd had it coming. He didn't like getting women involved. He didn't mind cheating them out of their money, but he'd never shoot one—not unless he had to.

"Still interested?" Newton shot out. Jenkins knew his pockets were to let, and he had only two dollars between his bare foot and his boot leather. Fifty dollars! That was almost two months' wages if he worked. After all, the money was for finding Wyatt. He could disappear while Newton's men dealt with the girl.

"All right, but I want the money up front!" Jenkins demanded almost aggressively.

Newton read Jenkins right. He took out his wallet and gave him twenty dollars. "You'll get the rest when the job is done."

Jenkins was satisfied and stuffed the money in his boot. Now the other two bills wouldn't be so lonely.

"Get some men together, Pete; at least twenty. Make sure they're good shots. Get Pinky and Frank Rawl."

Jenkins moved uncomfortably. He'd heard of Rawl. He was fast on the draw.

"You! What the hell's your name again?"

"Jenkins. Lee Jenkins," he said proudly.

"You can show them where to pick up Wyatt's trail. I'll give you those thirty extra dollars if my men catch up to him."

"But I thought—"

"You thought wrong! I pay for results. Find their trail—then you get the money." His voice was harsh.

"Reckon I can do that," Jenkins responded sulkily. He didn't know he'd have to do so much work. He figured all he'd have to do was tell them where to look for Wyatt. Nothing more contemptible than a man who won't part easily with his money. "I'm a bit hollow," Jenkins hinted slyly.

"You have time to eat before the men leave. Go see Rosa in the kitchen." Jenkins did just that. While he scraped up spoonfuls of beans and meat, Newton ordered his horse saddled. He was going to see Anne. She would want to hear about Wyatt.

When Newton got to town he tied his horse in front of the hotel. Anne had taken a room there while Newton ran her ranch. She couldn't stand being at the house now that her father was gone. Newton had urged her to marry him right away, but Anne had hung back. She wanted things "settled" first. Newton didn't know what that meant to Anne, but to him it meant getting Wyatt out of the picture by any means possible.

He stomped down the boardwalk while men dodged out of his way and entered the hotel's lobby with its seedy red plush settee and overstuffed chairs. A big oil painting of a woman in a purple low-cut gown hung on the wall. The hotel proprietor had painted it himself. It was supposed to be of his sister. The picture was terrible and several patrons had tried to burn it on a Saturday night drunk. The frame was a little charred around the edges.

Newton ignored the picture and went up the stairs, nodding curtly to the owner who sat behind the counter reading. He banged on Anne Garvey's door irritably after trying the knob first.

"Yes?" a soft voice spoke from the other side.

"It's March. May I come in?"

"Of course." He could hear the rustling of taffeta and then a dead bolt being drawn back. He had demanded the hotel's owner install it for Anne's protection. The idea of her living in a cheap hotel when her own mansion was unoccupied annoyed him. She opened the door and stepped aside, a dainty, slight figure in a pink ruffled dress.

Shutting the door with force, Newton leaned forward and kissed her on her soft lips. Every time he saw her, he couldn't believe how delicate and beautiful she was. Just five-feet-two, she looked like a child with her softly waving blond hair, light blue eyes, and small waist.

She was a woman who needed a man to lean on and Newton was that man. He didn't care that she was weak and vacillating. Newton was a man who liked to make all of the decisions and he didn't like a woman who had an opinion. He and Anne were ideally suited. Anne always took his advice and was grateful for it. The only thing she had mulishly refused to do was to marry him until Wyatt came home. He didn't believe for a moment that she loved Wyatt. Who could when he was around? But in her gentle way, he supposed she didn't want to hurt Wyatt even though she declared he had shot her father in the back. Newton hadn't minded her reticence. At the time he'd had pressing things to do and he could wait. Now it seemed the waiting was over.

"Jim Wyatt is out of prison," he said abruptly. It was too abrupt. The color drained from Anne's face. As she swayed on her feet Newton put his strong arm around her slender frame and helped her over to a chair.

"I knew it." She covered her face with her hands, her voice quavering. "I knew this day would come! I can't bear it!"

Newton pulled up a chair next to her and put his arm around her comfortingly. "There's no need for you to bear anything, honey. That's what I'm here for." There was a threat underlying his reassuring voice. Anne removed her hands and looked up at him, her eyes filled with tears.

"Thank you, March. I don't know what I'd do without you."

His chest swelled.

"Well, you don't have to. I have everything under control. There's somethin' else you don't know." Newton paused while Anne looked fearfully up into his face. "He's with the Bodine gang." She gasped.

"They robbed this here stage and shot Bud Harris. Or stabbed him. Anyway, the old boy is laid up pretty bad and may not live. He said there was a couple of pilgrims on the stage—a man and his niece or somethin'." Newton stopped and took a deep breath. "In all the ruckus, they killed the man. Then Jim Wyatt made off with the girl."

"Horrible! Horrible! I knew I couldn't trust him!"

"You'd better believe it, honey, I can. I always said he killed your pa—and the sheriff."

"But . . . but"—Anne dabbed at her face—"how could Jim have killed the sheriff? He was on his way to prison when it happened."

"That foreman of his, Laban Kettering, did it. Same difference." Newton didn't like his theory being tampered with. "They say the sheriff started asking questions. Next thing you know they'd have found Wyatt guilty of murder, not just rustling. Laban had to shut him up." There was disdain in his voice and intense dislike.

"If Wyatt comes back he'll probably try to clear his name."

"He won't get a chance. I've gotten a posse of my own men together to hunt him down. They're leaving now. Should be able to handle this mess. Can't have Wyatt comin' back here trying to point the finger at someone else. I won't have it. Who knows who he'll accuse?"

Anne seemed relieved. "I can't believe I was once engaged to him. I never took him for a womanizer. I guess I'd believe just about anything now." She looked up at Newton gratefully, her face stained with tears. Anne was all the more vulnerable and attractive for it. Newton's arm tightened about her. "Do you think you'll have to . . . oh, I can't even say it."

"I can say it," Newton responded tersely. "Kill him? But it's up to him," he lied, wanting to sound reasonable even if he was not. "If he gives himself up he can save his life. But you know him. He'd never admit he did anything wrong. Lyin' murderer!"

Anne sagged against him, breathing rapidly. "Do you think I'll be safe here?"

"I'll post a man here to be sure but I don't think he'll get this far."

Newton persuaded Anne to come and have a cup of tea with him downstairs. The hot drink seemed to revive her.

"I'll be going now. I'll send someone out here to guard you. He'll have orders to kill Wyatt if he comes near you."

"I don't know," she said slowly, regretfully.

"It's got to be done!" his voice exploded in the quiet room as anger mounted his face. "Men like Wyatt are trouble! He won't rest until he finds someone to pin those murders on! You can see that, can't you?"

Anne agreed because she saw he was riled up about it. After another kiss he left her, slamming on his hat and pushing through the doors to the outside.

Anne knew the kind of man Newton was. He would not let his authority on this issue be questioned. He was taking things into his own hands. Jim would be dealt with with ruthless thoroughness.

Anne watched him go, her hands clutched together. Jim had always protested his innocence. Many of the towns-people believed him but they were intimidated by Newton, who had sworn up and down that Jim had shot her father. The sheriff had believed Jim as well and had told Newton to his face. From the little the sheriff had let drop, it seemed he had a pretty good guess who had murdered Ralph Garvey. A few days later the sheriff was dead as well. This time there was no one to stand between Newton and his accusations.

Newton decided that Kettering had done it and assured Anne that he would take care of him. Almost one year later and Kettering was still holding on to the Flying W. It had angered Newton something awful. Perhaps something was protecting Kettering.

Anne's blue eyes strayed to the small church with the rudely made cross on top. Perhaps someone knew Jim was innocent. What if Jim could prove his innocence now that he was out of prison? Who would that leave to accuse? Anne's gaze left the wooden cross and fixed instead on Newton who had disappeared among the brakes along the creek. Who would that leave? Abruptly she turned away and went back up to her room.

"Let's get going there!" Newton yelled as his men slowly assembled. Gillens had gathered them together from all parts of the range. "There's a murderer that's got to be caught and it's gettin' late!"

Jenkins came out of the house wiping his mouth. He had enjoyed a nice time flirting with the plump Rosa, who had flashed her black eyes at him and provocatively swung her hips as she moved about the kitchen. Good-looking woman. She was bound to have money stashed away some place. In a jar or a sock or under her mattress, Jenkins figured.

"You still eatin'?" Newton growled as Jenkins sauntered to his horse.

"I got a ways to go yet today," he complained mildly.

"You're not getting there any faster. What's that crow bait you're ridin'?" He eyed the tired dun with distaste. "Put her in the corral. You can borrow one of my horses for now."

Jenkins' eyes brightened. "Yes sir!" Maybe in all the commotion he could just take the horse he loaned him and ride away. It was a fine-looking animal. Newton was the kind of man who made sure everything he had was the best. He figured he deserved it.

"What are your orders?" Rawl asked flatly. A morose-featured man, he had black hair that was slicked back off his long, sallow face. There was nothing flashy about him except his carefully clipped mustache and blue-checked shirt. The checks weren't washed out like Jenkins'. It showed the man had money. Apparently, killing paid well.

"This Jim Wyatt is a murderer. A few of you may know him," Newton announced, "so if he gives you any trouble— shoot him! He's a good shot." The last was added grudgingly. "So get him with your first bullet."

"I'm better," Rawl flipped out coldly. He had a reputation that he protected jealously.

"He kidnapped some girl, too," Newton pointed out to encourage them. All his men listened. Newton looked into each hard face, gauging their sentiments. He needed men who would stick and not turn squeamish at the last minute.

These riders wouldn't. They were primed and ready for action.

"Now I hope nothing happens to this girl." There were several snickers which Newton pretended not to hear. "But you've got to take care of Wyatt—*if* he gives you any trouble," he added scrupulously once more, just to clear himself. His men knew him. They wouldn't be paid for bringing anyone in alive—not all twenty of them. As for the girl, they were aware he was prepared to turn a blind eye to whatever they did. His men and he understood each other.

"Another thing. One thousand dollars to the man who kills Wyatt and brings me his body!"

All was silent. Newton let the amount sink in. It was a reminder of where their loyalty lay.

It was a lot of money. Even Jenkins licked his lips at the thought of it. One thousand dollars! He usually didn't kill for profit but sometimes a man had to make an exception. He hadn't had that much money since his wife died.

"Pete, you're in charge." Newton was satisfied with their sudden restlessness to get started. Then he spoke to them all. "You have a job to do, now do it well! Frank, Pinky, hold up a minute. The rest of you men—get to it!"

To shouts and whistles the riders went helling out of the ranch yard with Gillens in the lead. Then Newton turned to Pinky and Rawl.

"About this girl. I don't want any witnesses alive. You understand? Make sure you come back without her."

Both men nodded.

"Yeah, boss," Rawl answered with a laugh.

## Chapter Eleven

March Newton was already planning his next move as the men rode away. There were ten more hired hands scattered around the place including the cook and a few old-timers who did odd jobs and were good shots. That was enough to ride over to the Flying W and take it over. Before he took another step, however, he'd have to first get rid of Laban Kettering.

Newton rubbed his square chin thoughtfully. Much as he'd like to shoot him to bits, he had to admit grudgingly that Kettering had too good an aim with that Winchester of his. It never left his hands. The so-and-so probably slept with it tucked in beside him. If there was some way to lure the foreman away, he'd do it. Newton smiled. It was not a nice smile. Of course! He thought of the perfect bait to use. The next thing to do was to find that so-called preacher he'd seen knocking about town for the past few days.

Newton found Brother Arvel rollicking around the

saloons of Dautry looking for contributions for his cause. When money was refused he accepted drinks. Newton cornered him as he was about to enter the Spanish Spur to spread the Good Word. At first Brother Arvel was annoyed, but seeing how well-dressed Newton was and having been given to understand that his services were required, Brother Arvel's ears perked up.

"Ah yes, a fellow traveler on the road of life. How may I help you, good sir?" Arvel noticed the big silver belt buckle and was sure that the heavy clinking in the man's pockets betokened the presence of gold coins. His smile broadened ingratiatingly.

"I believe you were around here last year. Do you remember Laban Kettering?" Newton barked out.

"Ah yes, brother Laban," the preacher said vaguely. "May he rest in peace."

"He ain't dead—yet! You went to talk to him about giving himself up to the law a year back." Newton tried to revive Brother Arvel's defunct memory with the facts.

The preacher grimaced. He remembered. "Yes, sir, brother Laban. He just wouldn't take the Word to his heart. Put a bullet in my new hat," he admitted frankly. "Never met such an unrepentant soul in all my days as a minister."

"I got something for you to do," Newton interrupted. He had no interest in Kettering's soul or the preacher's hat.

The preacher looked interested. "A weddin', perhaps? I'm good at weddin's—and funerals."

"Yeah, well maybe I can use you later for that." The preacher brightened up. "Right now I want you to deliver a message."

"A sermon? Just let me git my Bible. I can give you a real hellfire sermon or sneak up on a person's soul careful-like." He was about to quote his fee when Newton broke in.

"I don't want a sermon! I want some information passed on. Reckon you're the one to do it."

"Oh? Why?"

"Because I figure he won't shoot a preacherman." The preacher didn't like the sound of that. He had been shot at—many times. Some people just didn't have respect for men of the cloth.

"If he's not ready to receive the Word, ya just cain't force it. The Almighty moves in mysterious ways. Mayhap he's a savin' Brother Laban for the ovens of hell. 'Sides, if my memory serves me correct, he's a mite too quick with that gun of his."

"I'll give you ten dollars to go up there and tell him something." Newton was impatient. "He won't kill you."

The preacher considered this carefully. Ten dollars was a lot of money and this good man obviously needed his help. "Make it twenty," he suggested. "Got me a lot of souls to convert and that takes money."

They finally agreed to fifteen dollars and the preacher was given the message. "Tell Laban that Jim Wyatt is out of prison and is being hunted by my men—March Newton's men, about twenty of them—for kidnapping a young girl."

"Ain't you March Newton?"

"That's right."

"And you want me to tell him that your men are hunting this Wyatt person?" At Newton's decisive nod he asked, "Why?"

"The 'why' of the matter just don't concern you, preacherman. You just deliver that message. Got it? Right now!"

"Some liquid refreshment would be most welcome—"

"Now!"

Brother Arvel sighed hugely. "Very well. The Lord's work never seems to be done." He looked up at the sky. "I'm goin', Lord. I'm a goin' to Brother Laban to try and reap his soul for your blessed harvest. But I won't be successful. Oh, no. Brother Laban will surely descend to the bottomless pit. And I hope, O Lord, that he don't take me with him." He clapped his hat on his head and mounted up. He had no choice. He could see that Brother Newton was not going to allow him to go to the saloon across the street to take a stiff drink of consolation before beginning his perilous journey.

"Fifteen bucks," he muttered to himself as he rode out of town. "I hope I have time to spend it!"

Unenthusiastically, the preacher took the trail to the Flying W. Last time he came this way, Brother Laban had told him that if he came back the buzzards would be dining on his hide. He sure hoped Brother Laban had a poor memory. Hours later, he reached the house. Prudently, he stayed outside of shooting distance and called out.

"Brother Laban, brother Laban! Can you hear my voice? Do you recognize it?" Brother Laban obviously could because a bullet came whining out of nowhere slamming into the tree under which the preacher sat.

"I came here bearing news, Brother. Not the glad tidings of hope and redemption, but ill tidings concerning a friend of yours." He was relieved that no more bullets came at him.

"I speak of a friend of yours, uh . . ."—the preacher groped about for the name—"Jim . . . Wyatt. Jim Wyatt." There was no sound. "Hello, there!" He waited a few minutes in silence. He knew someone must be there because the hairs at the base of his neck crawled in fear. Would they blow him out of his saddle? The preacher swallowed hard.

"What do you have to say?" The words were spoken from not more than ten feet away and were so loud and unexpected that the preacher's horse spooked and almost tossed him. He brought the frightened beast under control and peered into the shadows of some larger trees surrounded by rocks. He saw the metallic gleam of a rifle.

"I bring you some news I was told in town to deliver. Your friend, Jim Wyatt, is out of prison. He's being hunted by March Newton's men, about twenty of them they say, because your poor, misguided friend has seen fit to kidnap an innocent young girl against her will." The preacher lifted his hat and looked up at the sky. "Message delivered, Lord. I'm gettin' outta here!"

"Just a minute!" There was a sound of pebbles sliding, then a man appeared. He was in his forties with brown hair touched with gray. All five feet nine inches of him were solid and intimidating with a face that matched. He studied the preacher with suspicious eyes. He held his rifle lightly. Three other men were visible now—all well-armed.

"You alone?" he asked, his eyes darting behind and around the preacher.

"Alone except for the presence of the Almighty. Amen!"

"Why did you ride all the way here to deliver that message to me?" he questioned Brother Arvel narrowly.

"I won't lie to you, brother Laban. I was paid ten dollars to do it."

"Ten dollars?" Laban frowned.

"Fifteen, then, by Brother Newton who is mighty interested in cultivatin' your soul for the harvest."

"Ha! I'll bet he is! So, he paid you to tell me that, did he? And is it true? Is Wyatt out and did March send some men after him?" The brown eyes drilled into him. Fine, piercing eyes they were, too, that made the preacher's soul wither.

"It is true. I done heard it in town afore Brother Newton told me. 'Course, the story when first it entered my incredulous ears was that this Wyatt fella saved the stage driver and rescued this here Eastern girl from the Bodine gang. But Brother Newton put me on the straight and narrow of the matter. He seems mighty taken with the idea that Wyatt kidnapped the girl. Brother Newton appears to be a suspicious soul and could use a good sermonizing."

"And did he send twenty men after Jim?"

"That number was spotted leaving his ranch. Frank Rawl was one of them. He is a man who, I'm afraid, is altogether too handy with his gun. The hot coals of hell are awaitin' him. Three funerals in six months for people he'd had a disagreement with." He looked sad.

Rawl was bad enough by himself but there were twenty. Jim wouldn't have a chance. Laban swore long and hard.

The preacher looked pained. "Cursing is not the answer."

"You're right. Action is. You, preacher"—he pointed at the parson—"you git outta here! Didn't I tell you a year ago that if you ever set a foot on this land, the buzzards would be gnawin' on your hide?"

"You have been gifted with a remarkably good memory, Brother, much to my detriment. But I brave all to deliver this message to you. It is my duty."

"Well, you've delivered it. Now git out unless you want to stay around for the shootin'."

"I am a man of peace."

"Good. Stay that way and you'll live longer. Now you go down to town and tell March Newton that I heard the news, I got some men together and rode out of here. Got that?"

"You want me to lie?" He seemed taken aback. "I don't think I can do that." As an afterthought he asked, "What will you pay me? Savin' souls takes money."

"I'm not payin' you a red cent and you'll be saving your own soul. Because if you don't do it I'll come after you, and you'll be takin' that long-awaited journey to a higher sphere ahead of schedule." Laban lifted his rifle and aimed it at the parson's thin, washboard chest. "This time I mean it. I'm tired of making promises and not making good on them!"

The parson and his horse took several steps backwards. After a moment's deliberation he said, "Lyin's a sin, but dyin' is worse. And the Almighty won't hold it agin you for not followin' through on your promise to send me to the next world. I ain't ready for the land of milk and honey yet."

"Then git! And you tell Newton I took off. And don't you be tellin' him I told you to tell him, hear?"

"I hear you, Brother. Amen!"

"Did you tell him?"

"I told him, brother Newton, but he ain't forgiven me yet for the last time I tried to help his faltering soul down the path of righteousness."

"What happened?"

"He was aworried, Brother Newton. I could see the worry standing out plain on his face. Whilst I left, he was a gathering up his men to go find Brother Jim." A grin overspread Newton's face.

"Good! Now I can do what I've wanted to do for three years—get hold of the Flying W!"

The news the preacher brought back with him was just what Newton wanted to hear. Kettering would be off that ranch in a minute to save his friend. And that's when Newton would move in.

If Wyatt got himself out of his predicament, there would be no ranch to run to and no living to be made from it. It would all belong to Newton. He had a lawyer in his pocket in town. Once Wyatt was laid to rest 'neath the shade of the spreading willows up on boot hill, Newton would produce a bill of sale for the ranch. Yes, Newton grinned wickedly, life surely was looking good!

He'd take the rest of his men and just move onto the Flying W while Kettering was chasing all over the country looking for a corpse. Feeling superior, he headed for his horse. He figured Kettering had left by now. Newton would just ride up there and take over that piddling ranch house—take it right now—today!

Newton and about twelve men stopped for a moment to survey the Wyatt ranch and the green hills surrounding it. Nice setup, he had to admit. Wyatt was damn smart to get himself this place and all the water he needed. Now Newton would take it. He grinned when he saw the grain in the barn: Food for the cattle this winter. That would save him time and money.

"Come on," he said easily. "Six of you take the barn and we'll go up to the house." Newton turned his horse's head and started up the dirt trail. There was a corral to the left with several nice-looking horses. Newton's eyes alighted on one in particular. "I want that sorrel," he announced, his eyes going over it expertly. "Good breeding stock."

They were heading towards the corral when something whipped past Newton's ear. Incredulously, it sounded like a bullet. Newton whirled around in his saddle to look for the shooter.

"Horse thieves get hanged around here." Came Laban's laconic voice from a slope of boulders and rubble. He stood there easily, but his rifle was aimed at Newton.

"I'm no horse thief!" Newton growled angrily. It infuriated him that he had been caught in the act of committing what most would consider to be a common crime.

"You're nothin' but a thief!" Laban fired out contemptuously. Newton was irked. How dare he use that tone with him, the biggest landholder in these parts. "You steal people's land, you steal people's cattle, you steal people's lives." The words rolled coolly off Laban's tongue.

"And what do you think about murderers?" Newton asked, stung, thinking of Wyatt and Ralph Garvey.

"I think they're the scum of the earth," Laban affirmed pleasantly. "How many innocent people you reckon you've murdered, Newton? Not including Jim Wyatt, whom you sent twenty brave men after to hunt down and kill?"

Around Laban other men appeared, all holding guns aimed at Newton's men. The sight of them stopped Newton's riders dead in their tracks.

"That's far enough!" Laban's voice rang out. "I got my rifle trained on your boss' gut. Any move on your part and he catches lead!"

Slowly, Laban's men moved forward and disarmed Newton's. Newton was the last to unbuckle his belt and toss it disdainfully at the older man's feet.

"Next time—"

"Next time I'll shoot to kill! We'll all shoot to kill! You all understand that now! Any one of you sets foot on the Flying W and it'll be the last time you'll do anything. And don't think that doesn't include you, Newton! Maybe I'll put a bounty on your head like you did to Jim!"

Newton was so surprised that his hand jerked and the horse jumped nervously. It took him a few seconds to get him under control again. How in hell had Laban found out? But Laban had his own way of gathering information. Moreover, although Newton would find it hard to swallow, Jim had many friends around here. Several of them had come running to tell Laban the news. Newton wasn't admired and respected as much as he believed.

"I had nothing to do with that—if it's true," Newton shrugged noncommittally, "but whoever did, he's doing everyone hereabouts a favor." Then he added nastily, "He won't evade justice this time! He can't take on twenty men as easily as he did one man—and shot in the back yet!"

Laban's hand tightened alarmingly on the trigger. He replied smoothly, however. "Twenty men? Why, Jim can take them on easy! That's why I didn't bother goin' to help him. I'da just been in the way."

The matter-of-fact tone riled Newton as Laban hoped it would. "He's a goner. I know it and you know it! Now I'm givin' you some advice: Get out now while I let you live or else you'll be leavin' this ranch in a coffin—like Wyatt! I'll be back in a few days and I'll come in shootin' so you and your men better hightail it out of here while I'm still in a good mood! And another thing—"

"Get out of here," Laban said coldly. "Quick—all of you!" The men hesitated at first, then they started to move out. Newton remained sitting there, angry and frustrated.

"Wyatt's as good as dead and you know that!"

"Keep sayin' it, Newton, and maybe you'll believe it! Now you get on out. You and that other murderin' trash!" Newton reached for his guns—but they were lying on the ground. Laban watched him poker-faced, wondering what he'd try to do next.

"Let me have my guns and I'll fight you fair," he snapped.

Laban allowed himself to laugh scornfully. "Fair? I've seen lots of examples of your brand of fairness, Newton. Now you get goin' before I lose my temper. You've tried it sorely today and I'm pretty near the end of my rope."

Newton saw the icy glitter in the depths of those brown eyes and knew it would only take a little more prodding if he wanted to end up with a bullet in his chest.

"I'll go now but I'll be back," he threatened.

"Not without an invitation you won't," Laban said agreeably and signaled his men to follow them all until they were off Wyatt land.

Newton ripped out an oath and his men cringed. Then he rode in stony silence all the way back to his own ranch. This wasn't over—not at all! One of them, either he or Wyatt, would be leaving this town for good. And since Newton had no intention of moving on and no intention of allowing Wyatt to remain here, the choice was clear.

## Chapter Twelve

Shorty Reece was more dead than alive. He managed to open his eyes, then moved his limbs tentatively. They felt so heavy. Slowly, he rolled onto his side and sat up. He didn't remember crawling into this clump of cotton-woods. The last thing he recalled after being tossed around by the river, was lying on his back on a finger of rock that jutted into the water.

Groaning, he struggled to his knees, waited for the world to stop spinning, then staggered weakly to his feet. For a moment he leaned against a tree to catch his breath. His mind was a blur but he made his feet move.

Pushing away, he started walking. He didn't know where he was. One thing registered through the muzziness in his brain: He must stay on the trail so that Duncan will find him. Duncan was probably looking for him now. He shuf-fled along for what seemed like hours. When he could walk no more he sat down heavily on a rock. A vast blackness engulfed him.

With head lowered and eyes closed, he never heard the rider approach. He didn't know anyone was there until he felt the sun's warmth on his closed eyelids turn cool. A pebble rolled over and tapped his foot; a heel scraped. Nearby, a horse stamped restlessly.

"Duncan?" There was no answer.

Opening his eyes with difficulty, he saw the long shadow of a man blocking out the sun. His gaze followed wearily to the dusty, worn boots and legs braced apart. He saw the hard-worked jeans, the twin gunbelts strapped to narrow hips. A check shirt fitted loosely over the lean body and shoulders that were intimidating. A fighting-tough man, he towered over Shorty holding his rifle easily in one bruised, callused hand. Shorty knew his time was up when he looked into the man's face. It was Jim Wyatt—the very man they had been hunting!

Shorty flinched at the menace in the stony-green eyes, the grim set of his jaw. This was it. No use going on any farther. Wyatt had him in his sights, and Shorty couldn't even fight back. He didn't have a gun. His voice stuck in his throat. He swallowed hard and finally spoke.

"Ya gonna kill me, mister? I ain't got a gun so it'll be easy."

"You're right," Jim drawled. "But I don't shoot unarmed men. I'm no murderer. The question is: Should I help you?" A gleam of hope came into Shorty's dark eyes. Was he really considering taking him along? He doubted it. But, just maybe, he meant it. "You still intending to harm Miss Carter?"

"No sir, mister, I just wanna get outta this alive. I wanna live," he stammered out, wiping the perspiration from his brow.

"Where are the others?"

"I don't know. They was trackin' you. Then Bodine, he pushed me off my horse and took it." There was a long pause as if he still couldn't believe it. "He just pushed me into the water."

"Where's your brother, Duncan?" Jim's voice sliced through Shorty's confusion.

"He didn't come back. I thought for sure he would when he saw I was gone but he didn't. My own brother didn't come back to help me." He tasted the words like they were too hard to swallow yet. "He left me to die. He knowed how bad hurt I was but he never come back." His words trailed off. Too tired to speak anymore he rested his big, shaggy head against a rock. His eyes closed. Jim could see that he wouldn't make it if he didn't help him.

"All right, I'll help you," he said abruptly. "But get this through your skull, Reece. If you try anything I'll leave you how I found you: No horse, no water or food, no gun. Comprende?"

Shorty forced his lids open. "I won't do nothin', mister."

"What if we come on your friends? If you side with them, I'll take you out along with them, gun or no gun."

"They ain't no friends of mine."

"And your brother?"

"He left me to die. I reckon he's on his own now. I cain't trust him no more."

"No, you can't trust a dog that's bitten you. I would stay away from him in the future. If he lives," Jim added thoughtfully.

"You gonna kill him, mister?" Shorty did not seem upset at this; merely curious.

"If he comes asking for it he'll get it." Jim's voice was flat. "That goes for any man."

"Not me," Shorty protested quickly.

"Good." Jim knelt down, keeping his rifle well away from Shorty. He examined the wound. It was inflamed. He'd take him with him and tend to him later.

Pete Gillens led his men through the red-hot afternoon. Over twenty pairs of eyes roamed the countryside, looking for some sign of Wyatt.

Riding back and forth, the men searched for clues but found none. There were endless discussions of where Wyatt would go. Some favored Dautry; some liked the idea of Fort Ewell. Others felt he would make a run for his ranch. Every man was thinking of that thousand dollar prize. Most of them were cowpunchers and ranch hands who never saw more than thirty dollars at a time. All knew exactly what they would do with that money.

"What do you suppose this here Wyatt fella did?" one cowboy asked curiously of another. His companion shrugged.

"Don't rightly know, but Newton wants him dead so he musta done somethin'." The other nodded. No one really quite knew except Gillens and Pinky, but they didn't question the orders of the wealthy, powerful rancher. Besides, it wasn't as if anyone was objecting.

In camp that night Gillens spoke to his men. "Come daylight, we'll split into three groups. Fan out and search for him. Bring plenty of ammunition. You just might meet up with him."

"Is he that good?" Frank Rawl asked as he hunkered down with a cup of coffee.

"Yeah, he's that good," Gillens admitted sourly. "So watch it!" He didn't particularly like the gunfighter, but he was on their side so he felt obligated to warn him at least once.

"Fine." Rawl reached down and patted his Colt. "It's dull work to gun down someone who doesn't know one end of a gun from the other. I like a challenge. Makes the killin' that much more enjoyable."

Gillens threw him a disgusted look. "You're not invincible, Rawl."

Rawl pulled his gun so quickly, Gillens was taken aback and almost dropped his cup. Rawl laughed. "Ha! Think Wyatt is faster than that? I doubt it." He slammed his gun home and stood there confidently, thumbs hooked into his belt. "I like you, Pete," he said, taking out one of his guns again and looking at it. "That's why I'm letting you know now that I'm gettin' that thousand dollars!" He looked past the metal barrel to the foreman. "If anyone gets in my way I'm going to be mighty upset." He walked away still practicing with his guns.

Gillens watched him emotionlessly. Better him than me, he thought. Let him try to corner that cougar. Gillens was sure of one thing: The first man to come upon Wyatt would be the first man dead.

\* \* \*

In a small basin where rain washes down and collects on the shoulder of Radiant Butte, Jim made camp. He patched up Shorty's wound then handed him some coffee.

"Thanks." Shorty's voice was humble. "I sure am sorry for all I done to you and the girl. I ain't forgettin' that you saved my life, and when the shootin' comes I'll do my share."

Jim gave him a small smile. He believed him. "Good. We need every gun we can get," he said seriously.

"I ain't worth much, but I'm a pretty good shot." Shorty took a sip of coffee, savoring it. He didn't mention his brother and Jim didn't ask.

Jim went back to the fire. Julie came over to where he sat and settled herself next to him. She leaned her shoulder companionably against his. The wind flapped her hem so she drew up her knees and tucked her skirt around her legs.

"Do you trust him?" she asked softly.

"Yes. Even Shorty realizes that it would be useless for him to throw in with Bodine again, even if he wanted to. He knows he'd just be buying himself a bullet when it's all over. He has a better chance of survival with us."

"What about our chances of survival?"

"There's three of us and two of them. You see"—he smiled down at her—"I'm including you. With you packin' two guns, I figure you're a force to reckon with." She seemed pleased at this compliment.

"What will happen when you get home? With March Newton, I mean . . . and Anne." She sounded casual but Jim knew she was worried.

"Well"—he pushed up the rim of his hat—"I've been thinking on that for a long while—a whole year, in fact.

Like as not, Anne has hitched her star to Newton. I don't care so much about that though." He turned to watch for her reaction. She looked downward quickly, but Jim had seen a small smile of relief turn up the corners of her mouth. "But he's not stealing my place on me. He robbed me of a whole year of my life, ruined my reputation, and now he's making Laban's life miserable. I'd go after him for those three things alone."

"You wouldn't fight him for Anne?" she asked, suddenly absorbed in picking a speck off her dusty skirt.

"No, that's over with. A girl had a right to choose the man she wants to be with. Either a girl comes willingly or not at all."

"Very true." Her cheeks were pink from blushing. Jim made bold and took her hand in his, holding it gently.

"But I've got to get my reputation back if I'm ever to live in peace on my own ranch. I couldn't ask a woman to share my name if it's tarnished."

She seemed alarmed at this prospect. "What if you don't?"

"I will," he said confidently. "I'll find the evidence. If not, I'll force Newton to confess."

She studied him carefully. He could sell out and start over someplace else. It was a big country. There were plenty of places where people wouldn't have heard of him, but she knew he wouldn't. He was in the right, and he had to clear his name for his own peace of mind. There were some things a man had to do for himself before he could live with his own conscience. She could see his face set firmly with determination.

She squeezed his hand. "Then you give him hell, Jim

Wyatt! But," she added meaningfully, "come out of it in one piece."

"I aim to. I've been making a lot of plans in the last few days." His green eyes slanted towards her. "When this is all over I'll tell you about them."

Julie laughed lightly. It was the first time he'd heard her laugh and he liked the sound of it. "I'd like to hear them."


"What the hell's going on?" Jim exclaimed to himself the next morning as they prepared to leave. Far off in the distance he made out two small specks on the horizon: Bodine and Reece. Damn their souls to everlasting hell! They were sure hustling their bustles over those hills!

But there was something else to catch his attention; something even closer and much more disturbing. A party of riders was coming over the plains. Judging by the plumes of dust they sent up, it was a large party. Could it be a posse?

"What is it?" Both Julie and Shorty rode up to where Jim was just mounting. His face was set grimly.

"Riders." He indicated them.

"Maybe it's a posse comin' after me," Shorty observed gloomily. Jim glanced at him quickly.

"Don't worry, I won't let them hang you," Jim promised. Shorty gave a sigh of relief.

"Mighty kind of you," he muttered, ashamed. Then he made out the two horsemen. "Bodine and Duncan?"

"Probably."

"Maybe the posse will find them first!" The idea pleased him.

The large party of approximately twenty men had split

up and were frenziedly searching about for sign like a hound dog finding a scent. The sight of them just didn't sit well with him. Something big was going on. The best thing to do now was to get out of their way. His eyes turned to the jagged range of mountains that rose up from the plains far away. Rain King was directly ahead. It was a massive slab of a mountain, but it was no place to fort up. He looked to the lesser eminence next to it which was Grand Mesa.

"We'll head for that," Jim motioned. "If we go straight for my ranch anyone can follow the trail and even cut us off. The mountains will offer us some protection." He nudged his horse and the others followed. Long ago, an old Indian had told him about Grand Mesa. There was supposed to be water up there near the top, and an ancient trail that led down the far side of the mesa. Ordinarily, he wouldn't have banked on this information, but there was no place else to go. He'd better find water and that other trail or that old Indian had a lot to answer for!

## Chapter Thirteen

Jesse and Heddy were about to leave the shade of the cool trees and step into the sunlight when Jesse's hand stayed her. At the touch on her wrist she followed the line of his gaze. About a mile away they saw riders. Jesse counted them: Twenty at least.

"Who are they, Jesse? Do you know them?"

"No." A frown formed on his young forehead.

"Should we stop and talk to them?"

"No," he said with more force than before. "I don't like the looks of them. I wouldn't trust them, especially with a girl as nice looking as you are." Heddy blushed, but she saw that his expression was serious as he watched the men. "They have the look of hunters about them and I think they're hunting trouble. Let's not bring it on us." The man in the forefront was waving and gesturing. There was something oddly familiar about him. "Looks like they're coming from that box canyon."

"Do you think they're friends of the man who was killed?" Heddy asked worriedly. They, too, had come across Coolee's body.

"I don't think so. A man like that wouldn't have that many friends." Jesse's eyes narrowed. "Maybe they're following the others." He had an uneasy feeling and moved uncomfortably, suddenly chilled in the warm sun. "Let's get moving."

"Yes." Heddy breathed easier, glad to see the dark look leave his face. "It's such a nice day."

"The day isn't over yet," Jesse commented, moving out.

For several hours they traveled at a sedate pace. Neither saw the posse of men reappear. Jesse didn't relax. Something was going on. He could feel it deep down, and almost taste it in the dry wind that swept the dust into their mouths. It was not Indians, he was sure. It had something to do with those men and the way they had been tricked into going into the box canyon. Someone wanted those men off his trail. He couldn't say why, but his sympathies were not with the hunters.

That dead man now—Jesse was sure he recognized him. It was some gunslinger by the name of Coolee. He had been fast on the draw but now he was dead. And his gun hadn't saved him.

Jesse mulled over this, but kept coming up empty. He wondered what manner of man had killed Coolee. From all accounts Coolee had been pretty damn good with that knife of his too. Yet there he lay, dead, and although it wasn't clear what had killed him, the fact that Coolee had ended up dead with his own knife missing showed that he had tangled with the wrong man. This man had been wise to him which meant he either knew of Coolee or had been too smart for Coolee's own good.

Jesse and Heddy rode a few miles then Jesse called a halt. It was hotter than blazes in the sun. Taking off his hat, he wiped his forehead with the back of his sleeve. Up ahead he saw a small parting in the rocks. It was a good place to hole up for a while and rest the horses.

"Let's stop and have some coffee," he suggested. "I've got so much dust in my throat I can hardly swallow." Heddy agreed readily. It would be good to shake the dirt from her clothes.

Jesse helped her down, a courtesy her brother seldom practiced on her. As Heddy gathered bits of wood together Jesse unpacked the coffee and fixings.

"I was thinking, Jesse," she said, poking sticks into the fire as her companion put the pot on, "maybe when you take me home you could stay a while." His eyes slanted up to her face and she blushed slightly. "Pa and Joss would like the company, and Mama too. We don't get many visitors and you'd be real welcome."

His usually serious countenance lit up with a smile. "I'd like that. I'd like that a lot."

Heddy's face brightened. "Good. Then it's settled. You know, you might even stay the winter. With Joss down and Pa sick, we could use the help. We have an extra bedroom that's real comfortable."

"I'm sure it is." Jesse grinned as Heddy went to get the battered metal cups from the pack.

When the coffee was boiling hot, Jesse picked up the pot by its handle with his kerchief. Behind him a hoof crunched on rock.

Jesse flung the coffeepot away. As it clattered to the ground he spun on his heel, gun in hand. In that split second of recognition he saw one of the men from the posse mounted up and poised between the rocks. His gun was drawn so Jesse didn't hesitate. Jesse's gun bucked in his hand and spat lead just as the man's finger tightened on the trigger.

Jesse's bullet ripped through the man's hand. His gun flew in the air and landed in the dirt.

"What the hell!" he yelped furiously. Jesse ignored the outburst. Instead his eyes were rapidly scanning the narrow opening and beyond. For the moment the stranger seemed alone but Jesse knew he was not. His eyes came to rest once more on the intruder. He studied him with distaste.

"I still got five more bullets, mister, if you want some more!" His words cut through the man's rantings. It was not said boastingly, but in a cold, serious voice. It left the stranger in no doubt that he would get all the promised five if he made the wrong move.

The man was gripping his wrist as blood poured down his sleeve. He was mad clean through. It hadn't occurred to him he'd end up hurt himself. It had been such a nice, easy shot, and Chas Stewart had worn an expectant grin as he had leveled his gun right between the unsuspecting shoulder blades. The quickness of his enemy riled him. Now he was sitting under the gun with a useless shooting hand. His predicament didn't seem to dampen his anger any.

"You put your gun down now and tell your woman to do the same!" he snarled at Jesse. Chest heaving, he glared down at him from his horse. Stewart saw he was no more than a boy! His mouth clamped tight. If he could get to his shotgun fast enough he'd rip him open with one shot. He'd never grow to manhood.

Jesse's answer was to lift his gun and point it at Stewart's heart. In the back of his mind he knew that Heddy was doing the same.

"We're not bothering you none, mister. Now you git— afore I fill your sneaking hide full of bullets." Jesse's voice was even.

"Now you listen here. My name is Chas Stewart and I—"

The sound of pounding hoofs behind the man interrupted him. His cronies came rushing to see what was happening as the gunshot had echoed through the hills.

Jesse took a step back for a better aim but he did not retreat. Whatever happened, he wanted to keep the men bottled up in that small opening. Three more men suddenly were there, their horses packed tightly together as they vied to see what their friend had captured.

"What's going on here?" A big bull of a man pushed his way ahead of the other two. Jesse knew he was the leader. He had noticed that when he had spotted them a mile away. He was easily recognizable in a red shirt that had faded to pink. He had his gun in his hand when he saw the young man drawing bead on his own riders. A girl standing off to one side had a rifle on them as well. It angered the man to see they were both aiming at him now, especially since he knew he could never get a shot off without getting hit himself. The small black eyes swiveled around to Stewart. Pinky saw the bloody hand.

"Did you do that?" he rasped out. Jesse didn't answer which aggravated his hot temper even more. "I should kill you for that!"

"You can try," Jesse said in a menacingly calm voice. Heddy moved her rifle a little just so these men knew they were taking on the two of them. The black gaze flicked to the brown-haired girl and saw the message in her eyes. He quivered with impotent rage.

"Pinky, I figure him to be Wyatt," Stewart insisted. "Wyatt has a girl with him." They all looked at Pinky.

"Well? Are you Wyatt?" he demanded harshly.

Jesse didn't like the man's pushiness but he also knew he had Heddy to worry about. The man was already on a short fuse. To rile him further would do more harm than good. Right now they were ready to start shooting if he gave them half the chance.

"No, I ain't," he responded shortly.

"Who are you?" Pinky didn't like the boy's independent attitude. He was used to servility. Everyone knew of his temper and his talent with a gun. Obviously, this boy didn't know with whom he was dealing.

"My name isn't Wyatt. Who are *you*, and what do *you* want?" Jesse asked flatly.

"Never mind who we are, sonny boy. And what we're doin' is our own business!" His eyes sharpened. "Are you sure you're not Jim Wyatt?" He was not ready to relinquish the subject. Pinky's trigger finger was itching.

Another man who had stood impatiently in the back now edged his horse forward. Jesse recognized him: Lee Jenkins! He waited for Jenkins to recognize him but Jesse realized with a start that he didn't. It had been six years and Jesse had grown quite a bit now that he was a man. Jenkins' eyes held no sign of recollection.

"Can't you see he ain't Wyatt? He's too young. March Newton ain't never gonna pay you no thousand dollars for his hide! 'Sides, the girl is supposed to be an Easterner. A real lady." His eyes traveled disparagingly over the rifle-packing girl. From her too large shirt and boy's jeans to her worn boots and the way she held her Winchester, it was apparent even to the eager Stewart and Pinky that she was no Easterner.

"She's all sunburned and brown," Jenkins pointed out, "and she has freckles. Ladies back East take care of themselves." Jenkins prided himself on the fact that he knew women.

"I say we shoot them anyways. I don't like the boy's sass," Stewart growled. He wanted Jesse to pay for his bloody hand.

Pinky disliked the situation but he was no fool. Much as he wanted to beat the impudence out of Jesse, if any bullets started flying he'd get the first ones. He was not that anxious to lose his life. Besides, he had other business to take care of with no time to waste.

"Chas, if he bothers you that much, you can take care of him! I got no more time to waste." He shot one last look at Jesse. "But if you know anything about Jim Wyatt's whereabouts, you speak up now or you'll git what he's gonna git!" Pinky's warning was met by silence from Jesse. Annoyed, he turned his horse around and left.

The others hesitated a moment then turned to follow him. Jesse watched suspiciously as Stewart had to get down clumsily from the horse and pick up his gun. He gave Jesse a long look full of hate.

"This isn't over. When I'm finished with Wyatt, I'll come back and take care of you." His shifty eyes went to Heddy. "And you too, girlie," he promised, grinning evilly. Heaving himself up onto his saddle, he walked his horse slowly away, a sadder but no wiser man.

Jesse was hard pressed not to shoot him right then. He didn't mind his threats but it rankled him when he menaced Heddy. He looked at her but she was still watching the opening. One man lingered.

Jenkins sat his horse and stared at the tall young man in front of him.

"Do I know you?" He squinted at Jesse as if this would help his memory. That spunk and that boldness which he so disliked—he'd seen them before. They dredged up unpleasant memories.

"Maybe," Jesse paused, "maybe not."

"Durango?" He took a wild guess and Jesse laughed. Jenkins frowned. "I'll remember it. It'll come to me." He looked hard at the boy, but Jesse didn't seem worried by this possibility.

"You comin', Jenkins?" Pinky bellowed. "You're holdin' us up!"

"I'm comin'." He shot one last glance at Jesse. Shrugging, he left.

Jesse walked to the opening and watched for a long time until the men disappeared. When they had finally gone he turned back and saw Heddy making more coffee.

"Maybe we should be gettin' along. They may return."

"I'm havin' my coffee!" she said stubbornly. "They're not cheating me out of that. I could have cried when I saw it all spilled on the ground."

Jesse grinned. "I know what ya mean. I sure do have a hankerin' for some myself."

As they sipped their coffee later Heddy commented, "So they're looking for a man called Jim Wyatt and a girl. A girl from the East."

"Looks like it." He knew what was bothering her. "A girl without freckles." He smiled. Heddy looked up at him quickly. "Me, I always liked freckles. Only kind of girl I like is one with freckles. Wouldn't have any other kind."

Heddy smiled shyly. "Do you want some more coffee?"

He held out his cup. "Don't mind if I do." They drank in companionable silence.

Late in the day they climbed to a small ledge and stopped a moment to catch their breath. Jesse lifted his hat and let the breeze cool off his damp hair while Heddy fanned herself with the brim of her straw hat.

She looked at him and said seriously, "This sun is going to give me more freckles, for sure." He smiled slightly at the light dusting of them across her nose and rosy cheeks.

"You could use a few more. You hardly have them at all."

Her eyes sparkled with friendliness. "Those men seemed to notice—at least one of them did." She looked at him expectantly. "He thought that he knew you." Perhaps she shouldn't probe him but she was curious.

"That was Lee Jenkins, my—" He stopped, not wishing to use the word "stepfather" since he was no such thing and never would be. "My mother's second husband." Heddy's eyes widened in astonishment and sympathy. Jesse obviously didn't like the man.

"Your pa died?"

Jesse nodded.

"And your mother married *him*?"

As he nodded again she asked, "What happened to your mother? Do you still see her?"

"Ma died a while back." Even though he disliked her taste in men, she was still his mother. She had been a good mother until she married Jenkins.

"I'm sorry." And Heddy was. He could hear the sincerity in her voice. "What happened to your parents' ranch?" Jesse shrugged as if it didn't matter although it hurt like hell.

"I suppose Jenkins sold it. It's somethin' he'd do. He sure wouldn't work it." He jammed his hat back over his head. "Let's get going. Maybe we can make it to those hills before dark." He waved to the canyons and mesa farther on. One in particular seemed to hold sway over the others. It was tall and wide at its base and stretched up to the skies with its colors of red and orange. Even at this distance it looked formidable.

"I think that's Grand Mesa up ahead," he said eagerly. "I figure we can go up there a ways where it's safe and sit it out for a while. Whatever's gonna happen, I reckon it'll be all wrapped up either way in a few days." Heddy didn't look too happy.

"What about that other girl? I'd hate to see her at the mercy of those terrible men." Heddy had Jesse to protect her and she knew he would. Who did this girl have to help her? Heddy didn't know what kind of man this Wyatt was, but it was hard to believe he could be as thoughtful as Jesse Altman. "I hope this Mr. Wyatt takes care of her." Concern was in her voice.

"Remember now, that Wyatt fella took care of Ed Coolee pretty good. Coolee was a gunslinger. I'd say he knew what he was doin'. She's likely a lot safer with him than you are with me."

"I'd rather be with you," Heddy said softly.

Jesse looked away embarrassed but pleased. He cleared his throat. "I'm glad you think that." Cautiously, he looked at her from beneath his brim. She was smiling slightly. Jesse relaxed. "I figure going to Grand Mesa is a good idea. Ya know, Heddy, if I could help this Wyatt I would but who knows where he's at? Nobody seems to know. They keep on runnin' in circles chasing him. The way I see it, he's more'n likely taken that girl and is forting up some place. Seems like a good idea to me. Of course, it'll take longer to get to Dautry," he warned.

"It doesn't matter. My family wouldn't want me to risk my life." Deep inside she felt a bit guilty. Her parents probably believed she'd been scalped by Indians. Leastways, Joss was always warning her about it whenever she'd primp in front of the cloudy old mirror that hung on the parlor wall.

"Some Indian would sure like to get hold of that long brown hair one day," he had joked. "It would look good on a pole!" Her mother had hated such jesting. She'd bet mama was tearing strips off him right now for having said such nasty things. Heddy hoped so.

Jesse led the way and Heddy followed slowly in the

heat. They kept a friendly silence until they neared the foothills approaching the red-gold mesa. Close up, it was much larger and steeper than either of them had expected.

"It looked mighty attractive back a few miles," Jesse remarked, "now I'm not so sure." There seemed to be many trails crisscrossing Grand Mesa's lower portion, and the two spent hours reconnoitering the area in search of a trail leading to the summit. Feeling a little deflated, they came to a halt in some cottonwoods.

"I think we can go up here," Jesse decided when they finally found a narrow trail angling upward. "All the other trails we came across seem to lead nowhere. A man could waste his whole life trying to find an easy way to the top, and I'm beginning to think there isn't one." Each trail that had started off so promising soon whittled away into blank walls, sheer drops, or thin, unpassable ledges. If they hadn't wasted so much time here, he'd move on. But Jesse was ired. Damned if he'd leave this mountain without giving it a real try! Besides, the other, much taller one crushed in next to it was even less appealing.

Heddy didn't suggest moving along. Having lived with her father and brother, she recognized that note in their voices when they got a bee in their bonnet about something. Jesse, now, had taken a keen dislike to this mesa. It had become personal. He meant to scale it no matter what. Heddy could appreciate such single-mindedness. She got that way herself sometimes. Occasionally, you just had to hit your head against a rock to make yourself feel better. With this in mind, she gave Jesse an encouraging smile.

Jesse found a wide, flat area that was large enough to accommodate the horses. "I'll go up first," he said. "You wait here." He vaulted from the saddle and handed her the reins. "I'm going to go up a ways and have a look around. If you hear any shootin', you take off outta here!"

"I'll stay here and wait," Heddy stated firmly. "I don't run out on my friends."

A small grin tugged briefly at his mouth, then disappeared. "There may be nothin' to wait for."

"But the men are gone. We saw them. They couldn't possibly get back here before you, and be hiding up there."

"This land is just a lot of twists and turns. Don't know where you'll end up in these canyons. I'm thinkin' if they don't find what they want they may come back. They may remember what a pretty girl you are," he responded soberly. "I may be a while." Jesse checked for the knife strapped to his leg, then started up. Heddy watched sharply until he disappeared among some copper–flecked rocks.

Jesse moved deliberately and cautiously when he left Heddy. The way up was steep and narrow but he thought they could make it with the horses. His eyes were constantly darting about him checking not only what was ahead of him but what was above him, behind him and— his eyes slanted sideways—what was across from him. Even though it was some distance to the opposite side of the gorge, a man could get off a shot if he were good enough and careful enough. This was, he acknowledged grimly, a good place to be ambushed.

The bright sun glinted dully off something in his path for just a second. Jesse knelt down and touched the pink-ish stone protruding from the ground among a scattering of many other pieces that had broken loose over time. This one was different. Jesse frowned as he brushed it with his fingertips. It was a gash—the kind of gash a horseshoe would make and it looked to be a fresh break. Someone had passed this way ahead of him. More cautious now, he continued up.

Jesse wasn't much of a tracker, he knew, but he estimated that one person, maybe three at the most, had taken this trail, and recently. He had a pretty good notion that Jenkins and his crowd had not come this way. The ground they crossed would have been churned up by almost two dozen horses as they sailed boldly up the mesa. Their tracks would have been easy to follow. These were not.

Jesse smiled a little to himself. These people ahead of him were trying to hide. They were being smart. Jesse didn't know whether to worry about that or not. He decided to climb a bit farther, at least until he could see more of the mesa. It was green near the top. That meant water. He rubbed his dirty chin that was getting stubble on it. He could sure go for some water. Was it his imagination or did the top seem to flatten out in the wavering heat? Jesse took another step forward.

"Just stop right there!" a male voice rang out. Jesse froze. Immediately, he whipped up his rifle. He could see nothing to shoot at—impossible to tell from which direction the voice was coming. The canyon walls bounced sound off each other and the words echoed back and forth.

There was no cover to dive into so he stood still, waiting. They hadn't shot him yet and they could have, very easily.

"What do you want here?" The voice was hard-edged and didn't belong to any of Jenkins' men.

"Just passin' through, sir." Jesse thought the voice was coming from a small ledge packed with bushes just up ahead. His gray eyes dwelled there a moment, trying to detect motion.

"Where are you bound?" It was an educated voice, Jesse decided.

"Dautry." Jesse looked about him. He'd better start talking. People were less likely to kill you when you talked. They figured you had nothing to hide. "Name's Jesse Altman."

"Where's your horse?" Jesse started. The voice had moved and he hadn't even heard the whisper of movement!

"Down below. I was just tryin' to see if the horse could make it up here." He was still trying to locate the sound. It seemed to have moved off again. His eyes darted away in another direction.

"There's a canyon down there you could ride through," the voice suggested. No doubt about it, he was suspicious! He didn't seem convinced that Jesse was as harmless as he was trying to convey.

"Yes sir, there sure is. There's also the meanest bunch of critters you'd ever want to see roaming around these parts. Tried to shoot me, and me not even bothering them. Figured I'd leave them to themselves and find another way to get to Dautry." There was no reply. Jesse began to sweat. It ran under his collar and down his back. There was a small scraping sound that seemed to come from above. Jesse's eyes flew up there but he got nothing but an eyeful of sun. Swearing, he averted his gaze.

"Who are they?" This time he was sure it came from above.

"Don't rightly know. There was a man, Lee Jenkins, and a heavyset lout named Pinky, and another they called

Chas Stewart. They were lookin' for someone and figured me for him." Jesse looked sideways at a pile of boulders but saw nothing move.

"Who did they figure you for?" There was no give in the voice at all. It came out at you flat and cold. Still, if he had wanted to kill Jesse, Jesse reckoned he could have done it a dozen times by now.

"A man called Jim Wyatt." The silence was thick before, now it stretched out endlessly. Jesse stood there uncertainly as the minutes passed and no sound reached his ear. What had happened to the man? An awful thought suddenly flashed in his mind. What if he was going down to get Heddy? He spun on his heel, and took one panic-stricken step forward but was brought to an abrupt stop by the sight of a man standing there, rifle cradled in his arms. He was standing in the middle of the damned trail right behind him! Jesse cursed to himself. Fine lookout he was! If that were Jenkins, he'd have a bullet lodged in the spine right now!

The man poised in front of him seemed to read the chagrin on the boy's face because a small smile flittered across his features. He was studying Jesse, then, as carefully as Jesse was studying him.

Dangerous—that was the first word that came to Jesse. There was no doubt in his mind at all that if this man had wanted Jesse dead, he would be dead. There was a strength and intelligence in his handsome, chiseled face that told Jesse that this man was a hunter; he would never be the hunted. Just the way he held himself told any observer that you were looking for a hell of a fight if you were to pull his tail.

"Who's the girl?" the man probed. That set Jesse back a bit. It was then that he knew they had been watched the whole time; ever since he and Heddy had approached the mesa.

"Heddy Gibson," he finally got out with reluctance. "Saved her on the plains from some Cheyenne. I'm taking her back to her family. The cavalry moved them out before the attack." He looked back at the green eyes that seemed to lose a little of their iciness, but not enough to make him more comfortable.

"Now tell me about this Wyatt," he invited, but it was more of a command. Jesse told his story about how Heddy and he had been attacked at camp. He told of the men who had been offered a thousand dollars to find Wyatt and of the man, March Newton, who had hired them.

The rifle lowered a little. "So March Newton sent out a welcoming party, did he? Too bad he didn't come himself. I'd have liked that."

"Your name Jim Wyatt?"

"That's right. I own a ranch, the Flying W, near Dautry. Been away for a year and on my way home." At the question in Jesse's eyes he added slowly, "Been in prison." Jesse's eyes widened at this information. "Rustling," he added and watched for the reaction. Jesse's face did not betray his thoughts. For a young man he knew how to keep his own counsel. He'd learned it the hard way at a tender age. Jenkins had been his first teacher.

"Is that a fact?" Jesse said consideringly.

The dark-haired man seemed amused. "Yes, that's a fact. I didn't do it, but March Newton buffaloed the jury into convicting me. You can believe that or not if you like."

Jesse couldn't see a man like this stooping to rustling cattle. He also thought of the men who were hunting Wyatt. Mangy hounds like that were more likely to rustle.

"I believe you," Jesse's words came out slowly, thoughtfully. A man as angry as this Newton was wouldn't send out twenty armed polecats gunning for a man who'd rustled a few head of cattle. Not for a thousand dollars he wouldn't. Jesse was young but he sensed that something more personal was at the heart of it all.

"Miss Gibson and I were looking for a place to fort up for a time," Jesse continued. "We were goin' to look for someplace up here." The words held a question.

"I've found a place for the night up ahead." The dark head inclined to where the sun was getting lower in the sky. "You're welcome to share our camp if you like. But," he added to make his position crystal clear, "you may be cutting yourself in for trouble, being here with us."

"Mister, I never asked for trouble, but I keep gettin' it. I'd be obliged if we could camp with you. I'll get Heddy, er, Miss Gibson." He turned and hurried back down the trail. Heddy was worried, he could tell. Her face broke into a relieved smile when he came into view.

"Are you all right?" she asked sharply. He seemed to have all his limbs but he had been such a long time!

"Every part of my anatomy is accounted for." He grinned, then he became very serious. "I met up with that Wyatt fella. Jim Wyatt. He's got a camp up there and invited us to stay the night."

"Is he trustworthy? Is the girl there? Did you find out what became of her?" Heddy wanted to know first. She trusted Jesse's judgment yet she was still suspicious.

"She's fine, ma'am, and will be glad that you're asking after her," Wyatt's voice cut in deeply. Both young people gasped. "Sorry." Jim came down the last few steps into view and grinned ruefully. "I had to make sure you were to be trusted." At first, Heddy was inclined to be indignant with the eavesdropper's slyness. However, she knew very well that she would have done the same thing in his boots and never mind any apology.

"I suppose it's all right," she allowed. "Is it true? Is that girl from the East still with you and is she all right?"

There was humor in the guarded green depths of his eyes as the young girl in front of him brought him to book. She was like a pretty filly, young, but with a promise of becoming a beauty. Jesse was a lucky man.

"Yes, ma'am, I give you my word," Jim returned with mock humbleness. "You can see for yourself. Miss Carter will be glad for some female company for a change, I think."

"We would be pleasured to accompany you then." Heddy accepted his invitation primly as if she were being invited to a banquet served on Dresden china, or wherever the real fancy stuff came from, Jesse thought with unholy amusement. He could see that Jim felt the same way.

"I'll lead the way." He waited for Jesse to help Heddy dismount, then they led their horses slowly up.

When Jim entered their camp, he found only Shorty snoring softly in a corner. Julie was gone but the coffee was still boiling away. Jim leaned down and moved the pot to a cool rock.

"It's okay, Julie. You can put your derringer down. Come out and greet our guests." Julie was at once reassured by the amused lilt in his voice. She crawled out from where she had taken cover at the sound of approaching horses.

Smiling apologetically, she came forward placing her six-shooter down but slipping the derringer into her pocket. Jim would have been disappointed if she hadn't.

"I'm sorry. I heard the horses and didn't know who it was." With a welcoming look, she immediately extended her hand to Heddy. "I'm Julie Carter." She gave a shy nod to Jesse.

"This is Jesse Altman. He's taking Miss Gibson"—Jim gave a sketch of a bow towards Heddy—"to her family at Fort Ewell. They were moved off their ranch because a war party of Cheyenne was spotted nearby."

"Indians too?" Julie was dismayed. "We haven't seen any, thank heavens. We have enough trouble as it is." Then she looked at Jim as if she had been indiscreet. He smiled slightly.

"They already know about our trouble. In fact, they've given me more information." This news didn't seem to make her feel overjoyed.

"Good news?" she asked hopefully. Heddy averted her gaze while Jesse considered the toes of his boots. "I see. No good news," she said flatly. Seeing her shoulders sag a trifle, Heddy came up briskly.

"Let's get some supper going, shall we?" She took Julie by the arm and led her away. "I'll tell you all about it." While Heddy went off with Julie, Jesse took the horses to a narrow seep in the rocks that Jim showed him.

"What will you do?" he asked Jim, patting the dusty coats of the horses.

"I figure on going to the top of the mesa tomorrow. There's supposed to be a trail down the other side."

"Is that so? I didn't see any, but then I only went partway around, hit a dead end, and had to backtrack. This place would make a good fortress," Jesse remarked thoughtfully.

"It may have to be," Jim agreed grimly. "Newton's men are bound to find my trail soon so I may have to make a stand here."

"They may not find it. Had me a hell of a time gettin' up here."

Jim's smile was stiff. "They'll come. And if they don't, Bodine and Duncan Reece will." He indicated the sleeping man. "His brother." Jesse nodded, turning this over in his mind. "The way I see it, I can't keep dodging them forever; not with a sick man and Miss Carter along. I have to stop some place and this is the best I've found yet. You and Miss Gibson might want to go back down or try to find the trail down the other side before the shootin' starts. Maybe you can take both girls with you. Head to my ranch. The Flying W isn't that far from here." Jim sensed the young man's predicament: He would like to help but he had the young girl to think about. It was plain to see that Jesse was sweet on her.

"I don't know what to do," Jesse admitted, picketing the horses after they had drunk their fill. "I got no right to put Heddy into any more danger—"

"What's that? Who is putting me in danger?" Heddy had come up behind them to announce that supper was ready.

Jesse swept off his hat. "I will if we stay here." Heddy's eyes widened, startled.

"You're not thinking of leaving them, are you?" She put her small hand on Jesse's arm. "They need us," she insisted earnestly. Her brown eyes went to Jim. "You may not know this, but I'm a good shot." She stopped. "A fair shot," she corrected. "Anyway, one more gun is one more gun." Her voice was firm.

"I couldn't put you at risk, ma'am. I was asking Jesse, here, to take you and Julie—Miss Carter—to my ranch—"

But when Heddy had a bee in her bonnet she didn't allow anyone to finish his piece. "And leave you alone? We don't desert our friends, do we, Jesse?" Jesse grinned as she spoke for him as well.

"We certainly don't."

Heddy smiled back. "That's settled then. Supper's ready."

## Chapter Fourteen

Deep down, Jim knew they didn't have a hope in hell of making it to his ranch. Alone he might succeed but he couldn't make a run for it with a wounded man and two women. If it had been just Bodine and Reece after him, he would have left the others and gone gunning for them himself. But now, thanks to Jesse Altman, he knew that Newton's men were stalking him, too, making it impossible to leave the women here alone—just as it was impossible to make a stand here. Yet here they were and here they would have to stay because they had run out of options. Shorty couldn't go much farther and the women were sagging with fatigue.

Jim looked speculatively at Shorty. Even though he had helped him, that was still Shorty's brother out there. When it came to a showdown, would Reece side with Duncan? It was a possibility for which he had to plan.

Jim turned in his saddle to check on the others. His

green eyes met Julie's, and held. She was disheveled, her hair full of dust and her face red from the hot sun, yet she was still a beautiful woman. She managed to give him a smile.

He smiled back encouragingly. It occurred to him that Anne would never have come as far as Julie had. Certainly, she never would have smiled at him if he had dragged her mile after broiling mile over hills and through canyons.

Turning to the trail ahead, he led them through the parched morning over miles of terrain that lay like fractured bones, dry and broken in the endless heat.

An hour elapsed before they came to the U-shaped saddle slung low between Grand Mesa and Rain King mountain. Jim's eyes swept beyond the horizontal layers of sandstone up to the flat top of Grand Mesa. This was the place of which he had been told by an old Shoshone warrior some years ago. He hoped the old boy had been right about water being there even in the hottest weather. They could sure use it now. Their canteens were almost empty.

It was here that Jim had decided to make his stand. If the warrior had been right, there was also an ancient trail, never used anymore, that went down the other side. He had been warned that it was nearly impassable for most people. The warrior had looked at Jim consideringly. After weighing him for a few moments he had revealed that, for those with strength and wisdom, it was possible. Jim grinned cynically to himself. The old man had implied that Jim possessed such character traits. Too bad he couldn't ask him what the chances were with a wounded man and two tired women. He had a feeling the old man would have pared down his chances accordingly. Throw into the mix twenty hired killers eager to nail his hide to Newton's outhouse door, and the Indian trail was looking like a mighty poor proposition.

The small party crossed the saddle and began to mount the series of switchbacks that would take them to the top of the mesa.

As they approached a wide, overhanging shelf, he reined in. While the others sat motionless, Jesse and Jim went to inspect their back-trail. Shucking his rifle from its scabbard, Jim crawled to the edge of the shelf and flattened down across its surface. Farther back, Jesse took cover and waited.

From here, Jim could see most of the trail they had taken. It was empty. So far they hadn't been followed. He turned his attention to the wide plain that sprawled out below. At first when he slowly scanned it, he saw nothing. As his eyes restlessly moved about, he detected some movement far away. It was dust kicked up by many horses. Then he recognized the dark figures. Jim swore to himself softly. Jesse stiffened. He knew what it meant.

Pete Gillens, Newton's foreman, was known to Jim as being a damn good tracker. It would be only a matter of time before he found their camp and inevitably their trail leading into the high country.

"What is it?" Jesse asked urgently.

"March's men. A few miles away."

Suddenly, Jim looked straight down and surprised a flash of movement in the cottonwoods below. So close! He ducked quickly, then took another look at a deep ravine some eighty yards beneath him. This time he saw nothing. But something *was* down there. Whoever it was just might have been around to see them scaling Grand Mesa. Jim backed off the ledge silently until he came to where Jesse kneeled, a questioning look in his eyes.

"We got more company down below." Jim inclined his head towards the ravine.

"Couldn't be March's men," Jesse came back, his young brow furrowing with puzzlement.

"No, they're too far off." Jim's lips tightened with frustration. Heddy and Julie were watching the two men, scared looks on their faces. They knew something was wrong.

"I can go down," Jesse offered. "I'm good at treeing critters." Jim heard the humorous edge to his words and smiled back.

"No, this is my fight." Deliberately, he turned his back to the others. "I want you to take them to the top. If I don't show up or you hear shooting, you take the trail down the back of the mesa. I've heard it leads to the flats below. You'll probably have to search for it. It's not much used anymore. When you get to the flats, make a run for it to my place. You should be safe there. Tell Laban what happened."

"I don't like to leave you in a fix like this, Mr. Wyatt," Jesse said quietly. "I'm a fair hand with a gun. Nothin' to brag about, but good enough in a fight."

Jim's face relaxed. "Thanks, but they want me. And the girls need a man to take care of them. Shorty . . ."—he paused, then said softly—"well, I'm not too sure about him." Jesse nodded, needing no elaboration. He knew Jim wasn't just talking about Shorty's health.

"I'll keep an eye on him—and your girl too."

Jim stared, then turned red. "Thanks," he finally said.

Jesse grinned. "I'll take care of both our girls."

Jim nodded and Jesse backed away noiselessly from the slab and hurried back to the horses.

"Who's down there?" Shorty, who had been dozing, suddenly asked Jesse in a loud voice. Jesse saw his face was flushed with a slight fever. His eyes were bright yet almost vacant.

"We don't know yet," Jesse said quietly. His glance swept around to include the women.

"Shouldn't we stay?" Julie asked. "We could—"

"No, ma'am. I got orders. I'm to take you all to the summit, then try to find a way down."

"But Jim needs help," Julie insisted.

"Beggin' your pardon, ma'am, but by staying here we'll all just be in the way. Best to do what he says. That's a gentleman that knows what he's doin'." With that, Julie had to be satisfied.

As Jesse led the way, Julie kept looking back. The last she saw of Jim was as he stood there in the middle of the trail watching them ride off. Tall, tough, determined, he nevertheless looked alone to her as their eyes met for one last time.

Jim waited until the party was gone then turned to the job at hand. He bellied along to the edge of the shelf that was sticking out at a dizzying height. For a long while he studied the cottonwoods and the ravine but did not see a repeat movement. He was not deceived. They were still down there.

In a quick, fluid motion he went over the side of the shelf and hung there by one hand for a heart-stopping second. Even as the sharp edges began to cut into his fingers, he dropped down silently about fifteen feet to a debris-covered fan that extended from the base of the shelf.

Moving rapidly now, he almost lost his footing as a spray of loose pebbles carried him towards the edge and over the cliff. Grabbing a weedy but tough tree growing out of the rocks, he slammed to a halt just as the toe of his boot reached the shattered rim.

For a second he stood there, tottering on the edge, striving to regain his balance. The walls below jutted out in steep, fractured steps. If a man fell down there he would be smashed to pieces. At once, Jim felt about blindly for a secure footing. He found one and, inch by inch, he backed away from the jagged rim until he reached solid rock. Then he started scrambling down the hill, slipping and sliding as gravel and dust spurted out from under his heels.

There was an urgency in him now. Out in the open like this, he would be a fine target for anyone looking up. Not only did he have to get out of sight fast, but he had to make it down to the ravine's rim to cut off any intruders. He knew whoever was down there would head instinctively for the large, smooth shield of table rock gleaming white in the sun. It was just the place for both horses and men to rest.

Skittering down the slope, Jim could feel the razor-sharp edges grabbing at his clothes, and making small, painful incisions in his fingertips as he brushed his hand across them to steady himself.

As he reached the table rock his heel came down on a patch of rotted quartz, and he felt himself pitch forward. His foot shot out from under him and he fell sideways, landing hard. Jim's shoulder slammed into the ground and he grunted with pain. In a second he was up again and ghosting over to the thick, sage-colored brush where the ravine opened out onto the rock table. Swearing to himself he hunkered down, ignoring the throbbing in his shoulder and back.

He mopped the sweat from his face with the back of his sleeve, and remained motionless, rifle ready. For several minutes he crouched there in the dusty sun, getting his ragged breathing under control. When the blood stopped pounding in his ears he heard it: A shuffling sound as bits of gravel crunched under hoofs. It was a heavy, slow sound broken only by a rider as he swore at the horse's lack of energy. As Jim waited he saw the crown of a dirty gray hat appear a little below him.

"Get along there!" the horseman snarled unsympathetically to his mount. The tired animal was doing its best. The horse plodded closer. Jim's fingers tightened on his rifle. Then he recognized the face under the hat brim.

Lyle Bodine! Damn his rotten soul! How in hell's name had he found him here? Jim thought he'd had enough after prancing around in that devil's canyon back there. It seemed he hadn't.

Trembling with weariness, the horse now stopped of its own accord.

"C'mon, damn you!" he swore. But the poor creature was plumb played out and wasn't about to budge.

"Aw, the hell with you!" Bodine climbed off. He was hot, tired, and hungry. Only the thought of twelve thousand dollars had kept him going—that, and the pleasure of gunning down Wyatt. He was the author of all his misery.

If Wyatt had just minded his own business they'd have been in Mexico now, living it up royally. Instead, he was here in the baking sun, his tongue cleaving to the roof of his mouth from thirst, and only forty dollars to his name.

Jim observed Bodine as he tilted his head back and looked towards the top of the mesa. For a moment nothing showed in the hard, bitter face. Then, as Jim watched, he saw a smile start to twist his countenance. Bodine's eyes gleamed as an excitement seemed to catch hold of him. He'd seen something up there!

"I knew it!" he whispered hoarsely. For a second, Bodine's eyes snapped in the direction from which he had just come. Jim's followed. He saw nothing. Apparently, Bodine was alone. He didn't look like he was waiting for anyone as he once more swung up onto the back of his reluctant horse.

Jim couldn't allow that. He wouldn't let Bodine ride away. Hands gripping the rifle barrel, Jim vaulted from the brush and rushed him.

For once in his crafty life Bodine was startled. He felt a flurry of air. Glancing instantly over his shoulder, he saw Jim bearing down on him like a cyclone. There was no time to take aim. His rifle lay useless in the crook of his arm. Bodine could do nothing but bunch his shoulders as Jim swung wide his Winchester, slamming the stock across the side of Bodine's head.

Screaming with pain, Bodine slew around and lost his seat. Even as he fell onto the rocks, the horse spooked and reared up. Frantically, Bodine lurched to his feet and grabbed out for the reins. He snatched them but just couldn't hold on. The animal struck him hard with one powerful shoulder. Bodine staggered back with the wind knocked out of him. Then he collapsed. His horse fled, crashing through the underbrush.

For a second, Bodine lay panting on his back in the dust. Furiously, he watched his horse, his only means of escape, vanish back down the ravine.

Then his eyes lit on it: As Bodine had grappled for control of his horse, his rifle had clattered to the ground. He could see it. It lay only a few feet from his groping fingers.

Jim saw it too. He didn't give the other man a chance to act. Just as Bodine gathered himself to lunge for it, Jim was there slamming his fists into Bodine's face. Bodine fell back.

"You wanted me, Bodine? Well now you found me!" Jim ground out sarcastically as he straddled Bodine's chest on his knees. Still reeling from the blow to the side of his head, Bodine was pummeled unmercifully as he tried to push Jim off and fight.

This was not how he had planned it. He was supposed to have found Wyatt. For days now, he had been rehearsing how he would kill Wyatt, how he would dispose of the body, and what he would do with the money and the girl.

Blood was running from his face and down the front of his shirt, yet the outlaw's spirit was not broken. He had been dreaming of all that money. He could taste the lips of the pretty señoritas who would flock around him. Damn it! He wouldn't be cheated now! He was owed that money. Only one man stood in his way. If he took care of Wyatt, Mexico was just in reach!

With renewed strength, Bodine grabbed one of Wyatt's wrists just as he was ready to land another brutal blow to his broken face. In a frenzy he tried to twist it behind Wyatt's back. Bodine's other hand curled into a claw and swiped at those icy green eyes.

Jim dodged out of the way then threw his head forward and they butted skulls. Bodine's head jerked back. It smashed sickeningly against the pure white stone underneath, which pooled red with blood. Powerless now, Bodine released his hold. Any other plans now vanished.

Pulling roughly away from him, Jim stood above the prone body of the outlaw and watched as he tried to draw air into his lungs. Bodine's eyes dulled even as he rolled onto his side and strained to sit up. He struggled to focus on Wyatt's unforgiving face.

"You snake!" he slurred out. "I'd like to kill ya! I'd like to rip your heart out and—"

Jim thought the man was dead.

He was not. He was looking over Jim's shoulder, his eyes wide. As Jim watched, he saw the bloody lips stretch into a grin.

"Looks like . . ."—he gulped air—"looks like you're in trouble." Despite the intense pain pulsing through his wracked body, he managed to give a gurgling laugh.

Even as Jim whipped around, he heard the smooth sound of a gun being drawn from leather.

Duncan Reece stood behind him, starkly outlined against the sky. His gun was aimed at Jim and his finger tightening on the trigger. Jim's hand swept down and grabbed the gun at his side. Duncan wasn't that good a shot but he didn't have to be at this range. Jim knew he'd get that bullet even as he rolled to the side and aimed.

Before Duncan could get off a shot, a louder retort

shook the canyon. Jim froze, expecting to feel a bullet belting into him. Instead he saw Duncan incredibly rise high on his toes. There was a look of surprise on his face as he stared upwards, the gun slipping from his spastic fingers to fall into the dirt. His mouth tried to move, then he fell forward.

Gun still drawn, Jim turned and looked up to where Reece had been staring. He couldn't believe his eyes. There was Shorty standing there with his rifle in his hands. He was looking down at his brother where he lay, barely alive, on the ground. Suddenly his eyes shifted to meet Jim's.

"It wasn't me! I didn't shoot him!" Shorty shook his shaggy head.

A yankee war whoop came from down below. "I got him!" The words came faintly from the base of the mesa. "I got Wyatt!" Bedlam broke out as men shouted loudly to each other.

"I think we better get the hell out of here," Jim said mildly.

"Mount up!" someone bellowed.

Shorty's voice rasped hoarsely over the rising commotion. "Look out behind you, Wyatt!"

Lightning-quick, Jim swung sideways, gun drawn. Bodine had managed to drag himself over to where his rifle lay. Leaning against a rock, he was eagerly getting ready to blow Jim to kingdom come. Before he could get his shot off, Jim's gun blasted. Bodine's body recoiled with each thud.

This couldn't be happening, Bodine thought as the bullets tore at his flesh. He's the one who always walked away. He was fast—faster than anyone else! Faster than Coolee had ever been. The last bullet entered his chest.

"You cheated me!" he spat at Jim as blood foamed out of his mouth. "I hope they get you!" Then he pitched forward, dead. Jim kicked the rifle away just in case. There was no need. Black eyes looked sightlessly out from the hard, cold face. Jim quickly reloaded. Bodine would never make it to Mexico. There were no more señoritas for him.

Shorty stumbled over the ground to where his brother lay. Duncan had raised himself up on one elbow to stare at his brother as if unable to believe he was there. Heavily, Shorty fell to his knees while Duncan reached out to grasp his arm. As he felt the sturdy flesh underneath the ragged shirt he gave his brother a hopeful smile.

"Shorty! It's really you. I knew you'd make it!" he gasped, as a groan rose to his lips.

"I wasn't so sure," Shorty said soberly, looking closely at Duncan's face. Even now, he could see no affection in it. Duncan licked his lips and lowered his voice so Wyatt wouldn't hear.

"It's ours now, Shorty! Just you and me left."

"What ya talkin' about?" Shorty felt the hand that had clutched his arm so tightly lose its grip a little. Shorty put a supporting arm around him. He could feel warm blood soaking through his sleeve.

"The money is what I'm talkin' about! The money! Six thousand each. Bodine is dead. Coolee is dead." His voice was weak but exultant.

"And you're gonna be dead, too, Duncan," Shorty

blurted out flatly. Duncan's eyes dulled as he read the truth in Shorty's face. He suddenly realized that the coldness creeping over him was real. The weakness was not going away. The pain that had burst in his back was spreading. His hands and legs were trembling with pain.

"No, no! I ain't dead! I ain't dyin'. Help me, Shorty!" he shouted, scared.

"I cain't." Shorty shook his head. "Ya shoulda looked after me, Duncan. I'm your brother. You just left me alone out there on the trail to die."

Duncan looked at his brother as if he were speaking another language. "Who cares? Who gives a damn? You're alive, ain't ya? I'm dyin'!" He was silent a moment, then he said it again as if he couldn't quite believe it. "I'm a dyin'."

"Well, I'm sorry for you," Shorty said finally. "If you'd a helped me, you'd probably be alive now." As this bitter thought entered Duncan's mind, he sagged even more in Shorty's grip. It was the end of the line. He knew it now. He lifted his eyes to Shorty's face so close to his. Duncan actually saw sympathy there. He suddenly felt ashamed. "What will ya tell Ma?" Shorty's face began to waver before his fading eyes like a mirage in the desert heat. "What will ya tell Ma?" Ma in her old dresses, workin' hard on that dirt-poor ranch. Duncan never gave her any money. He only asked her for it. Ma: Old, gray, tired out. What would she think of him now?

"I'll tell her that you were a good man and tried to save my life."

Tears of thankfulness welled in Duncan's eyes. He couldn't see Shorty anymore, but he heard his voice.

"Thanks, Shorty. Appreciate it." Those were the last words he gasped out. His head fell backward and his body went limp in his brother's arms. Shorty gently lowered him onto the ground.

"Is he dead?" Jim's voice came from behind him. Shorty could only nod. Jim touched his shoulder in understanding. "March's men are coming up. We'd best get going. We can bury him another time."

Shorty took one more look at his brother's face. It was not peaceful in death. Grasping at the rocks with his hands, he shakily pulled himself up.

"He coulda been better, but then so could I," he admitted. Jim handed him Bodine's rifle. Shorty took it but used it more for a crutch than anything else as they made their way back up towards the trail. Jim brought up the rear, helping the wounded man when he stumbled and fell to his knees. When they reached a small plateau, Shorty collapsed. The bandage was soaked with blood, and his fever was so high Jim could feel it through the other man's shirt when he touched him on the shoulder.

"Ain't no use," he sobbed, eyes closed as he wearily leaned his head against the canyon wall. "I ain't gonna make it. I shoulda stayed down there with Duncan. It's where I belong."

"Come on." Jim pulled Shorty's arm around his neck and half carried him back to the trail. Shorty shuffled along dragging his feet. After a while his feet stopped moving and his knees almost touched the dirt. Without thinking twice, Jim heaved him across his broad shoulders. He winced as his sore shoulder took the brunt of Shorty's weight. He resumed the climb.

Was it his imagination or did he hear men's voices just below? Had they found Bodine's and Reece's bodies yet? If they did, they would know for certain he was here.

Jim's muscles bunched with strain. His jaw was set in stiff lines. He was breathing heavily now. He stopped once to wipe away the sweat that ran into his eyes so he could see. He had to hurry—faster! If he made it to the top, he had a chance. If they caught him carrying Shorty, he'd be defenseless. Shifting Shorty's weight, he steeled himself to climb up the last lap of trail. It was the most rugged section, strewn with boulders, and tilted almost upright along the face of the cliff.

Shorty stirred. "Leave me here, Wyatt. Save yourself. I ain't worth it."

"Just hold on. I haven't saved you yet. We may both end up at the bottom of this blasted mesa." When Shorty opened his eyes, Jim advised, "I wouldn't look if I were you." Shorty did, and gasped. He found himself hanging directly over the edge, head first. Down below he could just make out a sliver of water threading through some lost canyon. It looked like a long drop to the bottom.

"Let me down! I can walk!"

"Hold still!" Jim ordered sharply, his foot slipping from a precarious toe hold. Shorty's sudden jolt of movement made Jim sway backwards. He halted one second and righted himself.

"I can hear people talkin'." Shorty sounded calm and lucid all at once. It was true. Jim could hear them now. They were coming nearer and Jim could almost make out the words being spoken.

"Let's go!" Reaching deep down from within for the

last bit of strength he possessed, Jim pushed himself beyond his limits and forced himself to pick up speed.

He was near the summit when he heard more noise behind him. He put Shorty down and, with the agility of a wildcat, he slung around, guns drawn.

At the same time he heard the rushing sound of someone descending from above. In the next instant, Jesse came into view racing down the trail, rifle grasped tightly.

"They're right behind you!" he yelled and blew past Jim at full tilt. Jesse went careening down the trail and slammed into a pile of boulders that broke his stride. He took a position and threw his rifle to his shoulder.

Julie was suddenly there, helping Jim with Shorty. Between them, they soon had Shorty up on the summit of the mesa, sitting down under a shady overhang.

When Jim looked up he found Julie's eyes on him, filled with worry and questions. There was also something else: There was a warmth and love in them that he had never seen in Anne's.

"Jim, are you all right? We heard shooting. I thought you'd been killed! Is someone down there? Is—" Jim's hand came out to catch both of Julie's in his. He pressed them comfortingly.

"I'm fine. Right now, anyways. I've got to go help Jesse. They're comin'," he panted out.

Julie's face, so red from the sun, drained of color. "Who are they? Bodine and . . ."—she took a quick look at Shorty and lowered her voice—"Duncan?"

"No." He shook his head, then gave a quick smile as Heddy came up with a canteen.

"There's water up here, Mr. Wyatt," she rushed out

excitedly. Good. One problem was taken care of. He took a quick gulp then handed it to Julie.

"Those two won't be bothering us anymore." As his words sank in, Julie's face brightened.

"I'm glad. I was so afraid."

Jim nodded his thanks to Heddy who was also paying close attention. "They're gone, but there's twenty more to replace them. March's men. They're on their way up. You girls keep your guns handy."

In one lithe movement he was on his feet again. He hated to see how Julie's face darkened with even more stress. She shouldn't have to face this. She had seen too early what this savage land held for the innocent.

Before she could gather her thoughts together, he was gone seeking out Jesse. She turned to Heddy who watched her with a matching worry.

"What should we do, Heddy?"

Heddy smiled and handed the canteen to Julie. "Why don't you give Shorty something to drink? I'll look around up here."

Julie went over to Reece. He took the water gratefully, at the same time realizing that, but for him, none of this trouble would have happened.

"I'm sorry, ma'am. I truly am."

Julie was startled but said gracefully enough, "I'm sorry, too, about your brother."

"Duncan was a bad 'un, all right, but he was my only brother." He closed his eyes as if he had no strength left to continue. Julie waited a moment. She thought that he had fallen asleep but just as she was about to arise he spoke again without opening his eyes. "Yes, he were a bad 'un, and so am I. Can't think why your man toted me the whole, livelong way up the trail." Julie started and blushed. She was glad Heddy was not in hearing. He was about to say more, but apparently decided that he couldn't gather enough energy together to do it.

Julie left him to rest. She wondered where Jim and Jesse were. And what was down there . . .

Below, a few random shots rang out. Two minutes later, Jesse and Jim came scrambling to the top and took cover at the trail head. They were safe—for now.

*Chapter Fifteen*

Newton's men swarmed up the ravine, eagerly hacking their way over to the spot where they were sure Wyatt's body lay. If there was still some life in him, their rifles would finish the work.

Pandemonium broke loose when they spied the body lying in the dirt.

"There he is!" one man shouted gleefully as they all rushed over to take a look. That had been easy, real easy. It was almost like being paid for doing nothing. Pinky, the first one on the scene, saw the bullet hole that had punctured the man's back. Real neat shooting, he admired. And clear to see he was dead. Blood saturated his shirt. The man lay motionless.

With the toe of his boot Pinky kicked the body over. He leaned down and peered into the dead man's face. It was not Wyatt. Bewildered, he straightened up and scratched his head.

"Who the hell is this?" he asked of no one in particular. "'Cause it sure ain't Wyatt. Danged if we didn't shoot the wrong man." If there was regret in his voice it was for the expensive error they had made. Others crowded over to see what they had bagged. Gillens drew up in a flurry of dust and tersely ordered everyone to get out of the way.

"Hey, Pete," Pinky called over to him. "This ain't Wyatt."

"What?" Gillens flung himself angrily from the saddle and shouldered his way through the crowd of tired, sweaty riders to where the dead man lay. "Now who the hell is he?" Gillens bit out. "I coulda swore I seen Wyatt for just a second!"

"There's another one over here." One of the men had located Lyle Bodine. Gillens and Pinky hurried over.

"My, my. Looks like he went and cracked his head open," Pinky observed critically.

"I don't know him neither! And what's he doin' here?" Gillens fumed. "They're just gettin' in our way!" He turned and looked all around him. "Wyatt was here. I just know it!" Pinky was doubtful but said nothing.

"What do we do now?"

"What do you mean 'What do we do?' We keep goin' up the mesa. As for them"—he motioned at the bodies—"leave 'em lay. I got no time to bury the dead!"

Frank Rawl had come up. Gillens saw how he was staring at Bodine. Duncan, he gave a dismissive look.

"Do you know these men, Frank?"

"Sure do. That worthless trash over there is Duncan Reece. He and his brother are petty thieves." His voice held disdain. He nodded his head. "This one here is Lyle

Bodine." The intonation in his voice showed that he was impressed.

"Ya don't say?" Gillens was surprised. "I heard of him. Mean so-and-so. Killed a woman down in Mexico, I hear, for seein' another man. What do ya think happened here?"

"Clear to see. Bodine had a rifle, and someone beat him to the draw. Pumped four bullets into him. Very neat. Very neat indeed," Rawl purred. "He took them out in a very workmanlike manner."

Jenkins' face turned red. "What do ya mean?" He pushed up to Rawl. "I got that one. He's mine!" Jenkins pointed to Duncan's body.

"Who cares? You won't get a red cent for him," Gillens shot back. He turned away disgustedly and ordered them to mount up. As they did, Rawl spoke to Pinky.

"Who is this Wyatt, anyway? Why are we hunting him?"

"Don't you know?"

"I'm only hired to do a job. I don't make it a practice to learn about the men I'm paid to kill," he informed him coolly.

"I'll tell ya who he is!" Gillens spat out. "He's the snake who shot Ralph Garvey in the back—and got away with murder!"

Rawl's brows came together in puzzlement. "Why would he shoot Garvey in the back? He doesn't need to, a man as good with his guns as *that*."

Gillens was perplexed and it showed on his face. Rawl had a point there. It didn't add up. But it was all irrelevant because Newton had said it was true. "That's not the point here," he said gruffly. "Miss Anne Garvey, his daughter, said he did it, and March wants him dead. That's all you need to know."

Rawl said nothing, but he was very anxious to meet up with this Wyatt character. He enjoyed a good challenge, and Jim Wyatt presented him with one. Which one of them would win if they met? Rawl wondered. He thought about this with pleasure as everyone fell in behind and followed Gillens up Grand Mesa.

## Chapter Sixteen

It was late morning when Jim finally stood at the head of the trail that was their only chance of escape from Grand Mesa. One booted foot wedged securely in a crevice, he leaned forward to look down from the tall, rocky turrets to the desolate valley below.

So this was it. With one easy movement he swung himself over the edge and stood on a sheer precipice suspended in space. At once, the ancient stonework crumbled under his weight. It was a hell of a steep descent, and Jim could foresee danger in every treacherous twist of the trail. Soundly, he cursed that old Indian warrior who had told him of it.

Jesse came to stand above him.

He leaned down to examine the ruthlessly steep cliff face.

"Is that the trail?" he asked doubtfully and pointed towards a slim thread of white that cut through the rocks in the distance. It was barely visible against the gray granite.

"That's it," Jim affirmed grimly, shaking his head before turning to look up at Jesse. Jesse's mouth quivered a trifle.

"You say this Indian was your friend?"

Jim's green eyes turned humorous. "Claimed to be."

Jesse rubbed the side of his face as he considered the downward descent. "I'd like to have that Indian here right now."

"Me too."

"To point out the trail to us," Jesse added slowly.

"That's what I was thinking."

Both men looked at each other and started to grin.

"Hell, I don't know what I'm smilin' about," Jim said ruefully. "Going down isn't going to be any picnic." On a serious note he added, "We're going down at night." Jesse's face sobered. "Have to. Can't risk being seen in daylight."

Jesse expelled his breath. "Yeah, I can see that. Do you think we can make it in the dark?"

"Do you think we can make it in the daylight?"

Jesse saw his point. "Maybe there's another way down."

"Nope. I've been over the ground. Everything else is too sheer or cut inwards with nothing for a trail to hang onto."

"Except for that shallow gully over there." Jesse inclined his head towards the other side. The lad was sharp, all right.

"Yeah, I noticed it, but it leads nowhere. A man who tries to make his way down to the gully will just make himself a target."

"Still, somebody might try to come up that way. I'll tell Shorty to keep an eye on it," Jesse remarked. While he trotted off to talk to Shorty, Jim glanced quickly at the sky. The sun had passed the noon mark. They would have to keep Newton's men busy the whole day long to buy time.

Jim sketched out in his mind the terrain they would have to traverse to reach the remote plains below. A narrow path clung tenuously to the wall of Grand Mesa for about two hundred yards. It dipped then just as abruptly, took a vertical climb. He would have to watch so the horses didn't stumble there, he mentally noted to himself. After that was a bone-breaking plunge to the rim of a deep gorge. Once inside the gorge, the trail crossed over to the lower slope of the other mountain, Rain King. The ancient path traced the curve of the mountain's base and finally opened up onto the basin far below. Jim couldn't see it from here but he knew it existed. After that, it would be a race for the ranch across flat plains and hillocks.

He studied it for one last moment. If they had enough time they could make it, he was sure. If not—if the hired killers figured out his plan—well, it was a long, deadly fall to the valley floor. Those deep chasms and serrated rocks down there could be their graves.

Climbing back up, Jim took up his rifle. A shot rang out. Jim raced to Jesse's side. Behind a wall of boulders the two men took cover and waited. Jim looked questioningly at Jesse.

"I singed the seat of someone's pants over there. He didn't see anyone up top, so I guess he thought he'd charge us."

Nothing moved now. It was as if the sandy-colored

expanse glittering hot in the sun was void of life. Jim knew better. Newton's men were down there all right. Every one of them had his gun primed and ready to shoot.

Both men were silent. Both men were patient. They had nothing to gain by engaging the enemy's fire. The hired men did. They wanted to get their job done quickly. With the sun grilling down on their heads, their foreman would be hard pressed to hold his men back.

There was no avoiding a fight now. Jim hated having Jesse and the women involved but that was how the hand had played out. Right now, Jim held one ace: Gillens and his men believed Jim was up here alone with nowhere to go. They assumed he was trapped with a depleting supply of ammunition and his canteen almost empty. Hopefully, they would figure the longer they kept him bottled up at the summit, the easier it would be to pick him off in their own good time.

He'd guarantee they would be more than a little surprised to learn that he had deliberately chosen this ground to make a stand. And he had chosen it well. If anyone came for him, it would be straight up that trail. His rifle honed in on the exact spot. They would find out soon enough . . .

All at once a few men leaped from their cover and scrambled forward, trying to gain some ground toward the summit. Just as quickly they ducked out of sight. As one, Jim and Jesse took aim and fired. There was a muffled exclamation as a bullet tore past one man's cheek. Then there was silence again.

"Gettin' a mite closer," Jesse commented in a low voice.

"Yeah, but they've got some way to go." Jim scanned

the rocks again. His rifle paused at a shadow but it was nothing. He eased his finger off the trigger.

Jim glanced approvingly at the young man beside him. The determined strength in Jesse Altman's face belied his youth. The boy was smart, unruffled. There was a fight here, and he went about it coolly. Like Jim, he had a tough, no-nonsense attitude. If anything happened to him, Jim knew there was no better man to lead the women to safety.

Jim motioned that he was going to scout around and ghosted over to another rock. Craning his neck a little, he could see the elbow of Shorty Reece's shirt. He was perched in a V-shaped fissure about ten feet up. From that vantage point he could see the small gully and steep talus slide where the unwary might be daring enough to attempt a climb.

Shorty was turning out to be a good fighter. His fever had lessened a bit and he seemed anxious to do his share.

Jim turned his eyes back to the trail. There was a small, crunching noise as the heel of someone's boot stepped down on a pebble. He searched for the source of that sound. As his eyes once more went over a patch of ground littered with boulders, his attention sharpened.

Something was there that had not been there before. It was a scrap of faded plaid. There had to be some flesh underneath that fabric. Jim lifted his rifle. It was an easy shot, only seventy yards. He squeezed off the shot and the bullet slapped into its target. There followed a scream. For a second, a man rose to his knees, clapping a hand to his shoulder. Another dust-coated figure dodged forward to pull in his wounded friend. Jim fired again, and the bullet whipped a deep furrow in the second man's jaw. He swore loudly as he hauled the injured cowboy to safety.

A third man, thinking Jim was occupied, took advantage of the opportunity to crouch-run to the other side of the trail. Jesse fired, and he saw red spatter the man's pants leg as he half ran, half stumbled to cover.

Now there was a ruckus down below. What the hired killers had thought would be an easy day's work was turning mighty bloody. Four wounded already and they hadn't even got a good shot in yet. It was time to do some negotiating.

A commanding voice sliced over the fury-filled chorus.

"You up there! Wyatt! Can you hear me? This is Pete Gillens." Jim had recognized the terse voice even before he heard the name.

"Yeah, my hearing is pretty good," Jim shot back. Gillens held his hat up in the air, and Jim shot it a good one through the crown. "I can see you, too," Jim stated. He could feel that Gillens didn't like that either.

"Now, I'm here to talk some peace. I'm a reasonable man," Gillens lied, "I got some men down here, and I'm havin' a hard time keepin' them back. But you throw down your guns, and we'll let you live. We promise not to hurt the girl either."

There was a long pause. Jim saw Jesse open his mouth to speak but silenced him with a motion of his hand. It was clear he didn't want them to know he had help—not just yet.

"How do I know I can trust you?" Jim yelled.

"You have my word on it!" Even from here Jim knew

that Gillens' men were probably grinning at that. Gillens had been one of the men Newton had sent to ride roughshod on the small ranchers. He had shot innocent men, threatened their women, then torched their homes and stole their cattle. He was second only to Newton in viciousness.

Jim allowed a few minutes to pass to make Gillens believe he was actually considering his proposition.

"I gotta have time to think over your offer. After all, it's my life I'm dickering for and I'm pretty darned near scared."

Jesse smothered a laugh to hear the tough hombre sound as if he were trembling in his boots. He was surprised when Gillens, not doubting the fear at all, snapped back, "You got it!"

Gillens didn't seem surprised by his reception. After all, he was holding all of the high cards. When faced with so many men, he didn't think Wyatt would be so tough. Newton had been worried about him for nothing. Why, he was as soft as butter! Feeling that he was within an inch of winning, he called Chas Stewart over.

"Chas!" Gillens took out his tobacco and tore off a hunk with his teeth. "You go ride back to the ranch and tell Newton we got Wyatt cornered up on Grand Mesa." He chewed his tobacco with relish. His eyes gleamed as he spoke. "You tell him he's turnin' more yellow by the minute and is as good as dead." Stewart's stiff face split into a grin. "Tell him—you tell him I'll be bringin' his body back as soon as we've rested and had some coffee," Gillens added deliberately.

Stewart nodded with pure pleasure and turned away.

Keeping out of rifle range and moving from boulder to boulder, he clambered down until he reached the horses. He mounted up and rode away, glad that he was the one to bring the good tidings.

Jim heard the rider take off in one big hurry. It was a messenger to Newton, no doubt. Gillens was mighty sure of himself.

"Wyatt!" Gillens, down below, spat some tobacco juice onto the ground. "What's your answer?"

"I need more time. That girl is real scared of you and your men. How many have you got with you?"

"Only a few."

"Well, I still need time to talk some sense into her and take that gun away. She's that damn quick on the trigger."

Gillens didn't like the sound of that. He decided to let Wyatt handle it. Why should he or his men risk getting shot by some crazy woman toting a gun?

"All right," he decided, sounding magnanimous. "But talk fast! It's damn hot down here."

Jim knew it. Up here along the rimrock a strong breeze cooled them off. Down below with stonework all around them radiating heat, it could be like an oven.

Jim looked at Jesse and grinned. Then he motioned to him to keep watch while he moved soundlessly up the slope.

Julie was making coffee. While Heddy brought some over to Jesse, Julie handed Jim his. She settled down next to him. He smiled his thanks and took a grateful swallow. It was a bit weak but tasted good anyway.

"How are our chances of getting out of this?" she asked gravely.

"I think we have a good chance. Now that Jesse's here— and Shorty. Jesse's good in a fight. Shorty's not a bad shot either."

"What about me?" A dimple appeared in her cheek. "I can shoot too."

"Well, I heard a lot of boasting from you, but I only saw you shoot once—and you missed." He grinned, drinking down the rest of his coffee. "You never did get a chance to practice on me like you wanted to."

Julie blushed. "I'm sorry. I should have trusted you. If you hadn't helped me I would probably be dead by now." He reached out and took her hand in his, squeezing it gently.

"I always knew you wouldn't shoot me unless it was by accident. Every time you reached for your derringer, I thought it would go off. By the way, where is it?" She patted her pocket. "Good. Keep it handy. You may need it. If you see anything move at all, shoot it."

"I will."

"What about that rifle of Coolee's?"

She nodded to where it was propped up against a rock just a few feet away. "It's loaded."

"I'd better take that. I might need an extra weapon if they come at us in a rush." He came lightly to his feet, taking the rifle. She stood up as well. When he turned back to her, she was keenly aware of his closeness. She was not to know that he was aware as well.

"I'll be going back now." He pulled his hat lower on his head and gave her a searching look. She seemed suddenly shy, and he was satisfied. Touching her hair, he turned and left.

"How's it going?" Jim asked Jesse.

"Got me a few interesting things to shoot at." He pointed out a cowhand. "He's just settin' there, rollin' a cigareet." The man was in plain view, unaware that he could be seen clearly from above. Another man had his hand resting casually on a clump of rocks as if he was sitting on the parlor sofa. Still another had his leg sticking out from behind a small bush. "Didn't know if you wanted me to start shootin' or if you're still thinking of surrendering," Jesse said with mock soberness. "They seem mighty nice fellas."

"I had a feeling they were. Keep your eyes peeled. We'll wait until Gillens starts to get restless. I'm going to see if I can get hold of something just as interesting." Jesse nodded, and Jim, taking his two rifles with him, followed the ragged rim. He worked his way silently along until he was able to command a clearer view of the section of trail they had taken, then he settled down to watch.

He crouched there as long minutes ticked by. His keen eyes went to work, examining every inch of ground for something out of place. It was meticulous and time consuming, yet he searched relentlessly. His search finally paid off. Against one of those white surfaces Jim spotted a tinge of pink. It was a faded shirt cuff.

"Pinky Curtis!" Jim spat out the name under his breath. He strongly suspected Curtis of being the murderer who had shot Sheriff Lawton a year ago and put the blame on Jim. It was the sort of dirty work at which he excelled. Newton saved him for the worst jobs: Jobs that no one else would touch. Where the other men might balk at killing a woman, Pinky would not. It was important that he be gotten rid of first. When the shooting began, Pinky would be his first choice.

Jim raised his rifle and honed in on the scrap of pink. Suddenly there was a blur, and a dun-colored form separated itself from the cliff face. The man was only a foot from Curtis! Hell! He almost missed him. Jim wouldn't now.

A little way below the place where the two men were perched, a ranch hand slowly edged his way around a boulder to sit in the shade. Propping himself up, he took something from his pocket and put it into his mouth. He began to chew contentedly.

Carefully, Jim leveled his rifle at each target to get the feel of it. Yep, he could get in all three shots pretty easily and in good time.

The sun was still riding high in the western sky when Gillens got tired of waiting. He had gotten all he could out of his chaw, now he was ready to shoot. "Wyatt? You there?" His impatient words echoed through the walls.

"Where else would I be?" Jim's voice was dry.

"Have we got a deal?" There was silence. "Wyatt?"

"I'm still thinkin' on it." The answer floated back lazily.

"Why you son–of–a—!"

Twenty angry rifles responded to this insult. Jim's attention was elsewhere. He was aiming his rifle at the inviting pink cuff.

All at once, Pinky turned sideways facing Jim. He was in the process of lighting his cigarette, eyes intent on the burning match head. Through the acrid puff of smoke the small eyes lifted and squinted at something above him. He swatted away the smoke to focus. That's when he saw the muzzle of a rifle protruding from some rocks. At first, his face didn't change until he realized at last that he was looking death in in the face.

His eyes grew wide. The match, forgotten now, burned down to his fingertips and he dropped it with a yelp. Before he could grab for his Winchester, Jim's rifle belched flame. Coolly, Jim pulled the trigger two more times. The bullets slammed into Pinky's chest. Even at this distance Jim knew he was dead.

Jim swung his rifle and fired again. The dun-colored man tried to duck but he had nowhere to go. He crumpled, his Colt still holstered.

At the sound of shooting, the cowhand down the slope grabbed for his rifle. It flipped out of his nervous fingers and went clattering amongst the rocks. Futilely, he snatched at it, lost his balance, and went tumbling down the hill. Jim's bullet nicked his heel. When the smoke cleared, the man was crawling slowly back behind his rock.

More bullets rang out, and Jim leveled shots at the puffs of smoke. By the heavy thuds he knew some of them must have hit their mark. There were a few cries, and curses flew through the air. Then he reloaded.

From Jesse's position, Jim could hear rapid-fire shooting. Now was the time. In one blinding instant Jim dodged to the left and started firing. With brusque confidence he kneeled there, pumping out bullets.

His face set and savage, he laid down a field of fire that was hot and heavy, raking the ground before him with lead. Bullets slapped into stone, spattering deadly shards among the men where they hid. Shots riccocheted, then stabbed into flesh. A man leaped through the brush and bellowed with pain. Another scrambled a few feet before Jim's bullet burned him and he stopped moving. Guns pounded while frightened horses bucked and screamed.

When the rifle was empty Jim reached for the second and began strafing everything in sight. Bullets whipped past his head, and his hat went flying, but he kept firing till he had unloaded his rifle.

Then he dropped down, drew his twin Colts, and waited.

Would they attack? Jim crouched there breathing hard. The sharp pinging of bullets still rang in his head. Gun-smoke stung his eyes. He coughed to clear his throat. Shots still split the air, searching for the hidden shooter. They pelted the boulders all around him.

Jim could hear moaning from down below. Men shouted to each other. Jim sat back and reloaded the two rifles, satisfied that he could do no more at this time. He made his way back to Jesse and dived for cover just as a bullet clipped his hair.

The young man was shocked to see Jim alive. It was clearly written across his face. Jim looked past him and saw a body hanging from the tree up on a crag.

"Good shot," he commented.

Jesse exhaled long and hard. "That was somethin', Jim. You was like a wild man!"

"How many do you think we got?"

"I wounded one over here plus that yahoo in the tree yonder."

"Three that I know of. I wounded two earlier. That's seven—dead or wounded."

Nothing much was happening down below now. The

sun was beginning to pull back from the mesa's rim and shadows invaded the sun-bleached land.

The intense thrill of the fight was beginning to subside in Jim's chest. Taking his watch once more at the trail head, he considered Jesse's optimistic view of Newton's men with less enthusiasm than he showed.

Jim had seen Gillen's in action. Newton brought him along when he first came here and he brought him for a reason. Gillens was a stayer. Unyielding and unbending, he would do the job entrusted to him and he wouldn't stop doing it until it was finished to his satisfaction. He held his men together with an iron fist, something he had learned from Newton. They would stay and fight until Gillens told them they were done fighting—even the wounded. Gillens knew that if they didn't capture Jim on the summit of Grand Mesa, they'd have to corner him all over again.

Gillens must certainly realize by now that Jim was not alone. That would make him pause as nothing else would. Gillens had figured he knew who he was, where he was, and with whom he was dealing. Being shot at from three different directions would cool him off some. Jim knew it would cool off the eager mob he brought with him.

There was a rustling noise as someone's shoulder showed for a brief instant. Before Jim could let a bullet fly, it was yanked quickly back behind the rock. Good. They were being more careful now. Jim doubted whether Gillens could make them rush up the track like before.

For what seemed like hours Jim sat there. The sun was slipping from the sky, edging ever closer to the towering peak of Rain King directly to the southwest. Long shadows stretched across the face of Grand Mesa. Occasionally there was a retort as Jesse checked someone's hot blood with a judiciously placed bullet. They were still trying but now they saw how vulnerable they were. There were no more foolhardy chance-takers willing to make a wild race for the summit. Everyone seemed to have settled in for a lengthy wait.

Another long hour passed. Jim kept moving along the rim, trying to get some shots off and keeping them guessing below. A spate of bullets drilled into the spot where he had been sitting just two minutes ago. Jim returned fire, slid over, and poured ten rounds into the cluster of rocks from where some of those bullets had issued. Then the enemies' guns fell silent. Every fifteen minutes or so they tried again from a different angle and each time they were met by Jesse, Jim or Shorty, sometimes all three of them.

After a while, Jim told Jesse to take a break. Hot, dirty, and tired out, Jesse made his way back to the fire, glad to work out his cramped muscles. His spirits lifted when he saw how Heddy's face lit up when she saw him. Smiling, she handed him a plate.

"Did you get any of them?" Heddy asked worriedly.

"Got me a few," he replied, cleaning off his plate.

"How many do you think are out there yet?" Heddy handed him a cup of coffee.

Jesse considered this. "Don't rightly know. We hit a good many but it's hard to tell how bad."

"What are we going to do? Does Jim still plan to take us down at night?"

Jesse drank the coffee slowly, savoring it. "Yep. No

place else to go but down, and that place looks about the nearest we're gonna get to a trail."

"I don't see a trail," Heddy stated flatly.

"You gotta look hard, maybe squint a mite. It's a mere sketch of one but it's there."

"Do you think we'll make it down?"

Jesse looked surprised. "We've got to. Unless you plan to sprout some wings and fly. After all, an old Indian warrior—mighty reliable, too—told Jim about that trail. I'm thinkin' some old Indian can get down, we can."

"Did he have twenty men on his tail?"

"Might have. He didn't mention it. I'd better go relieve Jim." They smiled at each other.

Down below, Pete Gillens was organizing one last attack before the light faded. After carefully positioning his men all around, he gave the order to fire and to keep it up until he told them to stop.

Jesse was just kneeling down when gunfire boomed and rocked the ground on which he sat. Tossing his hat to one side, he began, like Jim, to systematically shoot at every breath of movement in front of him. Jim and Jesse gave as good as they got, firing at every stone, crevice, and shadow.

After five minutes of heavy barrage, Gillens waved his hat to cease firing. Now, he told them, they would have something to eat and get some rest. But Gillens wasn't through with Wyatt yet—not by a long shot. Around midnight, he intended to send a few scouts to the summit to see what was up there.

At the camp, Gillens' men were sitting around with filled supper plates.

"How many of them do you think they have up there?" Lee Jenkins asked, stuffing his mouth full of bacon and bread. Gillens shrugged.

"A lot less than we have."

"Two? Maybe four?"

Gillens didn't answer. Instead, he picked up his fork and ate in silence. Jenkins, however, kept on thinking. It occurred to him that that bold-faced kid and his girl might be there as well. That boy's face had bothered him for some days now, but Jenkins still couldn't remember who he was.

Strolling away from the fire and into the shadows, Jenkins looked up at the summit. It should be easygoing up there if it was just one man moving careful-like, he thought. He glanced quickly about, but no one was paying him any heed. It had been a grueling day, and the men were weary. If Jenkin's reached the summit and got to Wyatt first, he'd be the one to collect that reward. Why should he wait for Gillens' orders?

Shovelling down the rest of his beans, he made his decision. He was not going to wait for Gillens. He'd go up himself when the others had bedded down. He would be the first to the top! Having made his plans, he settled down away from the others. When he left it would be in secrecy.

Jim and Jesse kept watch for a while at the trail head. It wasn't until they heard murmurings below them and could smell the smoke from their cookfires that they figured Newton's men had quit for the moment.

Jesse remained while Jim loped over to organize their

departure. The girls were already packed up to go. Canteens were filled and the horses were well-fed and watered.

After another long look Jesse left his post and came up with an armful of brush. "I'll build the fire up."

Jim nodded. "I'll get Shorty down here. We're leaving now."

Shorty inched his way down and was helped to his horse. "I can make it," he assured Jim yet his smile was tight and painful.

Jesse jogged over to the trail head for one last look while Jim crossed over to help Julie mount.

Behind him the sun hurled its last rays, like bloodied Kiowa war lances, over the peak of Rain King and pierced the mighty heavens as if it didn't want to let go of the day. The sun was setting in a blaze of glory. The bulk of darkening clouds to the east bled crimson at their crests. It seeped across canyon walls until they were all drenched in the dying light.

Jim watched as Julie stood there in awe, taking in the grandeur of it all. Its fierce beauty was overwhelming. Jim was drawn to her like a magnet. He knew she belonged here in this land.

"It's not the time to say it, but the sunset is glorious," she told Jim as the big, round sun fell below the horizon, leaving only a reddish aura.

"You'll see other ones," he commented easily. She looked up at him.

"Will I?"

"I promise. We have some nice sunsets at my ranch too. I'll show them all to you." Julie turned pink at the implication.

"I'd like that," she admitted. Her heart was beating erratically at the way he was looking at her. Anne Garvey, she knew instinctively, was forgotten.

Suddenly Jim's eyes widened. His hands struck out, grabbing her hard by the shoulders. In an instant he was pulling her against his chest, almost knocking her over, as he swung her around and into his arms.

A bullet screamed past their ears, piercing the space where they stood just seconds ago. If Jim hadn't seen the dark figure looming on the shadowed rim they would both be dead.

As the gun exploded, Shorty and Jesse reacted. Shorty shot into the dark—but missed. Jesse didn't. A bullet slammed into the man's side. He stood there, tottering on his feet.

Jesse raced to the spot and saw what was happening. Jenkins, tired of waiting below and itching to do some killing, had thrashed through the ravine and somehow scaled the talus slide without being observed. He had seen Jesse but he wanted Wyatt. Wyatt was where the money was. It didn't bother him at all that he'd kill the girl with the same shot.

Again Jenkins aimed his rifle, and Jim's hand dropped for his gun. But Jim had wasted precious seconds getting that girl out of the way. Now their lives depended on the quickness of Jesse's gun.

As the man honed in on Jim, Jesse recognized him. It was Jenkins, his stepfather! Bitterness crawled in Jesse's throat when he saw the thousand dollar smile curl Jenkins' cruel lips.

Fury pulsed through him. All past wrongs seemed to rise

up in his mind like dead spirits crying out for vengeance. His father, his mother, the home they built together were all gone. Only Jenkins was left now. It wasn't fair. All those long, lonely years spent wandering aimlessly around this country because he wasn't welcome in his own home. Jesse threw the rifle to his shoulder and fired.

As the hand of death touched him, Jenkins wheeled and saw the boy raising his rifle. He saw the sober, black look behind the rifle and flinched. Afraid now, Jenkins rushed his shot and it only clipped Wyatt's shoulder.

Then Jesse was firing. He pumped three bullets into Jenkins. He could see him stagger with each shot but, damn it, he kept standing. Racked from the impact, the killer in him was alive. He still held onto that gun.

"Put it down, Lee, or so help me I'll kill ya!" Jesse snapped out.

Without wavering, Jesse walked steadily closer, firing on him as he approached. He struck Jenkins in the arm then pelted the ground around his worn boots with bullets. Jenkins still held onto his gun although he was sagging.

Jesse came up to him and stared into his eyes. Jenkins stared back, wondering how this kid knew his name. Jesse reached out and jerked the rifle from his grip. Jenkins was riddled with bullets yet he kept looking at the tough young man before him.

"Remember me, Lee?" Jesse asked with loathing. "And Ma?"

Through the fog that was slowly enveloping his brain, Jenkins finally remembered: Jesse Altman!

"Jesse!" he groaned. "If you ain't the devil's own whelp!"

If he could just get back his rifle, he'd shoot the kid. He

deserved it. But now he saw that Jesse was not a kid anymore; he was a man—and a very dangerous one.

"That ranch is yours! That fool of a mother of yours left it to you! Sneakin' off to see a lawyer behind my back! If I'd a known, I'd a never have taken care of her before she died. Scheming, double-crossin'—!" With his next breath Jenkins toppled over and sprawled on the ground.

Jesse let out his breath as if letting go of something he had held onto for a long time. Heddy came up to stand beside him. She put her hand in his and his fingers curled around hers.

Jim set Julie aside and went over. It was dusk now and the darkness, once it arrived, would be creeping over them fast.

"You know him, Jesse?" Jim asked, seeing the misery on the boy's face. Jim saw that it was tinged with relief.

"I know him. He married my mother after Pa was killed. I had to leave home because of him." Heddy rubbed her cheek against his arm in silent sympathy. Jim clapped Jesse on the arm. The best thing to do was to get out of this place.

"Let's go. Nothing more for us here."

It took Jesse a moment to shake himself back to the present. Looking down on Jenkins' weasel-like face, he wondered what he had ever feared from him. He was nothing—just a small-time crook and swindler who deserved to be exactly where he was. Jesse shrugged his shoulders and nodded.

"Yep, time to go."

"Jim, you're wounded!" Julie cried as she saw the crease across Jim's shoulder and the torn fabric covered with blood.

"It's nothing. I'll tend to it later. Right now, we have to get off this mesa—fast!"

Jesse helped Shorty and Heddy mount up. He went back over to Jenkins. Coldly, he dragged his body up to the rim and pushed him over the edge. "That's for Ma," he said softly, then he hurried over to get on his horse.

They started off down the trail and never looked back.

There was a startled crash as the body of Lee Jenkins tumbled from the high, dark cliff into Pete Gillens' camp.

Men, hunkered down by the fire, scattered instantly, their eyes wild with alarm. Then Rawl was there, his gun flying from its holster before the body could even roll to a stop. Jenkins' foot jerked and one booted heel scraped into the fire, shooting sparks every which way. Rawl held his fire—he recognized the dead man.

Slowly the men came out of the shadows, all on the torn edge of their jumpy nerves. "Is it Wyatt?" someone rasped out.

"No," Rawl returned soberly, easing his gun back. "It's Lee Jenkins." Gillens came over and looked at Rawl.

"Well?"

"Dead."

Gillens raised his eyes from Jenkins' broken body to look at his men. They were haggard—weary to the bone. It had been a brutal day and the sight of one of their own, all riddled with bullets made them even more jittery.

"He was a damned fool!" Gillens spat out. "When we go up, we'll go together! Until then, you men get some sleep. I'll wake you when it's time to leave." Jenkins' death was not in vain. Gillens now knew that they'd have to wait a long while before creeping up to the summit again. Wyatt would be wide awake after this. "We'll get him!" Gillens grated out. He stood there while Rawl and the others climbed uneasily into their blankets. His eyes traveled up the sheer wall to the very summit of the mesa where the wind howled. Nothing moved.

Wyatt was a cougar all right. And Gillens had called it: The first man to come upon Wyatt would be the first man dead.

## Chapter Seventeen

When night came to the high country, it came quickly, snuffing out everything familiar. Earlier, Jim had memorized landmarks they would be passing. Now they lay almost unrecognizable, covered in dark moonlight. Jim felt as if he was groping his way blindly down this remote trail. He cursed his own inadequacy to lead the group down safely.

Jim's horse had balked when it first headed over the mesa's rim. Almost at once the thin stratum of ancient rock crumbled underfoot. His horse halted, shifted fretfully, then slowly moved ahead. With uncertainty, it picked its way along the mighty spans of fractured ledges.

After traveling some distance, Jim threw a glance over his shoulder. The four riders behind him came along slowly. Above, the hulking summit of Grand Mesa hovered eerily some quarter mile away. All was quiet. His hands were tight as he held the reins. He dare not hurry over this three-foot-wide gash on which they were tottering, yet he strained to hear sounds of pursuit. All that met his ears were occasional snorts of their horses as they registered their complaints at the dangerous route their owners had taken.

The line of riders descended steadily while the very ground beneath them cracked and disintegrated. Bits of rock snapped like icicles and skittered noisily over the cliff's razor edge, the sound echoing loudly around them.

Jim's horse nickered softly. Further back another horse snorted in panic and shook its bridle as its hoofs scrabbled for a foothold. Instantly, Jim swung around and uncoiled his rope, ready to let fly a loop. He saw Jesse pulling firmly on the reins to steady the animal. His voice was unruffled as he spoke in a low tone to his horse. Under his calm hands the horse righted itself. Leather creaked as he leaned forward to pat the animal's neck.

"We're all right, Jim. Thanks. I can't believe that durn Indian coulda done as good as we are," his words floated back.

Jim smiled and it showed in his voice. "Now that I come to think on it, that Indian never did say that he actually used this trail. Just that he knew of it."

"I heard of the Red Sea being parted but I'd never recommend it to anyone tryin' to escape a necktie party," Jesse returned ruefully.

As they inched along the mesa's face, the western shoulder of Rain King, powerful and mighty, reared in brooding majesty.

Little by little the rotten surface beneath them began to firm. Unexpectedly, the trail took a sharp turn around a faulted column of basalt strapped to the mesa's uneven face. Jim reined in quickly.

Before the turn it appeared as if the end of the trail had loomed in front of his feet. It gave the illusion that one more step and his horse would have pitched off the cliff's edge into oblivion. Instantly, Jim raised his hand.

"Hold up!" He spoke quietly yet the order carried in the clear, thin air.

"Whoa, boy!" Heddy soothed as she reined in her fractious pony.

Jim dismounted and edged his way along the line of riders. There was barely enough room for him to pass by. He spoke to each one. When he came to Julie, he reached up and squeezed her hand gently. Her skin felt cold. Her fearful eyes stared back at him, black in a starkly white face. Her shoulders were squared stiffly.

"We'll be on solid ground soon. I'll be back to help you." She nodded slightly then he moved on to Jesse.

"Looks like there's no trail up ahead," Jesse pointed out pensively. "Sure hope there is."

"So do I. Everyone has to stop while I check on it. How's Shorty doing?"

"Pretty fair. He's sticking on his horse. I think his fever has let up. Leastways, he knows what's going on."

"Have you seen anyone on our back trail?"

"Not so far. And I don't think they'll try till daylight."

Jim made his way back to the cliff's edge and peered into the chasm below. It had no doubt claimed many victims through the ages. Would they be one of the lucky ones and escape?

A cold wind came rushing at Jim, yet his face was damp

with perspiration. He couldn't see where the trail wound along the column but he knew it was there. With a groping hand to the wall he took a deep breath and stepped out.

And came down on solid rock—black, hard basaltic rock. Jim exhaled. More confident now, he walked forward guiding himself with his hand. A few more yards and he had worked his way to the lighter side of Grand Mesa. Up above, he could see the moon, full and white. Stars appeared in the blue–black sky. They illuminated the nightscape and revealed the ghostly thread of trail unraveling down to the ravine then across to the base of Rain King. From here it looked to be a fairly gradual descent except for the last section.

Satisfied with what he saw, Jim scrambled back up to the overhang. He took the reins and walked his animal around the column into the light, then went back to lead the others over. When all were safely across he stepped into the saddle once again and took charge.

"Everything is all right up ahead," he said. "Just follow me. Shorty?" He had been awfully quiet. "Are you okay?"

"Yeah, Wyatt. I'm okay." Reece's voice sounded a bit hollow but he seemed lucid.

"Let's go." Jim's horse moved ahead warily, found his footing on solid ground for a change, and stepped forward more boldly.

For a stretch the trail straightened out and widened. Jim picked up their pace. They could see fairly well now as they descended below the treeline. Here, weird-shaped boulders rose up and cluttered the ground from centuries of landslides.

Up ahead, at the base of Rain King, Jim could see the

jagged tops of cottonwoods that lined the ravine in a crooked fringe. As he closed in on the ravine, he peered over the narrow ledge they were crossing to look down upon the treetops some fifty feet below. A constant breeze raced through them, rustling the leaves like scraps of paper caught in a high wind.

Jim took the rough trail at a fast clip, eager to get his party into the shelter that ravine afforded. He took the steep chute too quickly, and his horse slid dangerously. In a great rush of gravel and dirt it slammed to a halt at the bottom, coming to a welcome bed of soft sand. When all the riders were down, they slipped from their saddles, grateful to feel level land underneath their feet again.

Breathing hard now, they led their horses along the ravine on foot. Julie moved up to walk next to Jim. Without saying a word, she slipped her hand into his.

They stayed that way until they mounted up again. Then they began the twelve-mile trek across the plain to the Flying W. To home.

## Chapter Eighteen

A blush of pale rose hinted of the approaching sunrise.
Jim urged his horse forward eagerly. The animal nickered
playfully and shook his bridle. He knew he was home at
last. Into the foothills they rode, traveling the much worn
trail that uncoiled along Lodgepole Mountain. Halfway up
at its shoulder the party came to rest. The Flying W's
boundary began here at this rocky point. A meadow
stretching for two miles opened before them. In the middle
of this verdant oasis was the ranch and its outbuildings.

The riders came in cautiously. Jim wasn't sure in whose
hands the place was. The stone ranch house, a low-lying
gray rectangle, emerged in the softening light. A rocker
and other chairs sat on the wide porch. Roses bloomed on
the bush he had planted by the steps for Anne.

Jim surveyed the place fondly. He breathed in the fresh,
mile-high air and his tense muscles eased. Some of the
hardness that had etched sober lines in his face dissolved.

"Stop right there!" came a voice from a stand of firs on their left.

It was a man's voice, terse with a hint of menace behind the words. The figures were difficult for Laban to make out in the dim light, but there was no mistaking the sounds of five horsemen on the move. "You back again to try to ride roughshod over me, March? Last time you sent that preacher fella to carry your messages for you. Who are you bringing along to hide behind now?"

Jim answered whimsically, "I got two petticoats and a wounded man to hide behind, Laban." The silence stretched on.

Then Laban asked tentatively, "Jim?"

"Yeah, I'm home."

The next instant Laban slid from the trees, walked up to the party's leader and stuck out his hand. Jim took it heartily.

"Well," Laban said gruffly, "it's about time you came home! Come on, I'll take you up to the house."

Jim was in the lead. He was thinner now and more sun-browned than when Laban had last seen him, but the worried look was gone from his face. He looked a man in control again. Laban breathed a sigh of relief. He was afraid prison would have knocked the spirit out of him, but there was more decisiveness about Jim now than there had ever been before.

At the front door Jim took Julie by the waist and swung her down. "Are we home yet, Jim?" Fatigued, she stumbled forward clutching his arm. He swept her up in his arms and carried her into the lit interior. Walking straight through to the back, he shoved open the bedroom door with the toe of his boot. Crossing the room, he set Julie gently down on the wide bed. Then he left her.

"Heddy, you sleep in here with Julie." Shyly she passed by Jim and closed the door behind her, giving Jesse a wan smile. Laban helped Shorty into the second bedroom. Jim waved his arm around.

"Choose your ground, son," he said to Jesse.

Jim, his responsibilities fulfilled, kicked off his boots, shucked his gunbelts, and slung them over the back of a kitchen chair. He shook out his bedroll in an unoccupied corner. Dropping onto the floor heavily, he rolled up in his blanket and in an instant was asleep.

"Jesse, there's an empty bunk in the bunkhouse." Laban was just exiting Shorty's room.

"Man, I haven't slept in a real bed since . . . well, not for a long time. I'll just camp out in the hayloft if it's all the same to you."

Laban nodded. "I'll show you the way." Lantern in hand they moved toward the looming expanse of the barn. When Laban was certain Jim couldn't hear, he said casually, "Pretty girls. Is one of them your sister?" Laban already knew the answer.

"No." Jesse blushed. "Heddy is . . . her family is at the fort. I just met up with her. Promised to take her back to them."

"Is that so? That was nice of you." He smiled benignly. "And Julie?"

Laban noticed that Jesse breathed more easily. "Her uncle was killed back a ways. The Bodine gang killed him and—"

"Yeah, I heard. Bud Harris told everyone. So Jim faced down the Bodine gang, did he? Figures he'd get himself into trouble as soon as he . . . well, never mind about that, but it seems to me that wounded gent looks down right familiar. A friend of Bodine's, isn't he?"

"I don't know much about that. But Bodine sort of left him when he got shot, and Jim brought him along. He's been real useful. Helped us when March's men tried to attack us on top of Grand Mesa."

"Grand Mesa?" Laban chuckled. "So ya got off it, did ya? Using that old Indian trail?" At Jesse's nod he laughed again. "Damn Indian! Almost met up with him once." He showed him the loft. "Here it is."

Jesse took some forkfuls of hay and spread his blanket over them.

"Pretty girl," Laban said suddenly, thinking of Julie. "And he brought her home with him. Good! About time he settled down with some nice girl. Quit his bachelor ways. When a man has someone at home waitin' for him, he's a little more careful with his life." Jesse plopped down on the hay. "What happened to March's men?"

"Some were killed and hurt; the rest we left atop the mesa. But I reckon they're still comin'." He lay back and closed his eyes.

"Comin', are they? Well, we'll fix that. Ain't no one settin' foot on this ranch. I gotta tell the men."

"You do that," Jesse mumbled. He was more tired than he'd ever been in his life yet sleep didn't come to him right away. What Laban said about Julie made him think about Heddy. Maybe it was time he settled down with some nice girl. It seemed Pa's ranch still belonged to him. Heddy would like it. Nice to come home after working the cattle and find her there waiting—waiting for him. With this pleasant thought he fell asleep.

When Laban came in later he wondered at the boy smiling in his sleep.

## Chapter Nineteen

"He's as good as dead!" Chas Stewart exclaimed as he yanked out a chair and threw himself into it. He dropped his sombrero onto the red-checkered tablecloth. The other patrons at the Gay Paree Restaurant looked over curiously at the new arrival seated at March Newton's table.

"Who is dead?" Anne Garvey asked, bringing her hand daintily to her throat. Newton hoped she wouldn't faint at the news.

"Jim Wyatt!" Stewart spat out. He enjoyed watching her complexion turn from a delicate rose to white. Good! Women made Stewart nervous. You couldn't speak freely around them for fear of causing offense. Especially Anne Garvey. Pale and wan like a hothouse flower, she was continually clinging to Newton's arm, gasping at everything his rough men said or did. Well, Newton could have her!

"You better be sure about that!" There was a threatening undercurrent in Newton's words.

"Gillens has him holed up on top of Grand Mesa. That was about eight hours ago. He can't get down. The men should have stomped him to dust by now." The two men grinned at each other while Anne looked silently down at her plate. Their tough countenances glowed with self-congratulation. You couldn't see what Anne was thinking.

"That girl with him?"

" 'Pears to be."

Newton noticed Stewart's hand swollen with bandages. "What happened to you?"

"Some trigger-happy kid I ran across on the trail shot me."

"You kill him?"

"No!" Stewart answered shortly. He didn't want to talk about it.

"Too bad."

Stewart gave him a murderous look so Newton dropped that line of inquiry.

"Well, anyone else hurt?" Newton asked pointedly, thinking of the female passenger.

"Yeah, boss, two men were killed. Duncan Reece"—he stopped for effect—"and Lyle Bodine." The name hung in the air for breathless seconds.

"Bodine?! The hell you say!"

"Rawl identified them both."

"Rawl killed Bodine?"

"No. Wyatt did."

There was a significant pause as Newton digested this. Bodine had been a paid professional. Newton had even thought of hiring him at one time, but took Rawl on the payroll instead.

Newton didn't let the news affect him too long. Bodine was one gunman and, it was true, Wyatt had disposed of him efficiently. But there were twenty more Wyatt would have to deal with up on Grand Mesa all at once. Yes sir, Stewart was right: Wyatt was as good as dead!

When Stewart left, Newton moved his chair close to Anne and slid his arm around her shoulders.

"See that, honey? Just like I told you. I'll take care of everything. Wyatt won't come bothering you anymore." He pulled her close so that she laid her head tenderly on his shoulder.

As her eyes closed tightly she whispered, "I hope so, March. For both our sakes."

## Chapter Twenty

Down by the creek Jim stood in front of a mirror and shaved off the dark stubble covering his jawline. Shrugging into a clean shirt, he noticed someone leave the house and move with stealth to the stable. It was too far to make out who it was so Jim walked over to have a look. When he entered the stable's double doors he saw Shorty leading his horse from a stall.

"Goin' somewhere, Shorty?" A shamefaced Shorty jumped and turned slowly around to face Jim.

"I thought I'd better make a run for it. I won't have a chance once people start askin' questions about that holdup. I'm headin' for home. Back to Texas. Back to Ma. About time one of us helped her on that old place. I had enough of this kind of life. Duncan made it sound so exciting that I wanted to go with him more than anything. Now I'll sorta be glad to get home again. Stayin' put in one place, workin' your own farm . . . that sounds mighty

fine now. Ma's gettin' on, ya know. She needs help."
Shorty held out his hand and Jim took it. "Well, so long."
He mounted up.

"Good luck to you."

Shorty paused. "I ain't forgettin' that you saved my life.
It's somethin' when a stranger will risk his own life to
save yours, when your own kin won't. It's somethin' a
man remembers his whole life. Yep," he drawled softly,
"it sure is." He took a deep breath. "And good luck to you
too."

Shorty ducked his head and rode out of the stable. He
sat a little straighter now, a little more confident. Jim had
a pretty good idea that he would make out just fine now
that he was out from under Duncan's spell. In a little
while he was lost from sight up in the hills. He was Texas
bound. Jim turned and walked to the house.

Julie and Heddy were getting breakfast together when
Jim stepped through the door. Julie turned her head to
look, momentarily taken aback by the change in him.
Gone was the thick, black stubble that covered the lower
part of his face. Now she could see the clean-cut planes of
his lean features. He was a very handsome man. Julie met
his green gaze and blushed fiercely as she realized he was
taking in her appearance with the same lingering appreciation. At his openly interested stare, she quickly lowered
her eyes to the frying pan. "The food is almost ready.
Please take a seat," she invited primly.

Instead, Jim came across the room and stood close behind her, peering over her shoulder at the eggs in the pan.
She could feel his warm breath against the side of her

neck, his arm brushing her blouse. His nearness made her heart flutter.

"That looks good," he said quietly in her ear.

Julie's pulse raced. Her eyes slid away from his chiseled features and tanned skin. She tried not to notice how the gray flannel shirt fit snugly across his wide shoulders.

"Your hair looks like it's shot with fire." His voice was low as he touched an unruly curl.

Heddy grinned. That sounded as good as a proposal to her young ears. Jim saw the smile and winked. He moved away from Julie and poured himself a cup of coffee.

"Aren't you having any breakfast?" Julie was startled.

"I've got things to attend to." His mood became serious. After that, there was little said. He seemed silent and withdrawn. Julie once more became worried. Several times she screwed up her courage to ask him what he was going to do, but one look at his frowning concentration stopped her.

After a heart-wrenching stretch of silence, Jim reached for his guns. Inside, Julie turned cold. She looked into his face. It was set in determined lines as he strapped them on. Then he pulled his hat precisely into place. Tossing down the rest of his coffee, he turned quickly and crossed to the door, spurs jingling smartly.

Julie made no more pretense at cooking. Standing in the middle of the kitchen, she watched Jim head out. At the door he turned to her. Their eyes held.

"I'll be back in a little bit." He paused in the doorway as if feeling that those words sounded too stark, too bare. He groped about for something else to say. "Don't worry." Giving her a small, rueful smile, he turned on his heel and went down the stone steps. Julie rushed to the door and watched him head toward the stable. She wanted to stop him, run after him. He had survived everything they had thrown at him. Would this be when his luck ran out? She saw him saddle up and ride out of the ranch yard.

Julie whirled around to Heddy. "Jim's leaving! And he's alone!"

Without a word Heddy picked up her rifle and headed to the door. "Let's go." The two girls ran to get the horses.

"Good morning all!" Jesse called out cheerfully as he and Laban stepped into the kitchen. It was empty. Through the window Jesse spotted the dust of two riders far off. "They've skedaddled," he said resignedly. "Looks like they're headed for town. If I know Heddy, they're stalkin' Jim!"

Laban looked puzzled. "But Jim didn't go to town."

"I know," Jesse said thoughtfully. "I hope they don't find out where he went or there will be the hell to pay."

## Chapter Twenty-one

Only a little past daylight on Grand Mesa's summit, Pete Gillens and Frank Rawl discovered the trail Wyatt's party had taken. Rawl took one look and balked.

"We should backtrack," Rawl suggested, "go back down the way we came."

"You go down the way we came," Gillens dismissed the suggestion rudely. "I ain't got no time to waste."

"This trail will lead straight to hell! We can't go down it!" Rawl was angry.

"If Wyatt went down it, at night, women and all, we damn well can. Come on!" he ordered all of the others bunched around the trail head. Rawl went only because he didn't intend to be the last to reach Wyatt. He wanted him.

"We can't take these wounded men with us," Rawl spat out, trying to reason with Gillens as the horsemen started down. Several men were close to death, barely hanging

242

onto their horses. Others were swathed in bloody bandages.

"You tell 'em!" Gillens' stiff face cracked into a black grin and his dry throat coughed up grim laughter. Disgusted with it all, Rawl pushed on ahead, not looking back. Let the wounded take care of themselves!

Several grueling hours later they reached the plain. Wyatt wasn't hiding his prints now. "He's headin' for home! We got him on the run!" Gillens exclaimed with satisfaction. "We can send a few men ahead to cut him off. Then we'll come up behind them and shoot 'em to rags!"

"I'll be one of them," Rawl stated. "'Cause I'm gettin' Wyatt. I've waited too long for him—and that reward."

Gillens' eyes flew open wide, staring strangely at Rawl. Rawl looked back in angry puzzlement. "I'm getting that reward, Pete," he warned in a hard voice, a bit unnerved at the other man's silence.

Gillens tried to speak but started to choke. Rawl's horse jumped back as Gillens suddenly lost his balance and fell from his saddle onto his face in the dirt. Rawl turned cold: An Indian arrow was protruding from his back.

Over the empty saddle, Rawl saw them: About forty Cheyenne bucks boiled out from a brush-filled canyon and were thundering at them.

Rawl screamed like a woman. He kicked his heels into his horse's sides and beat a path for Dautry. He was still screaming when a hatchet descended on the gunfighter's head.

The attack was quick and brutal. The Cheyenne rifles decimated the small force before they could get off a shot. A few men tried to make a run for it but didn't get very far.

March Newton's army was gone.

## Chapter Twenty-two

March Newton sat alone in his office, comfortably studying the map in front of him. As soon as he added the Flying W to his property, this entire section of the Snake River range would be his. He already considered Anne's holdings as his own, and it never occurred to him that anyone else was entitled to Wyatt's ranch but him. Kettering would give up quick enough, Newton was sure, once Wyatt was dead.

That should be right about now, he grinned to himself. If Chas Stewart's report was correct, Wyatt's lifeless body should be lying on some lonely heap of rocks atop Grand Mesa this very minute. No matter how tough Kettering bragged his boss was, he could be brought down. Twenty guns against one? Newton figured those to be pretty discouraging odds—for Wyatt, anyway. And if something happened to that girl, no one in this town would care about Wyatt or how he died. It would be his fault that she was caught in the crossfire. Why, they'd probably regard Newton as some kind of hero.

Newton leaned back in his chair lacing his fingers behind his head, and sucked on his stogie. Yes sir, he had lots of plans for the Flying W. His men had reported that Kettering had already rounded up the cattle in one of the basins. Thank you kindly, Kettering, it will make my work that much easier after I throw you onto the next stage out of here!

The quietness of the ranch was disturbed when old Bill, the dog, gave a few barks. Through the window he saw the dog slink around the corner of the stable and disappear. A rider was coming. It must be Pete Gillens. That old hound always knew when to get out of his way. Stretching, Newton pulled himself up out of his chair. It squeaked complainingly from his weight. Newton was tall and heavy but he was all muscle. He walked through the ranch house to the front porch and stopped in the doorway, chewing on his cigar.

At first he couldn't make out who the rider was. Just a lone horseman coming quietly up out of the draw and through a stand of cottonwoods. He crossed the hard-packed ground of the ranch yard and reined in.

He did not dismount but remained motionless in the saddle, his back to the sun. Newton was irritated. With the blaze of the morning light in his eyes, he couldn't make out who the man was. All he could see was the tall outline and a battered hat pulled low over the face. It must be someone Gillens had sent back with a message.

Newton put his hand on the door to push it open, then suddenly dropped it. There was something eerie about the stranger. He didn't speak or move, he only turned his head to look to where Newton was standing. A breeze from the hills came through the screen door, lifting the damp hair at the base of Newton's neck like a chill warning.

Something was wrong here. There was an intensity about the figure that Newton could feel even from twenty feet away.

"Who are you?" Newton snapped out, moving his head so the sun was no longer glaring into his eyes. The man didn't respond. "Well?" He must see him through the screen yet he didn't answer. Wide-shouldered, slim-hipped, the rider sat easily in the saddle, one arm hanging down loosely at his side. From beneath the hat brim, the stranger's eyes never swerved from Newton's wooden face. Green, his eyes were, like the icy depths that hardened the Snake River solid during a midwinter deep freeze. The expression on his face was even harder. Then Newton knew.

"Wyatt!" Newton's eyes widened in shock. "What the hell are you doing here!"

Some small part of his thoughts recognized that Wyatt's shoulder was bandaged, and he rejoiced. All the rest of his attention was concentrated on the man in the saddle.

Newton was caught off guard for the first time in his life. Everything had been planned so carefully. How had Wyatt evaded the trap he had laid? What had happened to all of those gunmen he had sent? Frank Rawl had informed him that he could handle Wyatt all by himself. Then what was he doing here? Newton tensed. Why was he here, on *his* ranch? Wyatt was alone, it seemed, but damn it—so was he!

Wyatt didn't respond at first. Instead his steely eyes

flickered around the empty yard and bunkhouse, then returned to stab into Newton, still standing there behind the screen door.

"Where's everybody at?"

No doubt about it, the clever devil knew he was alone, Newton thought, clenching his teeth around his stogie. "They're out doing their work," he barked back, galled that Wyatt was even here, and brazening into his very yard acting as if nothing had happened.

"What kind of work would that be?" Jim asked coolly. "Heard you sent your men and a lot of hired guns to kill me for a thousand dollar reward." He considered Newton's stunned expression. "You must be mighty afraid of me."

"Afraid of you? Why you filthy murderer!" Down went his hand for the gun at his side. But the gun wasn't there. He had left it in his office. He lifted his startled eyes to see Wyatt's Colts drawn and pointed at his chest. Newton froze. Newton had gone for his gun and, even though he didn't have one on him, Wyatt could cut him down now and it would be considered a fair fight. His stony eyes met Wyatt's somber ones.

"You ought to be more careful, Newton. A man with as many enemies as you ought not leave his gunbelt hangin' on his chair."

Newton cursed himself. Wyatt had probably seen him through the window as he left his office. He hated Wyatt for being so shrewd.

Still targeting Newton, Jim looked about the place, weighing it up. "Thinkin' of taking this place for my own." He turned his head to meet Newton's furious eyes. "I could use the extra land."

"You can't take a man's land!" he shot out.

"Why not? Isn't that what you tried to do to me? And Laban? I figure if you, a law-abiding pillar of the community, can do it, why I guess anyone can."

"Any man who murders his neighbor deserves to be hanged and have his land taken away!" Newton smouldered, furious that he was unable to blast Wyatt out of his saddle. The guns were still held lightly in the other man's hands, but Newton was not fooled. One wrong move and Wyatt would drill him through.

"Exactly my sentiments. Now, let's take you, for instance. Ralph Garvey is found dead and what happens to his ranch and daughter? You get them both after framing me for rustling. That sure was a lucky day when Garvey was shot, wasn't it?"

"Don't try to turn the tables on me, Wyatt! I know it was you. If there had been any justice you'd been hangin' from a rope last year."

"But I wasn't. And why should I be? I was just about to be the happiest man alive, engaged to Anne, had my own ranch, a father-in-law who liked me. Nope, there was no reason for me to kill anyone. You now"—he pointed the muzzle of his pistol at Newton—"you weren't in such a happy position, were you? Seein' as Garvey didn't like you none."

Newton's face tightened. "He liked me well enough!"

"Well enough just isn't enough. He didn't want you to marry Anne. He told me he didn't trust you."

"That's a lie!"

"Let's suppose he found you putting my brand on his cattle. He sure wouldn't like you well enough then. My guess is he'd have gone straight to the law. You'd have been strung up then. That sure is a motive for killing." He summed it all up in a neat package.

Newton was simmering. "You damned upstart! You go passin' them lies around and I'll—"

"You'll what?" Jim asked, interested. "Put another price on my head? Or maybe one of these days you'll be a man and fight your own battles." The words jabbed at Newton's pride like the sharp point of a knife. "Or are you going to hide behind your door all day?"

Instantly, a red wave of fury rose up in Newton. Nobody talked to him like that! He kicked the door open with his booted foot. It slammed against the wall of the house and cracked from the force. Stepping out, he tore the cigar from his mouth and tossed it into the dirt. With the heel of his boot he ground it to a pulp. He seemed to be indicating that he would do the same to him.

"Come on, Wyatt. I'll fight you. Come on!" He held his hands out and beckoned to him tauntingly. "If you want to fight man to man with your fists, I'll do it. Either way, guns or fists, I aim to win. I always win! If you think you can get Anne back this way, forget it. We're already engaged. She don't want any part of you!" The bitter tirade was intended to rile Wyatt, but if it did, Newton could not detect any answering anger.

On the contrary, a mantle of dangerous calm lay upon Jim. He was in control of his emotions. A smarter man might have realized that he was not dealing with another hotheaded cowboy who would come recklessly on, fists swinging. Jim was not fighting out of pride. He was fighting for a deeper reason: His life.

"Is that so? Lucky Anne. Marrying her father's murderer."

Newton started impetuously towards him fists clenching and unclenching. "I'll tear you to pieces for that!"

"Think so? You brag an awful lot. Let's see you prove up on your boast."

"You sure picked on the wrong man!" He flexed his burly shoulders in anticipation of taking Wyatt apart. "All right, cowboy, you're on! Climb on down and shuck your guns. I don't want to get shot in the back like old man Garvey," he told Wyatt with deliberate pleasure.

Jim's mouth tightened at the mocking voice. Even now, the thickheaded rancher wouldn't admit to his crime. He was resolved to blame it all on Jim.

Slowly, keeping an eye on the big man, Jim dismounted on the far side of his horse. Newton sneered at the distrust in the clear, cool eyes. Jim came around his horse and unbuckled his gunbelts, slinging them over the pommel of his saddle. He tossed his old, beaten hat recklessly onto the grass and waited, hands resting lightly at his sides.

Newton rolled up the sleeves of his shirt. This would be a pleasure, a pure pleasure! And when it was finished, he'd have Wyatt's land as well. Once he gave Wyatt a good drubbing, he'd send him out of town by the seat of his pants! Anne wouldn't want to live near this man who had killed her father. Wyatt was going, and Newton was staying. There would be no other conclusion that Newton would accept.

"I wish Anne could see what I'm gonna do to you. She's been lookin' forward to it as much as I have." Without warning, Newton suddenly lowered his head and bolted for Wyatt's midsection.

Jim saw it coming and stepped out of the way. As Newton went sailing past and skidded to a halt, Jim was there waiting. At once a granite-hard fist slammed into Newton's jaw. The other one struck his stomach like a meat cleaver. Newton grunted both with pain and surprise at the unexpected swiftness of his adversary. Before Newton could straighten up, Jim clubbed him with both fists.

Stiff-lipped and sober, Newton backed away, more cautious now. Wyatt was younger and much lighter. Newton had figured on disposing of him with a few quick hits. He was still confident, however. Wyatt may have started with a few lucky punches but Newton knew he could give it back—and then some. He had beaten many a stronger man in his day. Why, he'd take him apart.

Even as he was thinking this, Wyatt boldly stepped in and hammered lightning-fast body punches one after another, aimed at Newton's stomach and ribs.

Like an infuriated bull who sees red, Newton dug his heels in and started swinging. Jim rolled his upper body to avoid some of Newton's wild strikes. Newton's fists could be murderous but he had a hard time connecting with the lithe figure in front of him. Finally, the older man drilled a right into Jim's jaw, stepped to the left and swung again. He grunted with pleasure at his success, but it was short-lived as Jim suddenly walked back in slamming a right into Newton's mouth, and a left hook that smashed the cartilage of his ear. A bareknuckled cross caught Newton's unprotected face. He swore long and hard.

Failing to fend off the brutal assault, Newton kicked out and caught Jim just below the kneecap, catapulting him into the dirt. Now that he was down, Newton moved in, aiming his boot viciously at Jim's head. Jim saw it, rolled away, and scrambled up again.

Before he could get to his feet Newton charged him, punching and jabbing with more precision this time. He was tired of this small-time, dirt-scratching cowpoke talking so big. He'd shut his dirty mouth!

Newton landed a leaden blow to Jim's chest that staggered him, then rammed his left into his stomach. Next he went for that bandaged shoulder. That was the weak point. Slamming his fist down onto the lump of bandages, he had the satisfaction of seeing Wyatt's face turn white. Feeling more in control now, Newton prepared to go for that shoulder again. Before he could ball up his big ham of a hand, Jim, grunting from the painful impact, threw a wicked uppercut that Newton didn't see coming. The force of it stunned him right down to his spurs.

Both men broke apart, exhausted and breathing hard. Their shirts stuck to their bodies, wringing with sweat. Newton's legs were feeling rubbery. Jim shook the damp hair off his forehead impatiently. He wanted to get on with it and be on his way. The savage pain in his shoulder prodded him on. He was aware of Newton's exultation when his fist had slammed into the wounded shoulder and Jim had flinched. He knew he'd keep aiming for it.

Newton poked at him a few more times, but Jim managed to dodge away. Without warning, Newton lunged forward, using all of his strength to plow into him. Instantly, he wrapped his big arms around Jim's waist and took him down. Jim landed on his bad shoulder just as Newton intended, with the force of his weight grinding it into the ground. Once down, Newton's hand grappled to get hold of Jim's throat. With the wind knocked out of him and reeling with pain, Jim still managed to knock away the fumbling hands and aim a fist right between Newton's eyes. Newton grunted and tried to roll Jim over. Hate poured out of him as he attempted to break Jim's arm by dint of his two hundred and forty pounds. Yanking his arm out of the vicelike grip that was bending it to an unnatural angle, Jim shoved him off with all of his strength. He slammed his fist into Newton's nose.

Newton howled. He rolled away while Jim, on all fours, climbed to his feet unsteadily. Turning around, Jim kicked back hard at the man still on the ground. The boot came crashing down toward Newton's face. Newton pawed it away but not before it scraped his cheek raw.

Jim backed away while Newton hauled himself up with effort. Both men were a little slower now, but still game. Blood dribbled down Newton's swollen lips and smeared up into his hair from a deep scalp wound.

Jim's eyes smarted from sweat. He ran his bloody knuckles down his pants legs before balling his fists for the next swing. Blood spotted his shirt where it seeped through the bandage. Hatred brewed in both men. Newton refused to lose and Jim couldn't afford to.

"C'mon, quit stallin'!" Newton yelled. He spat blood onto the ground and stared at Jim under lowered brows. Jim was dog-tired and Newton knew it. It infuriated him that the cowboy hadn't given up yet. Didn't he know that Newton was the better man? The sharp, black eyes noted that Jim was swaying on his feet. What he failed to notice was that he was doing the same.

Jim fell back on his last reserve of strength built up

from years of hard work. He had to have one more go at Newton. He had to take him down soon. Jim's head was already buzzing with pain. He knew he couldn't go through very many more rounds.

Suddenly Jim stepped in and swung at the big man. With clenched fists he drilled into Newton's stomach and ribs with every shred of power he had left in him. His arms heavy as lead, Jim walloped the side of Newton's head then shot a vicious uppercut between his arms that smashed the arrogant chin upwards. Newton's head jolted back and color burst inside his skull. Throbbing, blinding pain washed over him, wave after wave, until he lost his footing and fell with a crash to the ground.

Jim staggered away, watching the glassy eyes of his opponent for any signs of renewed life. There were none. All he managed to do was roll onto his side and retch. Newton was vanquished. For a while there, Jim had had his doubts whether he could finish the fight. Much as he detested Newton, he was a fierce fighter who actually believed he was in the right.

He stumbled over to the water trough and washed the blood from his face. He could feel his eye start to swell. He pulled the kerchief from around his neck and mopped his face, then he moved over to where Newton lay on his side.

"Well, Newton," Wyatt gasped out as his chest rose and fell with his exertions. "Now will ya admit it?"

"What the hell ya talkin' about?" Newton mumbled. He tried to focus on Jim's face above him, but his vision wavered. Everything was black around him. His jaw worked, but all he said was, "I won't admit to nothin' you did!" Then his eyes fluttered shut and he lay there unconscious.

Jim stared at him a moment, angry and baffled at why the stubborn side of beef still wouldn't admit his guilt. Perhaps he thought he was in the right when he killed Garvey. Men like him always manage to delude themselves into believing their motives are so noble.

Disgusted, Jim gave him a kick to get his attention. Newton only groaned, eyes still shut.

"Okay, Newton, I'm going, but I'll be back. I'm going to find out who killed Ralph Garvey and the sheriff, then you're the one who's going to pick out which tree you want to hang from. I know it was you or one of your men. I'm not going to give up until I clear my name. Comprende?"

Newton didn't seem to be comprehending anything. Jim staggered over to his horse and slung his guns back around his lean waist with bloody hands. All the while he watched Newton's inert form on the ground. The habit of being cautious never left him.

Jim heaved himself up onto his horse, who started moving off immediately. One last look showed Newton to be coming out of his daze. Jim turned his horse in the direction of home and rode out of the ranch yard.

Looking neither right nor left, Jim rode slowly into the cottonwoods, unaware that he was being watched by someone other than Newton.

Neither man had seen the dark, cloaked figure on the horse, sitting soundlessly behind a thick tangle of bushes and broken branches. All in black from head to foot the rider sat. Even the face was hidden with a concealing kerchief tied over the nose. Only the eyes, moving restlessly over the scene with a slightly mad expression, were visible.

Sounds of anger burst forth in smothered gasps as the two men fought and Jim Wyatt ultimately won. Jim couldn't see the eyes, like two daggers stabbing into his retreating back. He couldn't know that after March Newton had been dealt with, he would be next.

Coldly, a prodding spur moved the horse forward into the open. The rider came off the horse slowly, taking the long rifle with him. Relentlessly, the heels of the black boots came down on the ground, eating up the distance to Newton.

Into his groggy mind came the hollow thump of footsteps. It rang in his ears. Grunting, Newton managed to pull himself up on one elbow and turn around. As his eyes cleared he stared at the silent figure who stood there, feet apart, the rifle held menacingly in gloved hands.

While he watched, one hand lifted and yanked the kerchief down. Now the face was visible. Newton's eyes widened.

"What are you doing here?" His eyes went confusedly over the black duster, pants and shirt. "Why are you dressed like that?" The rifle lifted and pointed at Newton's chest. "No! What the hell are you doing?" The bullet blasted into his chest and March Newton fell back, a stunned look still on his face.

Jim's horse had covered only a mere quarter mile when two shots rang out from the direction of the ranch. Puzzled, he reined in and listened carefully. The shots were not repeated. He had half a mind not to go back, but a touch of uneasiness crept over him. Had Laban followed and tried to take Newton on? It wasn't his style to pull on a beaten man, but you never knew how much life was left in Newton even after that walloping he had taken.

Abruptly, Jim turned his horse and rode swiftly back up the draw. As he rode once more into the ranch yard, he saw that Newton was still lying on the ground. Holding himself still, Jim's eyes flickered towards the house, the barn and the bunkhouse. Nothing stirred. He let out his breath. Once again he looked at Newton. This time he stiffened. A dark stain was spreading out underneath him as he lay there. Blood!

Instantly, Jim flung himself from the saddle and ran towards the prone man. Kneeling down, he turned him over. The black eyes opened wide. There was blood all over his chest. Newton looked stunned.

"You—it's you," he barely whispered.

"What happened?" Jim's eyes scanned the area once more but nothing moved. He returned his attention to Newton. The man was dying—no doubt about that. "You killed Garvey, I know that, and branded his cattle. Did someone double-cross you? Talk, damn it!"

Newton was gasping for breath. "I—I did brand those cattle. You—you were too cocky. But I didn't kill Garvey." Jim believed him. He was a dying man.

"Who was it?" Jim shook him as the heavy lids began to close again. "Who shot you?!" The big chest took one last, strangling breath then stopped.

"I did." A brittle voice answered behind him. "Don't go for your gun or I'll kill you too!" Jim's hand that had automatically swept downward, stopped. He recognized that voice—but it couldn't be! Slowly, arms away from his side, he came to his feet and turned around.

"Anne?" His voice held disbelief. She was standing there with a Winchester in her hands, looking as if she knew exactly what to do with it. She was dressed all in black. The blond hair had been pushed under a flat-crowned hat and only her pale face, filled with animosity, was visible.

"What's the matter?" she spat out disdainfully, her sweet voice dissolving into a hard lump of anger. "Did you think I didn't know how to shoot? Why shouldn't I? My father taught me and I wanted to learn." She smiled coldly. "In time, he was sorry he taught me to be such a good shot." It took a few moments for her meaning to sink in. But that was impossible. Or was it?

"You killed Ralph? Your own father?" Jim was shocked. Anne had always been so dainty, professing a fear of guns. Now here she was, holding him under her barrel, and he had no doubt she'd drill him if he moved so much as an inch.

"He tried to cheat me!" she shrilled. "I wanted my name put on the title to the ranch and he only laughed. He laughed. He said he'd put it in your name when we were married! I tried to talk to him. I tried to be reasonable." And, indeed, her voice did sound calm and reasonable as she said it. Only the wildness of her blue eyes betrayed how far from sanity she really was. "I wanted my name on the deed so I could sell out, then get out! I gave him a chance but he wouldn't do it! I had to live in this hellhole. The only friends were a bunch of small-time ranchers and their dreary wives and their dreary lives."

"You have a fine ranch," he said carefully.

"I hate it! And I hate you! I thought if I married you I

could convince you to leave. But you were just as bad as my father!" She was becoming more incensed by the minute.

"So you killed your father," he interrupted calmly.

Her hands shook a little as she held the rifle on him.

"Yes, I killed him! I shot him in the back as he stood telling me how he's doing everything for my good. So I did something for my own good. I'll bet he was surprised!" This amused her. There was no touch of remorse to soften her damning statements. "And then you had to come riding up! I wonder if you know how close you were to seeing me that day!" she said aggrievedly.

"You told the sheriff you were home at the time."

"I know I did." A supercilious smile curved her lovely lips. "Then he started asking questions. I could see he was beginning to be suspicious of me. Oh yes, when he looked at me, I could tell. So of course, he had to die as well. Too bad you were already on your way to prison. You would have been blamed for that killing, too," she muttered with regret.

"Yeah, too bad," Jim said dryly.

Her fingers tightened on the stock. "And now you're going to be blamed for March's death."

Jim knew he had to keep her talking. She was too eager to shoot.

"Why kill March? You were engaged. He would have done whatever you wanted."

"But he didn't! He didn't kill you! That's what I wanted most of all!" Jim was shaken at the stark hatred on her face. "He promised he would. He sent all of those men after you and he still failed." She threw the dead man a contemptuous look.

"Why kill me?" he asked quietly.

"Why? Because so long as you were alive, you'd go on saying that you were innocent! People might actually start to believe you. Even March might have started to believe you! I saw his face when you accused him of shooting my father. I could see he was surprised by your accusations. Then he just might start thinking. Who would that leave for him to suspect? I wasn't having any of that!" She took a step closer.

"I thought for sure you'd be lynched. When that didn't happen, I prayed you would die in prison. Even when March sent out his men for you, you just didn't have the decency to die and go away." She was breathing hard from the intense emotions gripping her, but now she calmed down slightly. "I see now that if I want something done right, I'll have to do it myself." She lifted her rifle.

"So now you have to die. Then I can sell my ranch and go back East. Who knows, March might have even left his ranch to me. Then I'll really be a rich woman." She sounded pleased at the idea.

"No one will believe I killed March," Jim said. "All my friends—"

"I don't give a damn what your friends say!" she yelled, losing her patience once more. "I'll tell the sheriff you did it, and then I'll cry and cry and have hysterics and tell how the two of you fought over me." Her pretty lips formed a wavering smile. "And you won't be around to tell him any different."

"I think he will, miss," came a deep voice unexpectedly from behind Anne. Neither had seen the sheriff come out from among some rocks, his gun raised.

As Anne's head reared in astonishment, Jim, startled into action, took advantage of the moment to lunge for the horse trough. It was a good thing he did, because Anne instantly shot into the empty space where he had just stood.

Finding herself without a target, she slung around to face the strange voice behind her. Another shot rang out and before Anne could discharge her second round, the Winchester flew out of her hands and landed a few feet from her in the dirt. As she cried out, Jim saw Heddy standing there with a rifle in her hand, smoke coming from it. Julie, from behind her, came running up to grab Anne's rifle before she could think to go for it again. Taking it up, she moved a safe distance away.

The sheriff strode up to Anne and pulled the handcuffs from his back pocket. Before Anne knew it, her hands were cuffed behind her back.

"No! You got it all wrong!" she spat out angrily. "It was him! I came up and found March dead. Jim Wyatt—"

"Didn't kill anyone," the sheriff finished calmly. "Don't bother lying, Miss Garvey. I heard it all. So did both of my witnesses." His head inclined towards Julie and Heddy. "You confessed to three murders and was caught in the commission of a fourth. You've had a busy day."

Unsteadily, Jim rose to his feet, still woozy from the fist fight. As he stood up, Julie ran to him, dropping the rifle and throwing her arms around his waist. Jim felt a twinge of pain, but he didn't care. His arms drew around her and held her close.

Looking over her head, he smiled wryly at the sheriff. "It's a good thing you showed up, Sheriff. How did you know to come here?"

"Miss Carter and Miss Gibson were in town. They saw Anne Garvey sneak out the back of the hotel. They thought she looked suspicious all dressed in men's black clothes and toting a rifle. It didn't match with the description they had of her, so they stormed my office and rousted me out. I must confess, having heard so much about Anne Garvey, I was stunned to see her vault so effortlessly onto the back of that black stallion and tear out of Dautry with a rifle in her hand. I held my fire long enough to hear her confession."

Jim looked down into Julie's white face that was pressed against his good shoulder. "You did all of that, honey?" She nodded, and he ran his bruised hand over her hair. Jim knew that now was the time to speak.

"Julie, you've seen my place. It could sure use a woman's touch. Do you think you could do anything with it?"

Heddy smiled broadly as Julie's color mounted. Distraught or not, she knew a proposal when she heard one.

"I'd like to give it a try," she murmured.

"Do you think you could do anything with me?"

"You?" her voice strengthened. "Why, I wouldn't change a thing!"

"That's my girl!" A grin spread across Jim's face. He leaned down and kissed her. Reaching her arms around his shoulders, she returned the kiss.

"By the by," the sheriff remarked to no one in particular, "got us a new minister in town. Performs marriages and everything."

"Not Brother Arvel?" Jim asked skeptically. "I heard of him."

"Last I seen of Arvel, he was being escorted out of

town by your foreman, Laban. Said he made him feel tired all over. No—this is a real minister. You might want to pay him a visit on the way home." He looked pointedly at Julie and Jim.

"That's a good idea," Heddy said quickly. She liked to see things wrapped up neatly.

Anne, realizing for the first time that not only was she in serious trouble, but that her nemesis was actually preparing to enjoy the rest of his life with another woman, began kicking and screaming. The sheriff was treated to a stream of obscenities that made even an old hand like him blush. Shaking his head, he tossed her into the saddle and tied her down.

Jesse rode up just as the sheriff was leaving with his prisoner, still yelling. He looked relieved to see Jim.

"Glad to see you're all right. Who was that blond?"

"Anne Garvey."

"Is that a fact? I'm sure sorry I missed her." He turned his head and watched while she gave the sheriff grief.

"She tried to kill Jim," Julie said, pulling away self-consciously from Jim and smoothing down her hair. "She killed her own father—and Jim suffered for it!"

Jesse was surprised. "I figgered sure it was Newton." His eyes went to the body still laying in the middle of the yard.

"Anne shot March as well," Jim explained.

"Lord a mercy! You sure were better off goin' to prison than marryin' her!"

"You know something, Jesse? You're right. At least I'm still alive," Jim acknowledged with a half-smile.

"Jesse and I are pulling out now. He's going to take me

home," Heddy piped up. "But before we do, maybe we can stay for your weddin'?" The girls' eyes met. Julie tried not to smile.

"No need to prod me, Miss Heddy," Jim returned. "I aim to make an honest woman out of Miss Carter. What about it, Julie? Should we stop off and see that minister before we head back to the ranch?"

Julie gave him to understand that she would like it very much. As they all mounted up and swung down the trail, Jesse told him of the telegram that had been waiting for him at Dautry. "The sheriff was holding it for me. Bud Harris told him to. It seems my ma left the ranch to me just like Jenkins said. I thought we'd stop by and take a look at it. Heddy is that interested in seein' it."

"Is that a fact?" Jim's green eyes went to Heddy and it was her time to blush. "If that place of yours doesn't work out, you always have a job riding for me."

"Thanks, Jim, but I hope it does. Anyways, you're not the only one with prospects. Heddy wants me to meet her folks." He paused. "She thinks they'll like me!"

While the four of them rode towards Dautry together, old Bill, the dog, knowing where his bread was buttered, sniffed at Newton, then hurried down the trail after them.